HARD AS A ROCK COWBOY
ROCKY ROAD RANCH
BOOK 2

LEXI POST

All rights reserved.

No part of this publication may be sold, copied, distributed, reproduced or transmitted in any form or by any means, mechanical or digital, including photocopying and recording or by any information storage and retrieval system without the prior written permission of both the publisher, Oliver Heber Books and the author, Lexi Post, except in the case of brief quotations embodied in critical articles and reviews.

PUBLISHER'S NOTE: This is a work of fiction. Names, characters, places, and incidents either are the product of the author's imagination or are used fictitiously. Any resemblance to actual persons, living or dead, business establishments, events, or locales is entirely coincidental.

Hard as a Rock Cowboy Copyright 2025 © Lexi Post

Cover design by Dar Albert

Published by Oliver Heber Books

0 9 8 7 6 5 4 3 2 1

ACKNOWLEDGMENTS

For my husband, Bob Fabich, whose goals and ambitions are so in line with mine. I'm very happy to have a true partner in life.

Thank you to my sister Paige, who did double duty when this book was ready for beta reading. Only an awesome sister would patch and paint my house during the day and read my manuscript at night while I'm working on the epilogue.

Lexi's Legends, my reader group on Facebook, came through for me once again with names for everything from a bar to a baby. Thank you to Veronica Westfall, Beckie Lowe, Carey Sullivan, Tracy Jacobs, Pamela Reveal, and Patricia Way. You make this lonely profession so much more fun.

A special thank you to my wonderful critique partner, Marie Patrick. Her support and encouragement always get me through the tough times, even hurricanes.

Most of all, thank you for reading my stories. It's so wonderful to know that others enjoy a happily-ever-after as much as I do.

AUTHOR NOTE

Hard as a Rock Cowboy was inspired by the ancient Greek play, *Antigone*. This tragic play is about family and pride. It is Antigone's determination to honor her brother that pits her against the state, but family takes precedence for her. It is this idea of family against a greater entity that inspired the struggle for Hannah Kingsley. And it is Haemon's love for Antigone (the king's son) that inspired Brody's struggle between family and self.

In the play, Antigone is horrified that the king has decreed her brother not be buried, but that his body should rot for his attack on the city. Antigone devises a plan to bury her brother anyway, but the king hears of it and sentences her to being entombed alive. Though Haemon tries to reason with his father, the king refuses to listen. In the end, by time the king relents, Antigone, Haemon, and the queen have all committed suicide. Obviously, there can be a much happier ending to such themes as are portrayed in this play.

AUTHOR NOTE

Unlike the play, Brody's challenge is a bit harder than Hannah's. Like Haemon, it's a struggle between him and his family, whom he loves and respects. At first it appears that Hannah will be his way out, but she ends up complicating matters, eventually showing him what's most important.

CHAPTER 1

BRODY DUNN TOOK the outside stairs two at a time, heading for the third floor of the Phoenix apartment complex where the Harpers resided, at least according to his research. They were the only thing standing in his way of attending the academy in January to become a wildlife manager.

For years his father had been trying to get the Harpers to sell their land, which abutted the Rocky Road Ranch. The only way the Dunns could be a viable cattle ranch and compete with the larger operations was if they bought the Harpers' land next door. The problem was, the Harpers didn't want to sell.

With the family ranch on the brink of failure, his dad decided to invest in turning it into a dude ranch. Brody thought the idea inspired, but he wasn't as attached to the cattle ranch as his oldest brother, who wanted it to stay a cattle ranch. The dude ranch idea was a huge risk, since none of them knew how to run such an operation. So Dad still wanted the Harpers' land.

Now all Brody had to do is convince them to sell their land, and his father would release him from his promise to help with the ranch. That was what he needed to finally pursue his dream career at the age of twenty-seven. He was sure this was the job for him.

Confident in his ability to convince the older couple to sell, based on the public records, he reached the top of the stairs and looked for apartment 325. Walking around the west end of the building, he found the number directly across from the elevator. Stepping up to the door, he knocked.

He counted to thirty to make sure he gave the older folks a chance to get to the door. When no one answered, he knocked again. It was almost dinner time. Surely they would be home, unless they still worked. If they had to work to pay the rent, then his offer to buy their land could solve all their problems.

He counted to thirty again, while double-checking the floor and apartment number.

When no one answered, he knocked a third time. "Howdy. Is anyone home?"

After ten seconds, he received a response. "Who is it?"

"Howdy, ma'am. I'm Brody Dunn from Four Peaks and was hoping I could talk to you?"

The little cover on the peephole moved, and he smiled so she could see he was friendly.

"I'm sorry. I don't know a Brody Dunn."

She didn't sound that old, but it did make sense that she wouldn't know him. "Yes, ma'am. I understand. You probably know my father, Jeremiah Dunn. We're your neighbors in Four Peaks."

There was a sigh on the other side of the door. "I live here. I think you have the wrong apartment."

Did he? He pulled out his phone and looked at it. "Is this the Harpers' apartment?"

"It is. But we don't have a summer place in Four Peaks."

He rubbed the back of his neck, thoroughly confused. "Is this the home of Mrs. Norma Harper?"

"Do you know my grandmother?" The woman's voice sounded hopeful.

Ah, maybe the older woman was in a nursing home. "No, ma'am. But my father does. Could I speak to her?"

"I wish you could."

That didn't bode well. "Ma'am?"

"My grandmother passed six months ago. I'm the last of the family."

He looked directly at the peephole. If losing a grandmother felt the same as losing a mother, he could understand. "I'm terribly sorry. I didn't know."

"I'm still getting used to the fact she's gone."

His excitement of moments ago turned to sorrow for the woman as well as disappointment. "I understand. I lost my mother when I was a teenager. Losing someone you love leaves a hole in your heart. I'm sorry I bothered you." He turned away discouraged, but not beaten. He just needed to do more research.

"Don't go. I mean, you haven't told me why you wanted to see my grandmother."

He turned back at her request to find she'd opened the door as far as the chain lock would allow. She had a pretty, round face with an upturned nose, brown eyes the color of whiskey, and auburn hair framed her face. She'd obviously been eating cookies because there were crumbs near the corners of her full lips. He felt torn between being polite and finding out as much as he could. "Don't you wish to be alone?"

She gave him a crooked smile. "No. I've had quite enough alone time, and I love talking about my grandparents. Did you need to know something?"

He looked away not sure where to start. Finally, he decided. "Yes, there is, but I'm not sure talking in the hallway here is the best place."

She frowned, obviously not in a hurry to invite him in, which he could understand in the big city. "There's a little Mexican place on the north corner of this building. If you'd like to meet me there in about ten minutes, we could talk there."

Now, that sounded promising. "I would be pleased to meet you there, miss. If you're sure?"

She nodded. "Yes, I'm sure."

He smiled. Maybe he could find out everything he needed to know by talking to this relative. "I'll see you there shortly. Thank you." He tipped his cowboy hat and turned toward the stairway, forcing himself to mosey instead of run. But once he'd descended one flight, he raced down the rest.

As soon as he hit the sidewalk, he headed north. He didn't know the Harpers had children, or grandchildren for that matter. His father said they'd only visited the land on and off in the time he'd lived there, which made it odd that they didn't want to sell. But they must have left it to someone, maybe even this granddaughter.

His steps slowed as he looked for the restaurant. The red painted walls and large sign declaring *Mama Juanita's* told him he found the place. Walking in, he chose an orange booth where he could see the door and sat. He was pretty sure he'd know her when she walked in. She appeared older in the doorway than he would have thought for someone whose grandmother died. His own died before he was four.

He still felt a little guilty that she had just lost her grandmother. Maybe he'd get lucky, and she was the heir and would be happy to sell. If that was the case, he could be through the wild life manager training and physicals and in a new job by spring. He was almost afraid to hope. Every time he'd thought he'd be free of the ranch, something else happened to keep him there, whether it was his brother's deployment or his dad's stroke. He didn't resent it. He was happy he could help, but he was ready for it to be his turn.

―――――――

As the cowboy disappeared from sight, Hannah Kingsley finally closed the door. Wow—she hadn't expected to have a cowboy come knocking at her door. And not just any cowboy, but a dark-haired, broad-shouldered, drop-dead-handsome cowboy. No one should be allowed to look that good.

She made a beeline for the bathroom, and when she stepped in front of the mirror, she groaned. Crumbs from the peanut butter cookies she'd been munching on before going through the packet the estate lawyer had sent were visible around her mouth. Not the best impression. Then again, neither was the mess on top of her head. Unclipping her long hair, she quickly brushed it before pulling it back up into a ponytail. Reaching for her lipstick, she halted. What was she doing? This wasn't a date. In fact, it could very well be a scam of some kind. She turned and left the bathroom. Her face was fine and her jeans and tank top were good enough.

She strode back to the door and slipped on her sandals. Grabbing her keys and her phone, she left her purse, just in case. She may have become ultra cautious in the last six months, but her grandmother always said it was better to be safe than sorry. She stepped out into the outside hall and started to close the door, but paused. The packet from the lawyer lay open on the coffee table, making her feel guilty.

Quickly, she shut the door. She had all day tomorrow to read it. One more day wouldn't hurt anyone. As she took the short cut between the hallways of the apartment complex, she kept trying to remember if she'd ever heard Grandma mention anyone by the name of Dunn, but nothing came to mind. She was absolutely sure that they had never paid anyone by the name of Dunn, so the Dunn family was a complete mystery.

But not for long. She opened the door to Mama Juanita's and stepped inside. Immediately she saw him, being that he was the only man in the place with a brown cowboy hat on his head, sitting in one of the brightly-colored booths.

He noticed her as well and waved.

Had he really seen so much of her in the doorway that he knew it was her? She'd have to remember that next time a stranger knocked on her door.

As she approached, he stood and doffed his hat. "Thank you for meeting with me."

Her steps slowed, not because she was afraid, but because he was tall and so polite. She couldn't remember the last man, besides her grandpa, who had such charming manners. Finally, reaching him, she held out her hand. "I'm Hannah Kingsley."

He shook her hand and gave her the same devastating smile he'd given her when he promised to talk with her. "It's a real pleasure to meet you, Hannah. I'm Brody."

She returned his smile. He'd already told her his name, but she wouldn't mention that. When he released her hand, she slid into her side of the booth. "I have to say, Brody, that you have piqued my curiosity."

His smile faltered. "I imagine I have. If I had known of your loss, I promise I wouldn't have bothered you."

Now that she could see him in full, her estimation of his looks grew. Not only were his eyes a beautiful cobalt blue, but his nose was straight and his larger upper lip sported the hint of a mustache. His chin was square, with a five o'clock shadow that made him appear approachable. He was taller than her, and had very short hair that was a dark brown with blond highlights, no doubt from being out in the sun. "Actually, your timing is perfect as I was just looking for a distraction." Anything was better than going through the paperwork on her grandmother's estate.

"*Buenos dias*, Hannah. What are you doing here at this time of day with such a vaquero *guapo*?" Camila wiggled her brows before turning toward Brody. "What can I get you, cowboy?"

To his credit, Brody held his hand out toward her. "Hannah, do you know what you'd like?"

"I'll have a cup of coffee and your Tres Leches cake."

"You've got it. My abuela made a new one this morning." Camila turned to Brody again. "My grandmother makes the best Tres Leches cake in all of Arizona."

"That sounds good. I'll have a piece and some water."

Camila looked back at Hannah. "He's smart, too."

After Camila went back to put in their order, Brody hooked his thumb over his shoulder. "I'm guessing this is a regular spot for you?"

"It is. It's so close and has such great food. There's no reason to go much farther. Now please, I'm dying of curiosity. Why were you looking for my grandmother?"

"Your grandmother owns land in Four Peaks right next to my family's. It's—why are you shaking your head?"

She gave him a sad smile, because she'd really hoped that she would be able to see him again, but he had the wrong family. "My grandparents didn't own land in Four Peaks. I've been with them all my life. They raised me. Not once did they mention land there. In fact, we've lived in apartments in the city since I was a baby."

His brow furrowed. "But the public record shows Joseph and Norma Harper as the owners. It even has your apartment address as their address. You see, the land is pretty much empty."

Her address? That didn't make sense. "Would there be a need to pay taxes on the land? I took over my grandparents' finances eleven years ago. There was never a tax bill for any land in Four Peaks."

He sighed, his disappointment palpable. "I don't understand. I had hoped we were neighbors."

A spark of excitement hit her belly, surprising her. "I think maybe the deed office mixed up addresses. I can definitely check into it. I'm in the process of reading through the will and other paperwork since it was finalized in probate."

He opened his mouth to reply, but Camila came with their cake. Once she left, Hannah couldn't resist taking a bite before continuing their conversation. She closed her eyes and savored the first mouthful.

"Everything okay over there?"

She opened her eyes to find him giving her a crooked smile. "Sorry. I eat alone so often, I forget it might look weird. This cake is just so amazing. Go ahead, try it. But be sure to close your eyes and give the taste your full attention."

Humoring her, he took a forkful and looked at her as he put it in his mouth, then he closed his eyes. "Hmm." His eyes opened. "You're right. This is excellent. Do you think Camila's grandmother would share the recipe?"

She shook her head. "No. My grandmother asked many times. Does your wife bake?"

He coughed and covered his mouth as he'd just taken another bite. Holding up one finger, he took a gulp of water and cleared his throat. "Excuse me." He shook his head vigorously. "I'm not married."

He seemed to put emphasis on the word 'not.' Was that because he wanted her to know he was single or because the thought of being married freaked him out? She didn't expect that of a cowboy for some reason. "Then you want the recipe for your mother?"

"No, I want it for me. I enjoy baking. My oldest brother is an excellent cook, so I didn't want to be outdone, and became the family baker." He held up his fork with another piece of cake. "Don't get me wrong, I'm a good cook, but my baking skills are unsurpassed." He grinned before taking another bite. "I'm getting another piece to go. I'll figure this out."

"The recipe?" She stared at him in shock.

He nodded, then swallowed. "Yes. I do enjoy a challenge."

Learning that he could cook and bake made her wish more for a reason to see him again, but she could think of nothing. As lovely as it was to daydream about owning property north of the city, there was no way her grandparents could have ever afforded land. If they had, they would have lived there.

After they retired, they started to grow tired of city life. She'd always had the feeling they stayed for her. Yes, there were a lot of activities and places to go, but she'd love to live out on the Sonoran Desert. "Would you like me to let you know what I find out about the deed? They may give me more information about the property that could help, or—," she winked, "I may be able to get a hint as to where the owner is."

His eyes lit with pleasure. "You would do that for me?"

"Of course. I have the time. My days used to be filled with caring for my grandparents, but now..." She couldn't continue, not wanting to cry in front of a stranger.

He set down his fork and focused on her. "I'm very sorry for your loss and for bothering you at such a difficult time. I..." He looked past her. "I remember when we lost Mom. It tore me up inside. She'd always been my champion. and then she was gone." His gaze returned to her. "But that was long ago. I almost lost my father last year, but he's getting better. I think it must be even harder when you're older because you've known them for so long."

His remarks validated everything she felt and she wanted to reach across the table and hug him. "Thank you." Feeling far more comfortable with him than she should, she returned her attention to her half-eaten cake. "I do believe I'll consider this my dinner." She popped another piece into her mouth.

"I need to get back to the ranch. It's my turn to cook tonight." He shrugged. "I'm thinking barbeque hamburgers on the grill with a bit of potato salad on the side."

"Who are you cooking for?" She chastised herself for asking. It was none of her business.

"My father, my brother, myself, and my sister-in-law. And probably for Isaac, my dad's certified nursing assistant. He's always happy to help himself to leftovers, so we usually make sure there are leftovers." He grinned.

It sounded like he had a lot of family to get back to. She envied him that. "May I ask you why you were looking for the owner of the property next to yours?"

"Of course. I'm going to make an offer to buy it."

"Oh, why?" She waved off her comment. "Never mind. It's none of my business. If you can give me your phone number, I'll contact you after I get the mix-up figured out."

"I very much appreciate it."

After she added him to her phone, he took hers as well so he'd know who was contacting him. He typed her name into his phone. "H-a-n-n-a-h K-i-n-g-s-l-e-y T-r-e-s L-e-c-h-e-s. There. I'll remember you and our conversation now." He grinned confidently before pointing to her cake. "And if I figure out this recipe, I'm going to make a whole cake just for you as a thank you for helping me."

Her heart did a little dance at the thought that he would follow through, but she stomped down the feeling. He was probably just being nice. "And I'll be happy to eat it."

He rose, setting his hat back on his head. "It was a pleasure to meet you, Hannah. You made what could have been a disappointing trip a pleasure. Thank you."

She watched him walk up to the counter, get another piece of cake, and pay the bill before he turned toward her one more time, tipped his hat and exited Mama Juanita's.

Camila slipped into his empty seat. "Come, *chica*. Tell me all about this new man in your life."

Hannah took the final bite of her cake and wiped her mouth with her napkin. "Well, I met him about an hour ago and I'll never see him again."

"Say it ain't so!"

Standing, she shrugged. "It is. He was looking for someone else."

"Well, he's a catch. I'll wait on him any day." Camila waved her tip in the air.

"See you soon." Hannah turned and headed for the door.

"*Mañana*! Mama is making tamales!"

She waved as she strode out the door and headed back to her apartment. After climbing the three flights of stairs instead of taking the elevator, she opened the door and set her keys on the end table, closing the door with her hip. She locked it before kicking off her sandals.

The silence of the apartment had her halting. Grief made her turn off the television three days earlier, and the quiet still jarred her. It screamed that she was alone. She'd promised herself she'd turn it off when probate of her grandmother's estate was complete, giving herself those months to get used to the fact that the only two family members she had in the world were now gone.

She'd always lived with her grandparents, but after her grandfather passed away a year ago, Grandma kept the television on twenty-four-seven, claiming it was company. Hannah did have a part-time position working as a budget analyst, and she volunteered at the local food bank, but she wasn't gone that much. It wasn't lost on her that Grandma watched all the shows Grandpa used to watch, even though she'd ragged on him for watching them while he was alive.

Hannah had spent the last twenty years caring for them both, and now they were gone. She'd left the television going in hopes she could get used to being alone, but it hadn't helped. The silence didn't change that. It just made it more noticeable.

How nice it must be for Brody Dunn to have to rush home to cook for his family. Though he'd lost his mother, he still had everyone else, and some day he would have a wife and children of his own.

"You're not doing this, Hannah." Refusing to go down the dark hole of self-pity she'd been in for weeks after her grandmother died, she moved to the kitchen and pulled a bottle of water from the fridge; the chocolate-covered mints that her grandmother loved so much still sat on the second shelf. Quickly, she closed the door and opened the bottle. She could feel the burst of coolness from the water as it traveled down in her chest and settled in her stomach.

Determinedly, she walked into her bedroom and changed into a pair of leggings and a t-shirt. When she came back into the living room, the open folder with the will played with her conscience.

It wasn't as if she could call the state on the Kingsley mix-up as it was way too late in the day, so she might as well get everything read and filed away.

She turned toward the living room with the silent television and the folder on the coffee table she'd been avoiding for three days. She'd thought when her grandfather had passed, there would be a lawyer who would call her and her grandmother in to hear the reading of the will, like they showed on the family dramas her grandmother loved to watch. But that hadn't happened. Her grandmother had simply called their lawyer and everything was taken care of. She supposed that the reading of the will only happened with large, wealthy families.

Staring at the folder across the room, she tried to make her feet move, but she remained where she was. Something about reading the thin stack of papers made her grandparents' passing so final, as if their memories together would disappear and she'd be left completely alone. She shook her head and forced herself to walk the few feet to the couch and sit. Who was she kidding? She'd been completely alone since her grandmother breathed her last breath, quietly passing in her bed overnight. Reading a stack of legal papers wasn't going to change that or make it any worse...at least, that's what she hoped.

She basically knew what was in the folder. The will her grandparents had made over forty years before, the final probate papers, and the list of accounts she had made fourteen years earlier as she'd taken over the finances. With two Social Security checks and her job, they'd lived comfortably in the two-bedroom apartment. She had the paperwork to renew the lease for another year, but hadn't filled it out yet. She needed a one-bedroom unit on her part-time pay, but couldn't imagine leaving the last place she'd shared with her grandparents. But staying meant moving to full time, which her company would love her to do.

Either way she had a major life change ahead. Facing a whole year alone was too much to contemplate. Even so, maybe she should tackle that before the estate paperwork. *Hannah, never put off until tomorrow what you can do today.* She smiled sadly as one of her grandmother's many sayings flitted through her head.

She walked into the living room and flopped onto the old comfy couch before moving the television remote to the end table, resisting the urge to turn it on and lose herself in a sitcom for a while. Leaning forward, she opened the white folder with the lawyer's name embossed in gold on the outside. There were two pockets inside. On one side were copies of papers she'd sent him at his request, a letter from him, and a receipt of her final payment from the estate account. On the other side was the will. She'd never read it. Her grandmother had left instructions to turn everything over to the lawyer when the time came, and so she did.

Picking up the will, she set her feet on the coffee table and started to read. When she'd read the second paragraph and still wasn't sure what it all meant, she set it back on the table. Maybe she just needed to read something she understood first.

She pulled the pages from the other pocket that contained the lawyer's letter, receipt, and all the paperwork she'd handed over. As she separated her paperwork to put on the couch beside her, a check fell to the carpet. Had she paid the lawyer too much? Bending over she picked it up and stared. It was for $11,732.84. The check was made out to her. "What?"

Quickly, she read the memo of the generated check. "Tax remainder."

That wasn't right. Her grandparents didn't have to file taxes, because their Social Security wasn't high enough.

She set the check aside with everything else, but held onto the lawyer's letter. It started with the usual and thanked her for engaging him during her difficult time. Reading every word, she forced herself to stay focused.

Enclosed please find a check for $11,732.84, the remainder of the money Norma had with our firm for paying the property taxes on the land in Four Peaks. Since her will stated that everything was to go to you upon her passing, I have included the funds so you can choose how you wish to proceed. Though this is not a service we offer anymore, I would make an exception if you wish us to retain the money and pay the annual taxes.

Her heart leapt in her chest, making it hard to breathe. "Four Peaks?" That's what Brody Dunn had talked about.

She continued reading, but there was no other mention of the property.

She set the letter and check on the coffee table and started through the paperwork she'd given the lawyer, checking every page to make sure she didn't miss anything, but there was nothing about the property. Pulling the will from the coffee table, she focused on every word, but it simply mentioned that the land in Four Peaks was to go to her, not where it was, specifically.

Frustrated, she set the will aside and grabbed up the folder, shaking it. The corner of a white envelope peeked out from the pocket where the will had been. She pulled it out to find it sealed, her name on the front in her grandfather's handwriting. She blinked back tears and touched the lettering she hadn't seen in so long. Reverently, she opened the envelope, to find a letter, along with a faded document folded inside it.

She set the document aside and read.

> *My dearest, Hannah.*
>
> *If you are reading this, it means that your grandmother and I have left you, to be together for eternity. I don't want you to be sad. We lived fulfilling lives and were blessed with the opportunity to raise you and watch you grow into the intelligent and caring woman you are.*
>
> *Now, it's your time to live. We want you to be happy in your future, not stuck in our past. To that end, we are pleased to have left you our property in Four Peaks. We have owned it forever. In fact, we honeymooned there long*

ago and fell in love with it. We had planned to move there in our retirement, but then we lost your mother and father and decided you'd have more opportunities in Phoenix.

Now, the land is yours to do with as you wish. You can build there or sell it. All we ask is that you visit it and stay for a while before making a decision about it. This is our legacy to you. Our fervent hope is that someday you will find someone who will recognize the wonderful person you are and love you as you deserve. Maybe this property will be the start of a whole new life for you, no matter what you decide.

Remember, though you may feel alone, you will never be alone. We are with you always. We love you, Peach. Grandma and Grandpa.

She let the letter fall to her lap as she wiped at the tears falling down her cheeks. It was as if her grandparents had floated into the room to talk to her. Peace filled her. How could she think she was alone when their love was with her every day? Sniffing, she lifted the letter. She was amazed that her grandfather had kept the secret of the land her entire life. He was terrible at surprises. She couldn't count how many times he'd had to give her her birthday present days before her birthday, and Christmas was more like the twenty days of Christmas with him.

Sniffing again, she picked up the faded document, her vision still a bit blurry. "Eleven hundred acres?" That had to be wrong. It must be eleven acres. She wiped her eyes with her t-shirt and looked again. "Holy moly." It was eleven hundred acres! "What in the world?"

She couldn't seem to stop staring at the number, her heart pounding as she tried to wrap her head around the fact that she was the owner of a lot of land. She actually owned land. She'd never owned anything except her car, though she jointly owned it with the bank. But the land was hers. She could even live there!

As the reality settled, the possibilities exploded, and she jumped from the couch, sending the paperwork flying as she held the deed and danced. "I have property. I have property. I have—." She stopped and grinned. "I have a new neighbor."

CHAPTER 2

BRODY STUFFED the last bite of Tanner's three-cheese scrambled eggs in his mouth, chewing as he picked up his plate, and hopped off the stool at the counter. He set the dish on the floor and motioned Cami forward. His Great Pyrenees dog didn't hesitate, quickly lapping up the pieces he'd purposefully left.

"She's going to get fat." His older brother shook his head as if that would be the worst thing in the world.

"I wish." As far as he was concerned, she could still stand to gain a few more pounds, or ten. She'd been so malnourished when he found her in the hills, he'd probably never be satisfied with how much she weighed.

With the plate licked clean, he picked it up and walked around the kitchen island, dumping his dirty dish and coffee cup in the sink.

"What's the rush, Brody?"

He wouldn't let his oldest brother delay him. He washed

his hands as he answered. "I have to get out to Mesquite Road to meet our new neighbor."

Amanda, his sister-in-law, piped in. "He's meeting Miss Hannah Kingsley."

Her false sing-song voice, rubbed him the wrong way. "It's not a date, Mandy. This is important."

She sobered immediately. "I apologize. You're right."

Tanner stood, then came around the counter as well. "Good luck. If you can get her to sell, it means we'll be able to increase the herd and make the payments on the loans Dad took out for the new buildings. Then we will all be relieved."

He was well aware Tanner had doubts about the dude ranch thing paying off. "Not nearly as relieved as me." He grabbed two bottles of water and started for the front door. Cami followed him, her tail wagging. "Sorry, girl. I'll be out in the heat too long for you. When I get back, you can go for a swim."

Cami promptly sat on the entryway tile.

"Don't forget I'm meeting with the plumbers. You'll have to take the north fence-line run with Nash this afternoon."

Good thing Tanner reminded him. "Got it." Grabbing his hat from the entry table, he then crammed it on his head, gave Cami a pat on the back, and strode outside. The early morning heat hadn't yet reached triple digits, but he knew it would soon. He was counting on the heat to persuade the lovely Hannah that she was ill-suited for the land she'd inherited.

When he'd first seen her through the gap in her apartment door, he had been intrigued. But now having had cake with her and talking on the phone, he had a better idea of who she was—a city girl.

Striding into the stables, he stopped to give his horse Chaos a pat. "I'll be back soon." He continued down the row of stalls until he came to the ATV. He began to roll the machine out, when he stopped. He turned and grabbed a helmet from the hook. Hannah had auburn hair which would soak up the heat of the sun. The helmet would help protect her from that and if they had an accident, not that they would with him driving, but it didn't hurt to be careful.

Once outside, he started up the ATV and drove down the mile-long rocky road that served as the ranch's driveway. After getting Hannah's call, he'd stayed up late, excited. He doubted it would take long to convince her to sell. Then he would be free of the ranch. It wasn't such a bad place. He just needed a change and to spread his wings, as his mother always told him. He felt during the last five years as if his wings had been clipped and were finally growing back.

When he reached Mesquite Road, he turned off the ATV and waited. He was early, as usual, but he was anxious to show Miss Hannah Kingsley her land. Once she saw how far away it was and how empty it was, she'd be thrilled to have his family buy it from her. With the money from the sale, she could do anything, go anywhere. Part of him envied her that. He'd been trying to do that for years.

When Hannah had called him and said she'd just discovered she owned the land, he'd been hard-pressed not to let out a shout. Convincing an elderly couple to part with their land, even though they'd been asked several times before, would have been possible but difficult, even though he would offer more than it was worth. But with an attractive woman his age, like Hannah, getting her to sell should be a breeze. She was used to city life and had just discovered she owned the land, so she had no emotional attachment to it. That added up to success.

Dust in the distance on Mesquite Road had him stepping off the ATV. As the slow-going vehicle came closer, he felt as if the gates to his future were opening. Either that or the gates to his prison. He'd almost escaped twice before, but this time, his father was going to let him walk free to pursue his own dreams.

As excited as he was, he started to grow inpatient as it became obvious the vehicle wasn't just moving slowly but traveling at a snail's pace. If that's how she drove on dirt roads, what would she think of seeing her property on the ATV? Then again, the bumpy ride might make her more inclined to sell.

When they'd met at the restaurant, he'd found her to be pleasant and easy to look at, but she was a born-and-bred city girl. There was no walking to the corner Mexican spot for dinner out in the desert. Heck, from Rocky Road Ranch, the drive into town took almost a half-hour, though by the way she drove, he would estimate a good hour.

Finally, the car pulled into the driveway and under the sign above it that declared it Rocky Road Ranch. The door opened and Hannah stepped out in a pink tank top, white shorts, and tennis shoes.

Despite how inappropriate her outfit was for walking the desert, he appreciated how warm the pink top made her round face appear. She really did have attractive round, light-brown eyes. "Welcome to the Rocky Road Ranch."

She looked up at the sign and then at him. "Where's your ranch?"

He jerked his thumb over his shoulder. "It's right here. The house is about a mile in."

"A mile? Is your driveway better than this road. I don't think I've ever been on such a bumpy one."

He swallowed a chuckle. "Actually, our ranch is named for this mile drive."

"Oh." She walked toward him. "It's very different out here. Is my driveway the same, as in bumpy and long?"

"Not exactly. There really isn't a driveway onto your property."

"How can there not be a driveway?" She cocked her head to the side, causing her long hair to fall off her shoulder and behind her.

He spread his arms wide. "Out here, it's just desert, so unless you're using the land, nature does her own thing."

She smiled, appearing far more happy with his explanation than he would have liked. "I can't wait to see it. Should I follow you?"

She still didn't get it. The road ended at Rocky Road simply because no one had used her land in decades. "No. You'd better hop on the ATV with me. Your car wouldn't like the terrain."

"You want me to get on that with you and ride out into the deserted desert?"

It took him a moment to grasp her hesitancy, but understanding dawned. She was used to the city, where riding about alone with a man could be dangerous. "I know it seems a little strange to you, but out here, we all know each other and help each other. We're brought up to respect women and the land we make our living from. You could say it's in our soul."

Not sure what he'd said to make her relax, but she smiled, making her whole face glow with pleasure. "I forgot I'm not in the city anymore, though how I could in the middle of nowhere is beyond me." She clicked her car lock and pocketed the key. "Lead on."

He showed her where to sit and handed her the helmet. "You should probably wear this. Not only is it safer, but it will keep the sun from beating down on your head."

She nodded and obediently donned the helmet.

He climbed in front of her and patted his waist. "You'll also want to hold on." Then he started up the ATV.

Once her hands came around his waist tentatively, he started forward. By the first bump, she was holding tight.

He hoped that the path to her property would be enough for her to want to sell, but he wasn't going to place any bets. Sometimes what appeared to be an easy thing, turned out far harder than expected, like last week, when he'd forgotten that life lesson and brought a rope to pull Nash, his ranch hand and good friend, out of the muck, only to have the rope break and the ATV sink deeper.

It was over a mile to the Kingsley property, and for a first-timer on an ATV, he had no doubt she'd need a break, so he slowed the ATV down when they had gone almost a mile. He looked over his shoulder. "We still have about a half mile to go. How you doing?"

"I'm okay. Let's keep going."

A little surprised by that, he imagined she was anxious to see what she'd inherited. He was just glad she found out about it or he would have never had a chance to convince her to sell.

Finally, they hit the edge of her property. He slowed the ATV and stopped it just over the Rocky Road Ranch line. He turned off the engine and got off. Holding his hand out, he helped her down, steadying her as she caught her balance.

She unbuckled the helmet and pulled it off. He almost expected her to shake out her hair like they did in hair commercials, but she didn't. In fact, the helmet had matted her hair down and creased it where it had been blowing below the helmet. "Wow, I've never been on an ATV. That's fun. Do you ride it often in your work?"

Taken aback at her enthusiasm, he shook his head. "Sometimes, but we generally prefer to ride our horses, especially when driving the cattle. It's less stressful on them." He opened up the back of the ATV and pulled out the water bottles. "Here. You want to stay hydrated out here." He opened his and took a swallow, glad it was still a little cool.

"Thank you. You have horses? Of course you do. Does yours have a name?"

"Um, yeah. It's Chaos."

"Chaos? I bet there's a story behind that." She opened her bottle of water and took a sip.

Not entirely comfortable with that particular subject, he

pointed to the north. "Your property directly abuts two of the four peaks, the eastern ones. Ours abuts the western ones. The land after that is state land."

She lifted her hand to shade her eyes. "That seems a long way away. I really have no concept of what eleven-hundred acres looks like."

"Out here, it's enough for a medium-sized cattle ranch, but that's about it. If you look to the east," he pointed again, "you can see some powerlines in the distance. Your property ends just before them."

She turned in the direction he pointed. "I don't see any power lines. They must be very far." She turned back, looking at the mountains and then past him. "This is a bit overwhelming."

He nodded, pleased that she could see what a big responsibility it would be to own the land. "I understand. I'd be hard pressed to oversee that much land all by myself."

"If my land and your family's are up against the four mountains, then why is the town called Four Peaks? I would think it would be a different name."

It took him a minute to follow the switch in topic. "It's the view. Town is at a higher elevation than the valley we're in here, so all four peaks are visible. From here, it's difficult to see the outlying ones."

She took another sip of water, then raised her hand again to shade her eyes and looked to the east. "Now I get it." She dropped her hand and looked at him. "There's so much to learn."

Not if she sold. He kept his thought to himself. "Did you

want to see any more? Obviously, it would take a whole day to see it all, and you said you had to be back in Phoenix by early afternoon." He gulped down more of his water. The sun was already scorching the earth. It had to have reached over a hundred.

"I do, but I still have a couple of hours. Didn't you say there were buildings on the property? I'd like to see them."

He'd forgotten he'd mentioned that. "There were buildings. I know the shed blew down in a haboob about seven years ago. Honestly, I'm surprised it made it that long. I haven't been there in over a year, but last I knew the casita was still standing."

She squinched her face. "Would you be willing to take me to it? I know I'm imposing, but I really don't have anyone else I can ask."

Actually, that would be perfect. Once she saw how small the building was and there was nothing else out here but snakes and burrows, she'd be ready to sell in a heartbeat. "I'd be happy to. It's not too far. Just a couple more miles in." He downed the rest of his water and threw the empty bottle back in the compartment.

"Thank you. This means so much to me. To be able to see the property my grandparents honeymooned on really brings me full circle." Her smile was wide before she took another sip and put her half-empty bottle into the compartment as well.

At her gratefulness, he felt guilt crawling up his back. While today for him was about trying to purchase her land, for her it was about the memories of her grandparents. He did hope it brought her some closure. "Then let's see if we can complete that circle." He held his hand out to the ATV and she climbed on, before quickly pulling on the helmet.

He straddled the seat and her arms came around him.

"You can go faster this time. That is, if you don't mind me holding tight."

He nodded and turned the machine on. Though he was surprised she enjoyed the ride, he was more than willing to pick up the pace. As for her holding tight, he kind of liked that.

He didn't gun it, instead increasing their speed so she could get used to it. As he hit a straight spot without a ton of cacti and shrubs in the way, he gunned it. Her shout of pleasure reminded him of his first ATV ride at the age of four. They were definitely from completely different worlds.

He drove parallel to what was the Rocky Road Ranch driveway though they couldn't see it. When he got to the place where his house was, he turned toward the mountains. He didn't know the history of the casita, but he imagined it was built on the same longitudinal line as his family's house to make it easier to be neighborly, though no one had lived there his entire life and maybe even his father's life.

Taking down the speed a bit as he headed north, he kept scanning the landscape. He didn't know the property as well as his own and he didn't want to miss it.

Hannah's squeezed his waist and yelled in his ear. "Is that it to the right?"

He looked to where she pointed briefly before grabbing his waist again. "Yes." He adjusted their course a bit and brought them within fifty feet of the building before halting.

"Oh, I can't wait to see this!"

At Hannah's exclamation, alarm bells went off. He got off the ATV, and before he could say anything, she'd jumped off, only to stumble a bit. He grabbed her arm to help her regain her balance.

"Thank you. I didn't realize my equilibrium was so delicate."

He let go when she lifted her hands up to take off the helmet. She set it on the machine before turning to look at the adobe building, barely discernable from the cacti and Goat's Beard vines growing over it and against it.

"If it wasn't so flat out here, I would have never noticed this. I wonder if it was here even before my grandparents bought the land."

"My guess is it's been here at least sixty years." He'd hoped that would make her shy away, but that wasn't her reaction at all. In fact, her eyes widened with glee.

"Wow. That's just amazing." With that, she started forward.

Quickly, he grabbed her arm. "Whoa there, where you going?"

"I'm going inside, of course."

He planted his feet, still not letting go. "I wouldn't suggest it. That building has been abandoned to the desert. That means nature could have taken it over including animals, reptiles, and insects."

She blinked as if considering that for the first time. "Would any of them be dangerous? I mean, beside tarantulas. I do know they live out here."

He called on his patience, which he wasn't known for. She was simply ignorant of the dangers of the Sonoran

Desert. He let go of her arm and stepped between her and the building to face her. He wanted her to know how serious he was. "Yes, there could be tarantulas, but also rattlesnakes, raccoons, or even javelinas, not to mention the walls could cave in."

She eyed the building, hopefully seeing what he saw. "I didn't realize. I guess we'll have to investigate carefully."

As she stepped around him, he stood in shock for a moment before his senses caught on that he needed to protect her. Spinning around, he strode up next to her. "I wouldn't advise going inside."

She glanced at him, but kept her focus on the building. "Thank you. I still want to see it."

Beyond picking her up and carrying her back to the ATV, there was nothing he could do. It was her land and her old casita. Still, he wouldn't let her get hurt. Luckily, she started by walking around the structure. She stopped and pointed away from it to a pile of rotted wood on the ground. "Was that the shed?"

"Yes. There was more wood, but a lot has rotted back into the ground."

She didn't respond, instead continuing her walk around the building. Finally, she stopped at the front door, which was made of thick ironwood, being held on by rusty hinges. "It's beautiful."

He frowned, not sure he heard her right. "Did you say it's beautiful?"

She pulled out her phone and took a picture. "Yes, the way nature has wrapped its arms around this manmade structure as if to protect it. Don't you think it's poignant?"

Staring at the vine-covered walls and a mesquite that towered over the roof, he tried to see what she saw. But he couldn't. "It definitely makes a statement...to be careful."

She shook her head at him before moving forward toward the door.

His hand shot out before he could take it back, and she halted. "Is something wrong."

"Just go slow. I don't want you to get hurt."

Her warm brown gaze softened. "I promise, I'll be careful.

Nodding, he curled his fingers into fists as she pushed a few vines aside, ducked beneath them, and opened the door.

Hannah studied the room in front of her. She was well aware that Brody didn't want her to get hurt, but from the moment she saw the structure, she trusted it. He'd never understand because even she didn't. In fact, she was more than a little afraid of every critter he named.

Inside what must have once been white-washed walls was a very homey atmosphere, especially with the greenery crawling over the windows outside. There was a still brightly tiled counter that had an old-fashioned gas stove. Wood littered the kitchen area, which was probably formerly a table. It looked like it had been purposefully broken. There was no fridge, but there was a sink. Did plumbing rot? She had no idea. She'd lived in apartments her entire life.

She carefully stepped around the wood from the table. On the other wall was an old couch, though the material had dry-rotted in the heat, and some of the stuffing had been pulled out, probably by a small animal. She liked to think the critter used it to make a nest, preferably outside. The rattan coffee table that matched it had two collapsed legs, making it into a slide for mice, if the tiny black dots at the end were any indication. Mice droppings she knew, as they'd had a few apartments with mice.

At the back was an open doorway. Moving toward it, she heard something run under the wood behind her.

"Hannah, you probably don't want to go any further. I don't even know if this roof will hold for the next two minutes."

At Brody's words, she glanced up. The rafters didn't look rotten, and the wood above them showed no leakage from her to where he stood just inside the building. "I appreciate your concern, but I have to see the rest." How could she make someone, who lived in a house with family on a piece of land they owned, understand what it was like for her? He couldn't. This little place had belonged to her grandparents. It had been their dream, and they'd left their dream in her hands, for her, to become her dream if she wished it to be.

"Then let me go first. I'm wearing jeans and boots which are better protection from a snake bite than bare legs and tennis shoes."

To hear someone be concerned about her after being alone for six months had her eyes itching again. She really needed to hold it together. "Okay." She waited for him to step around the mess in the kitchen and move toward the open doorway. She followed and this time she saw a critter hop from a piece of wood to the wall. A gecko. She breathed easier since she was used to them.

"Wait here." He blocked the doorway, forcing her to stop.

She hadn't realized how bossy he could be, but she did as he commanded.

He moved into the room which was clearly a bedroom, then he disappeared through another doorway briefly before coming out. "Okay. It doesn't look like anything is living in this section."

As she stepped into the room, she could imagine how it had been when her grandparents had been young and in love. She'd seen pictures of them, so it was easy to envision her grandmother making the wooden bed that still dominated the room. She walked up to the bed and held onto the large ironwood bedpost. Had her grandfather built it or bought it? Either way, it still looked very sturdy. Though the mattress had the same holes as the couch cushions, the rest of the room seemed relatively untouched by the desert and its inhabitants.

Moving to the other doorway, she found a small bathroom. There was no mirror over the sink, and the shower was metal, but there was also no toilet. She stepped out to see where Brody was. He remained next to the bed watching her. "Do you think they had a toilet over that hole?"

"Of course. Sixty years ago isn't the stone age. Trespassers probably took it."

"A toilet? What would they want with that? I'd think the bed would be more worth their while?"

He shrugged, clearly not that interested. "It could be

campers wanting to embellish their campsite or college kids out on a dare."

Obviously, she had led a rather sheltered life that didn't include stealing toilets. "I imagine the fridge is missing for the same reason?"

He just shrugged.

She moved back to the bed, an irrational need to touch a place that her grandparents had been motivating her. Running her hand over the headboard, she marveled at how thick it was. Getting such a large piece of furniture out this far had to have been a labor of love.

A sound at the door to the casita had Brody immediately moving in that direction. She hurried after him to see what it was.

"Shoo! Get!"

She stepped outside to find a burro had pushed the helmet she'd worn off the ATV and was trying to step on it with his hoof. She'd never seen a burro in the wild. "He's so cute."

Brody sent her a glare before yelling once more. "Go on! That's not yours!"

The burro let out a loud bray, which struck her as funny. "I don't think he's happy with you."

"I'm not happy with him either." Brody scooped up the helmet and brushed it off.

The burro let out another loud bray before giving up on his prize.

She walked to the ATV. "Are there a lot of wild burros out here? Do you have any as pets?"

He stared at her for a long while, then finally answered.

"Yes, and absolutely not. They're ornery and think they own the desert."

She looked around them before turning back to him. "Well, they kind of do."

The tension left his shoulders and a crooked grin relaxed his face. "Yeah, I guess they do out here. Are you ready to go back? I do have to get back to the ranch soon."

"Oh yes, of course. I should have realized that." She held her hand out for the helmet, chastising herself for being so selfish. Was that part of living alone, forgetting others had lives too?

"I don't want to rush you. After all, who else is there to show you the land you inherited? As you can imagine, it's worth a lot to cattle ranchers like my family." He gave her the helmet.

"I'm very grateful. This has given me a lot to think about." She pulled the helmet on and buckled the strap before turning toward the casita once more. There was something about the little building that made her feel bad for leaving it. Shaking off the thought, she climbed onto the ATV. Once Brody sat and started the machine, she grasped him about the waist. She didn't mind in the least. Despite the heat of the day, he smelled good, like cut cedar.

As he drove them across the desert and back to her vehicle, she tried to enjoy the ride like she had when they'd come out, but her mind was a whirr of ideas and possibilities. When she said she had a lot to think about, she hadn't quite realized exactly how much there was. Her new land was the start of a new life, whether she sold it to the Dunns or kept it for herself. That feeling of being at a fork in the road with both paths leading to exciting newness and growth had her spirits almost jubilant by time Brody brought the ATV to a stop.

She practically jumped off the machine, unbuckling the helmet. Beyond grateful and happy for all he had done for her, she gave him a hug after he swung his leg off to stand next to her. "Thank you so much for everything." When she stepped back, she noticed a flush creeping up his neck.

"I'm happy I could help. Like I said, around here we just do that."

He may feel like it was nothing unusual, but for her, it was life-changing. "It was more than that. You're the one who told me about the property and then showed it to me. That's just plain kindness, and I appreciate that more than you know." The thought of how alone she was once again swept in like a thundercloud, and she swallowed hard to keep from tearing up. He'd think her a blubberhead.

"I'm happy I could help you." He hesitated as if he wasn't sure what to say next. "If you want to see it again, or more of it, just let me know. I'll check in on you in a few days."

She grinned, her good humor restored. "Because that's the neighborly thing to do?"

"Yeah." Once again, he looked uncomfortable, but at least no red colored his skin.

She dug her key fob out of her pocket and unlocked her car.

He immediately stepped up and opened the driver door for her.

A little surprised, it took her a moment to move. "Thank you." She sat on the driver's seat and turned the engine on, hot air blowing from the air conditioner vents. She pulled the sunshield off the window and grabbed the dishtowel from her console between her seats and laid it over the hot steering wheel.

Brody leaned over her open door, his denim shirt protecting him from the hot metal. "Have a safe drive home."

She nodded, and he shut the door for her. She waved.

He tipped his hat before striding toward the ATV.

How had she not noticed what a cute butt he had? "Hannah, you stop that right now. He's either your neighbor or your buyer."

Stepping on the accelerator, she started down the long dirt track called Mesquite Road, which would lead to Black Spur Road and then to Main Street. She really should explore the town of Four Peaks to see what it offered, but she needed to get back and change. She'd promised her grandmother's friend she'd help her and her husband with their taxes for their small business. She was an expert with budgets, not taxes, but she'd been helping them for years as a favor to her grandparents. So far, everything had worked out.

As she pulled onto the highway heading west before going south to Phoenix, she contemplated going back to school for another degree. She loved learning and debating, and was probably in the minority as she enjoyed doing research. If she sold the land, she could afford a master's degree. Yet even as the thought occurred to her, the image of the little casita standing out in the middle of the desert all alone filled her head.

The casita was like her, alone in a big world with no purpose anymore.

What was she thinking? A building didn't feel. People felt. She was imposing feelings on the casita because it belonged to her grandparents. That's all it was. Still, keeping the land was the other option. She needed to look at both options fully. The only way to do that was type up the pros and cons of each. Yes, that's what she'd do and look at the options logically.

"Sure you will."

CHAPTER 3

BRODY YANKED the fence wire up. "Get her under!"

"I'm trying." Nash held his arms out and waved at the stubborn calf, but she decided to lie down rather than move back into the field.

"Forget it." He let go, straightened, and yanked his gloves off. He pulled his bandana out of his back pocket and wiped the sweat from his neck. A loud moo sounded behind him. Turning, he faced Lulabelle, Tanner's cow crush and mother to the errant calf. "Why'd you let her go out there in the first place?"

The cow just stared at him as if he were worthless.

He opened his arms toward the mom. "What? She's your kid. Takes after you, too, you stubborn prima donna."

"I don't think she's impressed." Nash, his best friend and a ranch hand on the Rocky Road, ducked between the temporary wire before stepping up next to Lulabell. "What do you want to try next? There's always food."

Brody stuffed his bandana back in his pocket. "Great idea, but I don't have any, do you?"

"Whoa, what's got your panties in an uproar? You've been snapping all day, and don't tell me it's the heat. That's a daily occurrence." As if to accent his statement, he pulled off his hat and wiped the sleeve of his forearm across the light brown hair plastered to his forehead before placing his hat back on.

Shit. Nash was right. "Sorry, just got other crap on my mind that's frustrating the heck out of me."

Nash left off soothing Lulabell and came to stand next to him. "Is it that Kingsley property?"

"Yeah. I showed it to Miss Hannah last week and called her a few days ago, but she hasn't called back." He pulled his phone from his other back pocket and looked at it. "I even texted her this morning and nothing."

"She's ghosting you?"

He gripped his phone at that. "She better not be. I know where she lives. I can always go knock on her door and ask what's going on."

Nash resettled his hat on his head, something he always did when thinking. "I know you're anxious to move on, but you said she just found out she owns the land. She may simply need some time."

"But she could at least respond. I didn't even mention buying the land last I saw her. I'm not that selfish."

"You're not selfish at all or you wouldn't still be on this ranch. You have a point, but I still say give her a few more days before showing up on her doorstep. Discovering she owns a bunch of desert with burros and geckos is one thing, but having a handsome cowboy trying to buy it from her is a whole other ball game." Nash nudged him with his shoulder.

"You have a good point. This handsome face probably sent her heart a-flutter." He fluttered his lashes.

Nash groaned before walking away. "That may be, but it's doing nothing for Lulabell here. Save the face for tomorrow night at The Stampede pool tournament, and put what's under that hat of yours to work on how to get this calf back in here. You know if you lasso her, Lulabell will have you on your back in three seconds."

He did know that and it wasn't something he wanted to experience...again. "We just need to corral her so she—wait, I wonder if Cami could help."

"It's worth a try. Why don't you go get her and I'll stay here. I know your brother doesn't like us out here alone, but you're coming right back."

It was a good plan and if it worked, he might be able to use Cami more often. The dog was still an unknown, but he connected with her immediately when he'd found her. Some asshole had abandoned her. Now, she slept on his bed every night and loved learning new things. "Let's do it."

He mounted Chaos and headed for the house. Cami was better suited to colder climes, which is why he made her stay indoors during the day. His father certainly didn't mind, though Jeremiah Dunn would never admit it, after having forbidden pets decades ago. Mandy had even incorporated Cami into his dad's therapies, now that he was doing a lot more.

He was glad his brother married Amanda. She brought his father a lot further than he'd expected after the massive stroke. Once Dad was as good as he was going to get, then Amanda could help on the ranch, which would make it even easier for him to leave.

As he drew closer to the house, the three bunk houses set in a U for their new dude ranch operation came into view. They were done and ready for guests, but from what he understood, there was a lot more to be done, including finishing the club house and marking new trails. There would be more employees, too, which made him that much more dispensable. His future was calling him, and it wasn't on the ranch. Too bad Hannah wasn't calling him, too.

He dismounted at the porch of his dad's three-thousand-foot adobe ranch house, and looped Chaos's reins over the hook to let him munch at the hay feeder there. As soon as he opened the front door, he heard Cami's paws racing across the travertine tile. He stopped and braced himself. In the next instant his arms were full of ninety-five pounds of white fur. "Did you miss me?"

Cami licked at his face, and he strained his neck to avoided being slobbered on the mouth. Letting her down, he ruffled her neck. "How'd you like to come work with me?"

She cocked her head as if trying to understand.

"You want to go out?"

This time she jumped up on him again and he laughed. "Okay." He stepped to the kitchen doorway but no one was in sight, so he yelled. "I'm taking Cami with me!"

"Okay." The muffled reply came from his father's office, which surprised him. Either Amanda was working in there, or she had his dad in there. Though curious, he let the matter go. Tanner would give him shit if he knew Nash was out on the north line alone.

As he stepped outside, he realized Cami would need the ATV. He wasn't going to let her run all the way out there. "Come on, girl. We're going for a ride." He took Chaos with them and settled him in his stall, then patted the seat of the ATV. Immediately. Cami jumped up.

Settling in behind his large dog, he was on his way back in no time, but he took it slow. He needed to figure out a way to strap Cami in. Maybe there was something he could pull behind him. He'd go online later and see what he could find.

As he drew closer, he could see Nash no longer stood within the boundary. In fact, he seemed to be hiding behind the large boulder they had moved, when it had crashed through their wooden fence. It wasn't until Lulabell turned at the sound of the ATV that he realized his mistake. "Shit."

Quickly, he drove the ATV to the fence fifty yards from the mad cow and shut it off. "Come on, Cami." He coaxed his dog down off the seat and ducking, led her between the rails of the wooden fence just as he heard the steps of a running cow. What was he thinking, to bring the very dog that had scared Lulabell so badly that to protect her calf, she'd knocked down half the birthing enclosure two months ago?

"Come, girl." He patted his thigh and Cami obediently followed him down the fence line. He stopped before the wire fencing started, just in case. "Nash, are you hiding?"

"Damn right." He pointed to Lulabelle. "She charged me."

He swallowed a chuckle. "That's because you weren't helping. Where's the calf?"

"Over there by that saguaro."

The little calf had wandered at least twenty yards away. No wonder her mother was beside herself. He crouched down next to Cami, who sat watching the little calf. "Okay, girl. I want you to herd that little one this way. Can you do it?"

Cami didn't look at him, her gaze locked on the baby.

He had no idea if she'd hurt the little one. Lulabell obviously thought her a threat. In fact, mama was starting to make a racket with strong bellows.

The little calf turned its head toward mom. Did it get that Lulabell was upset?

He kept his hand on Cami, not sure if letting her go towards the cow would be a good thing. The last thing he needed was for Lulabell to charge the wire fence and get cut. "Nash, can you move behind the calf?"

"Sure." Nash walked slowly toward the calf.

The little thing looked at Nash then back at mom, but didn't move.

"I need you to call Cami to you. I'm going to lift the wire in case the calf runs for mom or mom runs for the calf. Got it?"

At Nash's nod, he let go of Cami. "Go see Nash, girl."

She hesitated until Nash yelled for her. As soon as she ran toward him, Brody strode to the wire.

Lulabell immediately bellowed and started for the fence. He stretched the wire as high as he could, but if mama didn't duck, she was going to get caught.

"Here she comes!"

At Nash's yell, Brody looked over his shoulder to see the calf running toward him, Cami jogging behind. "Good girl!"

The wire jerked out of his hands as Lulabell hit it. She backed up a step ready to make another go, but he grabbed it again and lifted just as the little calf ran under to her mother. Immediately, he dropped the line, his hands burning and bleeding.

Cami ran up and sat in front of him. "Well done, girl." He folded his fingers in and stroked her with his knuckles, not wanting to turn her white coat red because he was an idiot and forgot to put his gloves on again.

Lulabell had stopped her bawling and was now making soft humming noises even as she nudged her calf away from the fence.

Nash strode toward him. "Well, that worked. Whoever said animals don't feel emotions has never met Lulabell."

Too impressed with how Cami handled herself to spare much thought on Tanner's lovesick cow, he wiped his hands on his jeans.

"Where're your gloves?"

He scowled, ignoring the question. "We need to get that new fencing up tomorrow. It was put on the back burner because of the dude ranch build, but we can't afford to lose any cows while that thing gets up and running."

"I'll let you tell Tanner it's a priority. When I talk to him about the herd, he seems to only be half listening." Nash shook his head as if thinking about anything beyond cattle was a serious defect in personality.

Brody ducked under the wire and back into the field, now

that Lulabell was far enough away. "Yeah. He's really nervous about this new dude ranch enterprise working and keeping the ranch alive. Tells you what he thinks of my persuasion skills." He couldn't help the resentment that colored his tone.

Nash slapped him on the back. "Well, he's obviously lost touch with your skills. I've seen you convince a woman with no rhythm to dance with you, and an old woman who never gives samples of her baked goods at the fair to let you have a taste. I'd bet a hundred bucks you could get a thirsty man to give you his last beer."

His friend's words did soothe his ego. Nash knew him even better than his big brother. So there was that. He stopped at the ATV. "I appreciate it, though to be fair, the young woman who had no rhythm didn't need it for that slow dance."

Nash laughed as he continued to his horse. "See, and that was your luck. The band at Boots n' Brew suddenly slowing it down like that. If I didn't know better, I'd say you paid them to do that."

He grinned as he remembered that spring night. "To be honest, the thought had crossed my mind. She really had no dance moves at all, but she was a great kisser." He started up the ATV. "See you back at the barn. Come on, Cami." He patted the seat in front of him and she jumped up.

As Nash mounted up, Brody headed back toward the house. He was halfway there when he felt his phone vibrate. Stopping the ATV, he adjusted Cami so he could look at the caller. Seeing Hannah's name, he quickly shut the machine off. "Howdy, Hannah."

"Oh, Brody. I'm so relieved it's you."

Now that made no sense at all since she called him. "Who did you think you called?"

A soft chuckle came across the phone. "I'm just relieved. My phone fell in a pot of boiling pasta at the Community Dine-in Center. Not only did we have to throw the whole batch out, but when I went to get a new phone, they were having a hard time transferring all my contacts. It took days."

So that was why she didn't get back to him. "You didn't get my text this morning?"

"You texted? Hold on."

He clamped his mouth shut, not really caring anymore that she hadn't responded. He just wanted to know what she planned to do next, specifically with the land.

"Well, sugar. My notifications were muted. I'm sorry."

"No problem. I was just texting to see if you had any more questions about the property."

"You're so thoughtful. Thank you. I've been doing some research. In fact, I've booked a room at the Lucky Lasso Saloon and Hotel in Four Peaks for the weekend. Do you know where that is?"

"I do." Everyone did. There were only two hotels in town, and then the campgrounds and an RV park.

"Wonderful. Would you be able to meet me there on Friday sometime? I'd like your input on some ideas I have."

Excitement and nervousness collided in his gut. On one hand, he was thrilled she was looking at him as a friend she could listen to, but the word 'ideas' made him nervous. Was she hoping to start ranching herself or some other enterprise? "I'd be happy to help. Is seven too early?"

"Seven PM?"

He patted Cami as he grinned. "No, AM. If that's too early, I can come later."

"No, no. That's fine. I'll buy you breakfast."

"I accept. I'll see you Friday then."

As she thanked him and hung up, Cami turned her head and slobbered a wet one on his cheek. "Ugh, really?" He wiped his face with his sleeve. "Let's get you home." He started up the ATV again, held onto Cami, and headed for the barn.

Even in that short conversation, he learned a bit more about Miss Hannah Kingsley. He didn't know anyone who used 'sugar' instead of 'shit.' So she obviously didn't swear. She'd dropped her phone while volunteering, which meant she had a kind heart. She wasn't afraid to learn, as she'd done research and had ideas. It could all help him persuade her to sell.

He pulled up to the barn, and no sooner had he stopped the machine than Cami jumped down. As he rolled the ATV back into its spot, his conscience started to niggle at him.

The fact was, Hannah had called him for help, as someone she trusted. She would be taking him into her confidence. He sighed, knowing he'd have to remind her he wanted to buy the property. He needed to be upfront with his motives.

Still, as he walked toward the house, Cami running ahead of him, he couldn't wait until Friday morning.

CHAPTER 4

HANNAH GRABBED her purse and exited her hotel room. Even coming in the night before so she wouldn't be late, she was barely going to make it downstairs before Brody arrived. Was he an on-time kind of person or a five-minutes-late type of person? It was weird how little she knew about him and yet how much she trusted him. He had gone out of his way to help her, plus he was a cowboy. Those two reasons alone had her guard down.

She rushed down the grand stairs of the Old West-themed hotel. When she'd looked it up online, she knew she had to stay there. It was toward one end of the Main Street of Four Peaks, so a great place for exploring the town. Plus, the 1800s décor was adorable, with its curved grand staircase into the lobby, the pale pink wallpaper with red roses, clawfoot tubs, and four-posted beds. The owner, Mrs. Ava Gutierrez, who was not much older than she was, was a sweetheart. She had an aquiline nose, thin shaped eyebrows, and long, straight black hair that she kept in a bun at the nape of her neck. Though she let her staff dress more casually, she always appeared incredibly neat, not a hair out of place.

Once on the first floor, Hannah started to walk past the front desk toward the large window that looked onto the street, so she could watch for Brody.

"Miss Kingsley, Brody is waiting for you in the dining room."

She stopped in midstride and looked at Ava. "He is?"

The woman nodded. "Yes, he is. That man is always early, especially when a woman is involved." Ava rolled her eyes as if with Brody, there was always a woman involved.

That gave Hannah pause. "You know him well?" Now, that was a stupid question.

Ava chuckled even as she moved to the ringing phone. "We all do. This is a small town, Miss Kingsley. Everyone knows everyone." The woman answered the call. "Good morning. The Lucky Lasso Hotel and Saloon. This is Ava Gutierrez. How may I make your day wonderful?"

For some reason, Ava's answer made her feel better. If everyone knew everyone, then she could find out a lot about Brody, the Dunns, the other landowners, and even the best place for enchiladas. It would also be hard to be dishonest and have no one know, which would fit her own needs perfectly.

Quickly, she made her way to the dining room. As she stepped past the small arched entry, she barely had time to notice the pale pink drapes on the windows or the white tablecloths on the small round tables, before Brody waved his arm and caught her attention. Smiling, she made her way across the ironwood floor, stepping in-between the tables, over half of them filled already. Either the room had a lot of locals who got up early, or the guests were anxious to get on with their day.

Brody stood and held out a chair for her. "Good morning."

His smile warmed her while his manners charmed her. "Thank you." He slid her chair in as she sat. "Good morning to you, too. If I had known you're always early, I would have been down sooner. I had the most wonderful sleep."

His brows raised as he took his seat. "Now you have me doubly curious. How do you know I'm always early and—oh, Ava. Never mind. I'm glad you had a good rest. I rarely sleep well if not in my own bed." He picked up a carafe on the table. "Coffee?"

"Absolutely. I can barely think without some caffeine in the morning."

He poured hers, then topped off his own.

How long had he been waiting? "I'm so glad you could make time to meet with me today. I have so much I want to talk with you about. Ever since I discovered I inherited the land next to Rocky Road Ranch, my mind has been spinning with possibilities. I'd very much appreciate your honest opinion and experienced knowledge."

He set his cup down and opened his mouth to reply when the waitress came over. "Well, Brody Dunn. I haven't seen you in here since New Year's Day." The young blonde woman paused. "Funny, you don't look hungover."

Hannah pursed her lips to keep from laughing, because from the looks of the red flush creeping up Brody's neck, he was not amused.

"I'm not. I'm here meeting a friend." He gestured toward her. "Hannah, this is Stacy Mitchell."

The woman's too-large-for-her red Lucky Lasso Hotel t-shirt fell to her thighs, barely showing her short black skirt beneath. "Hello, Stacy. Nice to meet you."

Stacy's blue gaze studied her. "You must be from Phoenix. Wait until you taste our French toast. Texas Toast has nothing on ours."

"Then I must try it. Could I have a side of bacon with that?"

Brody chuckled. "All the breakfasts come with bacon. Ava's cousins raise pigs."

"Ahh, so then it must be the best bacon north of Phoenix."

Stacy nodded vigorously. "Got that right. You know, if you're looking for another 'friend,' I have a brother—"

"Stacy, she's not here to date anyone."

The waitress raised her hand as if held up at gun point. "I was just sayin'. What do you want, Brody, besides a new haircut?"

"I'll have the chorizo scramble."

With that, Stacy turned and headed for the kitchen.

Brody shook his head. "Sorry about that. You were saying?"

She looked at him, still trying to wrap her head around how small the town really was, if the waitress wanted to set up her brother with a guest at the hotel. "Honestly, I've completely lost track. Oh wait, no, I do remember. I've been thinking a lot about the land. I have so many ideas, they keep me up at night. So I've made a couple of decisions and wanted to get your input."

His whole body seemed to freeze as if he were afraid of what she might say. "Of course. I promise to give you my honest opinion."

Not sure why he seemed wary, she continued. "The first decision I have made is to not make a decision on the land right away. My grandparents left me a letter and asked me to visit it. Which I have done. I can see why they fell in love with it and spent their honeymoon there."

"They spent their honeymoon on the land?"

"They did." She took a sip of her coffee, a bit hesitant to tell him her second decision, but truly wanting his honest opinion. "My grandparents also asked me to stay on the land for a while before making any decision about selling it or keeping it. And I've decided to do just that."

His eyes rounded before he lowered his brows. "You want to stay on the land? Where?"

"In the casita." She grinned. "I know it's small, but it's just me now. I don't need two bedrooms anymore. Plus, I can carry out my grandparents' wishes. It's perfect."

"But the roof is rusted, the appliances are worthless, and…and there isn't even electricity out there."

His voice had risen with each point and she could see he wasn't happy. "I've already contacted someone about the roof, which is one of the questions I had for you. Do you think I need to replace the tin roof or can the rust be treated?"

He stared at her, his mouth open.

She glanced around at the other tables to see if anyone

was watching them, and a few people quickly glanced away. "Why are you so shocked?"

His brows rose as his mouth snapped shut, before it opened once again. "Where do I start? The casita is uninhabitable. It's in the middle of nowhere. You're a woman alone. There are a number of dangerous critters out there. And again. There is no electricity. Not to mention the commute to your job and to your volunteer work would be over an hour. I understand that your grandparents wanted you to stay on the land for a bit, but I doubt they realized the conditions there now. There isn't even a road."

She knew he would have some misgivings, but didn't expect such a strong argument. After all, she had asked his opinion as a courtesy. But before she could respond, Stacy came back with their food.

Since she wasn't happy, and didn't wish to appear ungrateful, she cut a slice of her French toast and took a bite, letting her temper cool. That was easy to do because the French toast was so unique, she found herself attempting to decipher the flavors. It definitely had an almond hint to it, but there was another flavor she knew but couldn't put her finger on.

"Do you like it?"

At his question, she cocked her head. "I do. It's different."

"Yeah. It's got coconut in it. Not my favorite."

"Coconut, of course. Very unusual. I would have never thought of that in French toast."

"The cook vacationed in the Caribbean last winter, and added some island flavors to a few of the dishes. For me, I prefer the same old eggs and meat." He held up a forkful of chorizo and stuffed it in his mouth.

"That makes sense. You do seem to be a traditionalist." She took another bite, liking it even more now that she understood what she was tasting.

"You say that like it's a bad thing."

"No, it works well for many people. It also explains why you can't see my vision. That's okay. It's not like you'll have to live in the casita. I was just curious about your opinion on a few choices I have to make, since if I sell it, it would be yours. Or rather, your family's. But if you're not interested. That's fine." She shrugged, more than a little irritated, and stuffed another piece of French toast in her mouth to avoid saying something downright rude.

He had a forkful of eggs and chorizo halfway to his mouth, and stopped at her response. He put the fork down on his plate. "I apologize. I just didn't realize you would contemplate living in the desert, roughing it. How long do you plan to stay? That should impact your decision on how much to put into it."

Though his words were soothing, he didn't look pleased at all. "Maybe this was a bad idea to ask your opinion. I'm sure you have to milk the cows or spread the hay or do whatever it is you do. You don't need me bothering you." She took a sip of coffee before taking another bite.

This time his fork did make it to his mouth, and as he chewed, he studied her, so she took another bite as soon as she swallowed. Was she being rude? Not really. Was she being nice? Not really. It's why her grandparents called her a peach. They said she was fuzzy and soft on the outside, but had a hard pit if pushed.

Then Brody smiled, and she found herself distracted by how warm and friendly he seemed when he relaxed. "Actually, our herd are meat cows, so no milking involved. And since we hired two new ranch hands this summer, they can handle mucking out the stalls while I enjoy my breakfast with you."

So now he was being nice, or was he laughing because she knew nothing about ranching. "Thank you for telling me. I've never visited a ranch before, though I've seen them on television."

"Well then, we need to change that. You need to come out to the Rocky Road so you can see a working ranch in person."

Her belly flipflopped at the thought of visiting a real ranch. "I'd like that. I love learning new things."

"Good, you can come out tomorrow."

"Actually, I can't. I'm meeting a mason at the end of Mesquite Road to bring him to the casita to patch up any holes in the walls. Those mice got in somewhere. Then later, I have a plumber coming to install a new toilet. Today, I plan to go out there and clean out the entire building, except that bed."

"You really plan to stay there, don't you."

"I do." She took her last bite of French toast and wiped her lips with her napkin. "I want to stay at least six months."

He coughed, quickly covering his mouth before clearing his throat. "Six months? In that little place?"

"Brody, it's just me. I don't even have any pets. Which is

a little sad, now that I think of it. Maybe I'll get a pet. Anyway, I don't need a lot of room. It will be perfect." She smiled, truly excited by the prospect of living is such a quiet, beautiful landscape.

He set down his utensils, his food growing cold on his plate. "You're really serious about this, aren't you?"

She gave a nod, not sure if she could truly explain what it felt like to actually own a home and a family legacy. "I am. I owe it to my grandparents. They raised me. I was only four months old when I lost my parents. My grandparents sacrificed so much for me. Then to learn they had this place all along, but never lived here so I could have all that the city offered—well, I feel I owe it to them to seriously consider their gift."

Even as she spoke, she could see he had made up his mind to argue the point further, so she switched her tactic. "Have you always lived on the Rocky Road Ranch?"

"Of course. My great-great-grandfather bought the land. My whole family has grown up there, which is why I know how hard life can be out here."

She held up her hand to forestall what she was sure to be a long explanation of why she wasn't up for it. "I'm most certain you do. I admire how much knowledge you have of this area, which is why I had hoped for your opinion on a few things, but you should also understand that living on *my* property is something I will do no matter what you say. What you can't understand is what it is like to have never owned a home, or even your parents or grandparents having not owned a home. This is my very first home, and I'm going to live in it."

He stared at her a long moment before he actually nodded. "I can't say I truly understand what it's like to never own a home."

She raised her brows and cocked her head. "You can't? Do you own a home?"

"I...I guess I don't, actually." He gave her a sheepish smile. "It's not a tin roof."

His switch in topic caught her off guard. "Excuse me?"

"You asked me about your tin roof. It's not tin. It's a metal roof, and the color actually provides added protection. It will last a long time and is low maintenance. No need for a new roof. What else did you want my opinion on?"

Beyond thrilled that he was willing to help, she pushed her plate aside and took out her phone from her purse to jot down some notes. "I'm going to need a driveway if I'm to get anything delivered out there, like a mattress to sleep on. Do I have someone lay down pavement, or have stone trucked in?"

He was back to looking at her as if she had three heads and fangs. "No and no. You're talking about six months. Your best bet is to simply decide the most direct route to the casita from Mesquite Road and drive it every day. If you want to put in the work, you can dig up some shrubs and cacti, but I'd just drive around them."

Surprised it could be so easy and so inexpensive, she grew excited. "How would I remember the route? Do I stake it out or just remember to bear left at the saguaro?"

He shrugged. "Either way works. But you'll want a truck or something. That desert dust will eat away at your little car in no time."

She waved off his comment. Why was it that men

thought women knew nothing about cars. "I already took care of that. I traded in my car for a used Jeep. Now, what do you think is best for power out there—solar, wind, propane, or electric?"

"Hmm, I need to think about that." He picked up his fork and plopped another bite of food in his mouth.

As he continued to eat and ponder, she warmed up her coffee and took a sip. Part of why she'd wanted his opinion was because she'd already done her research and made some educated guesses, but upon talking to people in the various trades in Phoenix, she'd found herself at odds with them. But Brody appeared to think along the same lines that she did. Maybe it was because he'd seen exactly where and what her casita was.

Finally, he finished his meal and set his fork down. "I'm no expert, but if it were my place, I'd put up a few solar panels nearby and have a propane generator for back-up. We get so much sun in this valley that you would have plenty to power that little place. But you never know with monsoons and animals, so there could be times you need a back-up. I wouldn't go with wind, as we don't get enough, and getting the power company to put poles out that far might just be a study in frustration, not to mention expensive."

Her heart leapt at his answer. She'd noticed that the stove had been propane, so there had to be an underground tank somewhere. Deciding between solar or propane had been her sticking point, so to have him suggest combining them told her she was on the right track. "Thank you. That's what I needed to know."

"What about water?"

"Water? Isn't there water to the casita? It had a sink, shower, and toilet."

He shook his head even as he waved at Stacy. "It had water when those were put in. You will want to have the well checked, as well as the pipes. A lot can happen in sixty years."

"Of course. I hadn't thought about that. Can you recommend anyone?"

"I haven't had a need to put in a well, but I have a friend who did, so I'll contact him and let you know."

Before she could respond, Stacy came over and took their plates. "What did you think of the French toast?"

"I enjoyed it. It's very different, but I'd order it again."

The woman gave her an odd look. "Are you sure you wouldn't like to meet my brother? He also likes the French toast."

Hannah chuckled as she shook her head. "Not right now, but maybe once I get settled in, I'll contact you."

"Settled in?" Stacy's eyes lit with curiosity. "Are you moving here?"

A warm excitement filled her with confidence and excitement as she answered. "I am."

Stacy looked to Brody. "Tell me you're not moving in with him."

"What? No. Into my own place. We're just friends."

Stacy didn't take her eyes off Brody as she shook her head. "Well, that's good. The Dunns are known for having heads as hard as a rock." With that, Stacy dropped the bill on the table and strode off with the dirty dishes.

Hannah expected Brody to take umbrage to Stacy's words, but he didn't. In fact, he seemed quite pleased.

"At least we're not pushovers like her brothers. Trust me Hannah, to live out here, you need backbone."

Oh, she had backbone aplenty, but he didn't know that... yet. She picked up the bill and pulled out a pen, quickly adding a tip and her room number. "I appreciate all your advice. I know you have a lot to do on the Rocky Road, and I need to get over to the casita." She wrinkled her nose. "As much as I like the casita, I need to come up with a name for it."

He smirked. "You probably don't want to call it what we've called it all these years."

"I can just imagine. What did you call it?"

"The dump."

She barely kept from rolling her eyes. Not because of the name, but from the glee with which he said it. "No, I won't call it the dump. I was thinking something along the lines of "heaven" or "oasis.""

This time it was his nose that wrinkled. "Maybe you should wait until you're in it to decide."

She rose from the table, knowing full well she wouldn't. "Thank you again."

He stood and held his arm out for her to precede him. "Thank you for breakfast. If you need any more opinions, please call me."

As they walked into the lobby, he stopped. "Wait, you wanted to see Rocky Road Ranch. If you are busy today and tomorrow, how about Sunday, before you head back to the city?"

"That sounds lovely. What time should I be there?"

"Come by around seven in the morning. We're done with breakfast by then and it will be cooler."

"I'm not a great morning person, but if you provide the coffee, I can be there."

"Will do. See you then." Brody tipped his hat before striding for the door.

She watched him as he exited the hotel and walked by the large window, giving a wave as he passed. "Well, that was interesting."

"Ms. Kingsley, anything having to do with Brody Dunn is going to be interesting."

Hannah spun around to see Ava leaning on the counter, obviously eavesdropping. "Why is that?"

Ava waved her hand toward the street. "That Dunn changes by the hour. One day he's trick riding, the next he's getting his pilot's license. I pity the woman he sets his sights on. I get dizzy just hearing about his next adventure."

Hmm, that could be a good thing. Maybe once she was settled, he'd leave off challenging her decisions. Then again, she was the one who asked for his opinion. She wouldn't do that again. "Luckily for me, he's only interested in my land."

Ignoring Ava's raised brows, she quickly exited the building herself, anxious to get to the hardware store for a few tools to tackle the dirt in the casita. Brody Dunn may not be able to see the potential of the casita, but she did. And if she had her way, she'd be moved in by the time her apartment lease expired at the end of the month.

Her quick stop in at the hardware store ended up taking a good thirty minutes after the store owner, Mr. Hardy, found out she was cleaning up the Harper House, as he called it. Her grandparents had often stopped in to chat with him and to have some of the popcorn he kept popping all day long. It was worth every minute to her because she was able to talk about her grandparents.

By time she hit Mesquite Road, it was mid-morning, and she still had a lot to do. As she headed for the casita, she could see a black pick-up truck was already there. The well-inspection wasn't until two in the afternoon, and the mason wasn't coming until tomorrow, along with the plumber. Could Brody have come to help her clean?

Even as she parked her Jeep, she dismissed that idea. He had work on the ranch to do. Besides, the truck was too clean to be Brody's. She had ordered satellite internet, but they were supposed to text her a timeframe of when they would arrive, and she'd received nothing yet.

Opening the door, she called out. "Hello? Is someone here?"

"Sure am." The male voice that came from her bedroom was not one she recognized. For the first time she understood Brody's concerns about her living alone.

She didn't venture in any farther, seriously contemplating running for her Jeep.

"Miss Kingsley? Is that you?"

Okay, it was someone who knew she owned the place. That had to be a good sign. "Yes, it's me."

Footsteps sounded in her bedroom before a large shadow crossed the threshold into the main area followed by an equally large man who wiped his hands on a lavender hand towel that was definitely not hers. "I hope you don't mind, but my morning appointment cancelled, and since it's so dang hot in the middle of the day, I didn't think you'd mind if I installed your toilet a day early."

Relief washed through her at the realization it was the plumber she'd contacted over the phone, and she let out an uncomfortable laugh. "Of course not, Mr. Lawerence. Who wouldn't want a toilet a day early?" She continued into her home with the bag from the hardware store, setting it on the dust-covered kitchen counter. "I hope it's not too unpleasant in there. I haven't had a chance to clean up yet."

Mr. Lawerence, who had a full head of long salt-and-pepper hair tied back in a ponytail, shook his head. "Not too bad, considering."

She wasn't sure what that meant, but at least he seemed able to work in the bathroom. "I need to get my cleaning supplies out of my car, but I can get things cleaned up for you before you continue."

He waved his large hand. "No need. I'm just going to make a mess anyway. I've already finished getting the bolts out of the floor. Whoever stole your toilet must have broken it into a hundred pieces to get it out." He shook his head. "People."

She held back a smile until he'd turned around and returned to the bathroom. People? Wasn't he "people" too? Grinning now, she returned to the Jeep and pulled out her box of cleaning supplies. She needed to add getting a lock for the door to her to-do list. She didn't want another worker just walking in on her unexpected.

After depositing the supplies on top of the small counter next to her hardware bag, she went back for the five-gallon jug of water she'd bought, not knowing if the rest of the plumbing worked. She set it down on the floor next to the sink. Maybe she could get Mr. Lawerence to lift it up on the counter for her, once she made room for it.

While Brody had said the casita had been abandoned for sixty years, that couldn't be. If Mr. Hardy had seen her grandparents, then it would have only been abandoned less than thirty, since they took her in when she was an infant. Still, did pipes stop working after that long?

Maybe she should find out. It was her home, after all. Reaching for the cold knob on the sink, she turned it. Nothing happened. Disappointed but not giving up, she turned the hot water knob. Still nothing. Well, at least she had her jug of water which would help her get started.

Looking around the place, she decided to start by hauling the broken wood outside. She didn't imagine there was trash pick-up so far out. Did she bring it to a dump or could she burn it? There was so much to learn.

Once the coffee table had joined the pieces of wood from the kitchen, she added the couch cushions, finding many more mouse turds. Obviously, they'd been living inside, not outside. "Okay, I'm giving you fair warning. You need to leave the premises or I'll have to take stronger measures." She grinned as she imagined the mice listening to her and thinking her loco.

After dumping all the cushions on the pile, she walked to her Jeep and took out the broom she'd bought at Mr. Hardy's. She also had a vacuum in her vehicle that she'd brought from home, but when she saw the brooms, she remembered there was no electricity.

She had just stepped into the casita, when a thought occurred. Continuing into the bedroom, she stopped in the bathroom doorway. "Excuse me."

"Sorry, this bathroom is occupied." Mr. Lawerence, who knelt on the ground, turned his head and grinned at her.

She grinned right back. "I'm sorry. I didn't realize you were paying homage to the porcelain god."

He sat back on his heels and laughed. "Not today, anyway."

She decided to ask her question while she had his attention. "I noticed there's no electricity out here, yet there is a well, a split unit in this bedroom, and even lights and outlets."

"Propane."

She frowned. "How can propane make an outlet work?"

He shook his head. "No, the propane runs a generator that powers the electrical panel. From the size of this place, I imagine it wasn't a very big generator. The well pump would be the biggest draw. That and the split unit air conditioner in the heat of the summer."

"Oh. Thank you. How's it going in here?"

He rose from the floor, practically filling the only floor space in the tiny bathroom. "I've got the floor cleared and checked the plumbing. It looks good. I just need to get the toilet from my truck. I should have it installed in no time."

Excited that her little house was already being fixed up, she stepped back to allow him the space to get by. Once he left, she eyed the old mattress. She'd wait to take that out. She might get in the way of her new toilet.

She shook her head as she returned to the kitchen. She'd

always taken bathrooms for granted. Who knew getting a new toilet could be so exciting? Chuckling at herself, she opened one of the kitchen drawers to see if there was anything left in it.

Surprised, she stared at the drawer full of receipts. Pushing the box of cleaning supplies to the end of the counter, which gave her a foot of space, she pulled a handful of receipts out of the drawer and started looking through them. There were receipts from a bakery and an ice cream shop, as well as from a western wear store, a place called the Stampede, and the hardware store. She perused the handwritten hardware store receipt for a date and stilled. It was only three years ago.

"What?"

"It's just me bringing in the commode." Mr. Lawerence walked past her and disappeared into the bedroom.

She turned her attention back to the receipt. It was dated March. In March that year she'd gone to California for a four-day training for work. She'd invited her grandparents, but they declined.

She widened her eyes. "They were here!"

"I can't hear you. You'll have to come in here if you have a question." Mr. Lawerence's response to her shout had her taking a deep breath.

"Just talking to myself!"

When he didn't say anything more, she returned to the receipts. She found about a dozen more for that date, but before then she found plenty of others. Every date was when she was away from home for one reason or another. The implication was clear. Her grandparents had continued to use the casita as a love nest, keeping it as their secret hideaway.

Part of her felt a little betrayed, but the other part, the part that loved them more than she loved herself, melted with happiness. Now the surprise inheritance made sense, as did her grandfather's ability to keep the secret. A single tear rolled down her cheek at how beautiful their love had been.

At the sound of footsteps, she turned.

"All done." Mr. Lawerence continued to wipe his hands on his lavender towel as he studied her. His smile faded. "Hey, you don't have to get all teary on me. It's just a toilet."

She sniffed. "Oh, but I'm so grateful to have one."

He studied her for a moment. "Yeah, I get it. It's home sweet home."

Her throat closed at his understanding and she simply nodded.

"Tell you what, since I'm here. Why don't I check out all the plumbing? You know, just to be sure it works."

She swallowed hard. "Thank you. I'd like that. And I'd best get back cleaning. I'll start over there in the living room so I'm out of your way."

As she moved toward the couch with her broom, a feeling of comfort filling her. She was going to enjoy making the little house into a home.

CHAPTER 5

BRODY SHOVED the last coffee mug into the dishwasher before practically slamming it shut.

"Hey, son. Don't break it. What's your hurry?"

He looked behind him to discover his father in his wheelchair at the entry between the kitchen and what used to be the den, but was now his dad's therapy room. His dad wheeling himself around the house was new. "Hannah Kingsley, the granddaughter of the Harpers, is coming this morning to see what a real ranch is like. I'm hoping to show her how hard it is living out here, so she sells us her property."

"Why? Does she want to build a house on her land? If she does, she'd only need an acre near Mesquite Road, and we could buy the rest. Tell her we'll even pay for the subdividing."

Before he could explain why his dad was completely off target, his father had rolled himself past the kitchen and living room and was halfway down the hall. It was just as well, since he didn't have time. Hannah would be arriving soon, and he wanted to roll the ATV out before she did. He very much doubted she'd ever ridden a horse, so taking Chaos and Havoc, his brother's horse, was out of the question.

Grabbing up his hat, he left the house and strode to the barn. He drove the ATV around in time to see a Jeep making its way over the ranch's very rocky driveway. He halted in the middle of the dirt parking area and watched as all four tires left the ground before the front ones came down. He grinned, quite sure she wouldn't be excited about her own driveway either. It had to be as rocky as his.

When she pulled in, he swung his leg over the machine like he was getting off a horse before striding forward, ready to assure her that desert roads weren't so bad when taken slow.

The door opened and she jumped out of the Jeep in a pair of blue jeans, brown boots, a white button-down shirt tied at her pale waist, and a straw cowboy hat atop her head. "Hey, Brody. Your driveway is a blast. Do you think mine will eventually turn that rocky?"

He halted in his tracks. What happened to her? He'd just seen her two days ago, and now she looked like she could rope a calf in seven seconds. The woman had gone from being a city-dweller to a hot cowgirl in hours. "I'm sorry. What did you say?"

She strode forward looking as at home on the ranch as any rancher's daughter he knew, including his sister-in-law. "I asked if you think my driveway to the casita will get as rocky as yours. That was fun."

"Fun?"

She stopped in front of him. "Yeah. Is something wrong, Brody?"

He shook his head as much to clear it as to answer her. "No. It's just that usually people complain about our driveway."

"Then I guess no one has driven it in a Jeep before. It's better than a roller coaster."

"Roller coaster. Right." He needed to get his equilibrium back and stop staring at the button on her shirt that seemed to be straining to keep it closed between her breasts. He forced his gaze back to her face. "I see you've been shopping."

"Oh, yes. Everyone in town is so lovely. No wonder you enjoy living out here. People are super friendly and really go out of their way to be helpful. I didn't realize when we met that you were just the tip of the iceberg for Four Peaks."

He really shouldn't be proud of her vision of him, but he still was. "It's just how we all are out here. Are you ready to see the ranch?"

"I am. I was afraid I wouldn't be able to sleep last night for thinking about seeing your operation and how it all works. It must be so wonderful, waking up every morning knowing you get to work right here at home. I only get to do that sometimes. I would love to be able to do it all the time. I'm not sure I'd ever leave."

He held his hand out toward the ATV. "Then let's get started, unless of course, you know how to ride a horse."

She stopped in her tracks. "Oh, I'd love to ride a horse. Can we?"

He widened his eyes. Had she been holding out on him? "You know how to ride?"

Her shoulders lifted in a short shrug. "Don't you just sit on the horse and pull the reins to the right and left?"

"And how do you get it to gallop or slow down?"

Her smile disappeared. "I don't know. I imagine that would be important to learn."

She imagined? "Riding a horse starts with taking care of a horse. You need to feed it, give it water, rub it down, give it medicine, trim its hooves, and a million other things to ensure it stays healthy as long as possible."

"That sounds fitting and you know all that, plus you take care of cattle, right? Is it just your family working here or do you hire ranch hands?"

"Come, I'll explain everything." They settled onto the ATV, and he waited for her hands to come around his waist before he put the machine in motion. As soon as they passed the barn, one hand let go of him and she pointed to the guest bunkhouses. "Is that where your ranch hands live?"

He slowed the ATV to explain. "No. Our ranch hands live in town or in the area. This is actually the guest bunkhouses for when we open up Rocky Road as a dude ranch. We have to because we don't have enough land to compete with the bigger ranchers in the area."

"So that's why you want to buy my land. Would it be enough to help you compete?"

"That's really a question for my brother, Tanner. But my guess is yes, because he wanted to do anything else but turn us into a dude ranch to save the Rocky Road."

Her hand came back around his waist as he accelerated

again. "Really? I think becoming a dude ranch is a great idea. Of course, you'll need people who know how to run one. I imagine you'll hire food service workers and a cleaning service and even entertainers. I may just have to come when you open and be a guest."

His sister-in-law liked the idea as well. Maybe they should market it to women more than families. They could even come up with a creative name for it instead of just Rocky Road that would appeal to ladies. It was definitely something to think about. If the dude ranch was successful, he'd feel a lot better about leaving the ranch.

He slowed the ATV and brought it to a stop. "This is what we call the birthing enclosure. When a number of cows are from seven to eight months pregnant, we move them in here. There are always a few stragglers, but we add them as they get further along."

"Is it too dangerous for them to be roaming the land at that stage?"

That thought had never occurred to him. "Not really. We just move them here to be able to keep a better eye on them as they get closer to birthing. We had cameras up, but a monsoon came through and wreaked havoc with our roof and wires. We had tarps up, but after one of our cows pulled one down, we decided to take them down after all the calves were born. You can see the lumber and metal we'll be using to rebuild over there." He pointed to the pile on the right. It had been sitting there for two months now, but like everything else, was on the back burner. He probably should bring it up to Tanner.

"Why do you need to keep an eye on the pregnant cows? Do they need help with their babies being born?"

"Sometimes. We hate losing a calf, so if we know a dam is struggling, we'll help." He felt her hand on his shoulder before she spoke.

"So you must know a lot of veterinary science as well."

"I don't know about that. We send for a vet when we need to, but some situations we've had over and over, so we just know what to do. We have to, because by the time a vet gets here, it could be too late."

"Oh, how sad. I couldn't imagine losing one of your baby cows."

He was about to remind her that all the cows were slaughtered for meat, but decided not to. "We haven't lost one in over five years, so we're doing well." He started the ATV moving forward again, and when he felt her hands around his waist once more, he accelerated. He took her down to the south field to explain how they let the grasses grow, keeping the cows in the north and why they did that. Then he took her to where the cows were in the north range.

As he pulled up, he found Nash and their oldest ranch hand, Layne, with ropes around one of their bulls. He turned off the ATV and jumped off. "What happened?"

Layne kept his eye on the bull as he answered. "He decided to pick a fight with Old Glory. We got him this far, but if you could open the gate, that'd be real helpful."

"Damn. Glad I pulled up when I did." Quickly, he ran over to the gate and opened it. Stepping inside, he used his presence to keep the other cows from exiting. It wasn't easy keeping an eye on the cows and the approaching bull, who was not happy about being escorted out of the range area. Once the men had the animal outside the fencing, he closed the gate then walked toward the bull.

"You keep the tension on until I say, got it?"

Once he had agreement, he stepped up to the bull. Luckily, it was one of their younger ones and his horns weren't that long. "Okay, buddy. I'm going to let you loose, so be nice." Grabbing the ropes where he could pull them quickly, he readied himself. "Now!" As the tension left the ropes, he pulled them free and the bull bounded forward before stopping and turning to face him, its head lowering. Well, shit.

"Hey, sweetie."

At Hannah's voice he spared her a glance. What the heck? "Hannah, don't draw attention to yourself. He's pissed."

"Oh, sorry." She still smiled at the bull as if he were a puppy.

When the bull turned toward her, he swore. "Shit. Hannah, don't move."

She ignored him and leaned back against the ATV.

His heart started to pound as the bull began to walk toward her.

Slowly he turned toward her as well, preparing to run interference.

"Brody, wait."

He didn't dare look over his shoulder at Layne. If the man thought to keep him from Hannah, he had another thing coming, so he just shook his head.

"Look at the bull. He's not a threat." Layne's words were

quiet, but they all heard him. "Miss, go ahead and talk to the animal."

Brody wanted to shove his fist into Layne's face at that, but the man was behind him and on a horse, while a bull stood no more than three yards from Hannah.

"Hello Mr. Bull. I'm Hannah Kingsley. It's a pleasure to meet you. I haven't met a bull before. You're quite handsome."

The animal walked forward slowly, a soft grunt issuing forth.

Now he didn't move because he was in shock. He could count on one hand how many times he'd heard a happy grunt from a bull the entire year.

Hannah clasped her hands together in front of her. "You have such a beautiful place to live and such knowledgeable cowboys taking care of you. You must be very happy here."

The bull stopped and sniffed the air, then turned and ambled down the dirt road between the north and south pastures.

Dropping the rope from his sweaty fingers, he strode to Hannah. "Are you okay?"

"Of course. After all the activity of getting him out of the gate, he was agitated. He just needed a calming presence and a non-threatening one. That's why I made myself appear as small as possible."

A hand clapped him on the shoulder from behind before he could respond.

"See, Brody, this young lady is smarter than you." Layne walked forward. "Howdy, Miss Kingsley. I'm Layne, the head ranch hand under Tanner."

"It's a pleasure to meet you, Layne. I thought Brody would be in charge." She looked past Layne's broad shoulders at him.

He quickly strode forward and waved off the assumption. "Absolutely not. I'm the youngest, and don't plan on having that kind of responsibility here on the ranch."

Her brow furrowed for a moment, but then Nash had to step up and introduce himself. It was if they were at a barbeque and the band was going to start up again.

Hannah gave Nash a beautiful smile. "Do you have a specific rank as well?"

His best friend laughed. "Not me, miss. I'm just a simple cowboy, happy to do what I'm told. That and keeping him out of trouble is plenty of work." Nash hooked a thumb at him.

"Really? I think I need to hear more." Her tone was far too enthusiastic.

Nash looked about ready to launch into a good long story, obviously bent on charming Hannah.

That wasn't happening. "Sorry, Nash. I still have a lot to show our new neighbor. Hannah, are you ready to move on?"

Damn if her brown eyes didn't twinkle with mischief. "And here it was just getting interesting." She favored Nash with a wink before facing him. "Where to next?"

"The peaks." He straddled the ATV and waited for her to settle in behind him.

"See you later, gentlemen."

He started up the ATV before Layne or Nash could respond, and headed down the same road the bull had wandered. When they caught up to the animal, it was holding court through the fence with three heifers.

"What will happen to the bull?"

He waited until they were a safe distance past before stopping to answer her. "The men will round him up and put him in a different section. This guy has been a royal pain, but he's good for, um, good for the cows, so we put up with his shenanigans." He accelerated again, more determined than ever to show her the dangers of living in the desert.

Finally, he brought them to the gate at the north range and stopped. He spoke over his shoulder. "Would you like to open the gate?"

"Sure." She climbed off and walked to the gate. Lifting the latch, she pulled and it moved about a foot. "These are heavier than they look."

His instinct was to help, but he was hoping to show her how hard living was in such an unforgiving climate. She didn't give up, but it took her longer than he usually had patience for. Once it was open, he drove the ATV through then got off. "I'll close it."

She didn't say anything, but she definitely looked relieved, which lightened his mood, especially after all the flirting that had been going on before with the ranch hands. After latching the gate, he returned to the ATV and drove them to the spot where the boulder had come down earlier in the summer and where Lulabell's calf escaped. He and Nash had added more wire as a quick fix, but they really needed to get the wood out to the spot and permanently fix it. He turned off the machine and waited for Hannah to get off before joining her.

"Wow, this is a huge boulder." She examined it and the space around it, walking completely around the large rock that was far taller than her. "How long ago did this roll down here? It can't have been that long."

He had to acknowledge she was observant and quick at assessing the situation. "Early in the summer. My sister-in-law convinced Tanner that we should leave it here to make it more interesting, so we strung wire until we can rebuild the fencing it took out."

She looked up at the rocky side of the mountain where the boulder had been for who knew how many centuries. "Does that happen often?"

"Boulders rolling down? Yes. A lot. Do they usually hit our fence? No. They get stuck in the small valley at the bottom of this rocky area, but this one had so much steam, it just kept coming. I'm glad no one and no cows were in the way."

She shivered at that. "Me, too. I imagine I have similar areas on my property. That must be why the fence is so far from this part of the mountain, while where we were earlier, it was right at the base. Does everyone fence their property? I mean, even if they aren't ranching?"

That was a good question. "I don't know. Most people who have this amount of land are using it for ranching."

She shrugged off his answer. "I'll just ask in town when I get back to the hotel. Everyone is so willing to share their knowledge."

He had to ask. "Is that how you learned about facing a bull?"

"Oh no, that never came up. No, I did research on

ranching in Arizona on the internet. There are some amazing videos that show what it's like, but being here is so much more impressive. Thank you for having me."

He wasn't sure if her good impression was exactly what he'd hoped for. "I'm glad you enjoyed your visit."

Her face sobered. "We're done? But what about the horses?"

"You want to see the horses?"

"If it's not too much trouble. I know I've kept you from your work for half the day already."

He could imagine her walking into the barn and petting his horse and a few others like a child at a petting zoo, which would just make life on the ranch seem even more idyllic. He needed something else to prove that the city life was better—of course. "Actually, I do have to get the fencing materials out here. How about if next time you visit Four Peaks, we care for the horses?"

Her smile lit up her entire face. "I would love that. Thank you. I'm coming back next Friday, but I have a few items being delivered. Can we do it on Saturday?"

All he could picture was cardboard boxes showing up at the hotel for her, but that was fine. As long as she helped with mucking out the stalls, he was sure she'd re-evaluate life in the desert. "That will work. Now we best get back to the house. I do need to get that lumber loaded up." He walked to the ATV and straddled it, waiting for her to get on and wrap her hands around his waist, but when she didn't, he looked behind him. "You okay?"

"I am. I just can't believe how impressive these mountains look from here. They really are amazing."

He had to keep himself from rolling his eyes. If she reacted like that, then the dude ranch would be a huge success. For himself, the mountains were simply part of a familiar scenery that he noticed once in a while when the sun set.

As soon as her hands came around him, he set the machine in motion. By time they arrived back at the house, they were hot, sweaty, and dirty from their ride. He felt rather good about that as he waited for her to get off the machine.

Once she was off, she came to stand next to him. "I've learned so much today. I can't wait to help care for the horses next weekend. This week is going to crawl by. I really can't thank you enough." She leaned forward and brushed a kiss on his cheek.

Two impressions hit him in those few seconds. One, she smelled damn good, and two, her lips were soft. "It was my pleasure."

"No, really. It was mine. See you next week." With that, she twirled around and walked to her Jeep, her hips swaying. She opened the door and swung herself inside, then waved before closing the door.

He waved back out of habit, trying to wrap his mind around who Hannah Kingsley really was. Not that it mattered, as he just needed her to sell her land, but knowing her better definitely would help. He'd thought he'd figured her out, but now...

The Jeep backed up then pulled forward. She honked the horn then stuck her arm out to wave again. Finally, she headed down the Rocky Road drive just as fast as she'd arrived.

He got off the ATV. Next weekend might be helpful to his cause, but just in case, he needed a backup plan. That, and to talk to Nash about flirting with Hannah.

The last thing he needed was for her to have a relationship with anyone in Four Peaks, especially with his best friend.

CHAPTER 6

"YOU CAN JUST SET that down against the wall." Hannah wasn't sure if she'd leave the couch there, but it was the easiest place for the men who had offered to help her move. She'd been absolutely thrilled last weekend when not only Ava, the owner of the Lucky Lasso Hotel and Saloon, but also Stacy, the waitress, had offered up their brothers to help her move. She really didn't want to bother Brody anymore, as she had the feeling she'd taken up a bit too much of his time.

Then when she'd run into Nash at the hardware store and told him what was happening, he'd made himself available. She couldn't believe how wonderful everyone was in Four Peaks.

"Where would you like this?" Nash held a large cardboard box labeled 'stuff.'"

No wonder he had no clue where it should go. "You can put that in the closet in the bedroom."

He shook his head, his eyes crinkling under his cowboy

hat. "That's full to the top. I can probably squeeze it in on the floor next to the bed if you like."

"Oh dear. I thought I had culled out enough items, but it looks like I may have to rent a storage unit."

He readjusted the heavy box. "Not necessarily. Once you know how much you need to store, you could order a storage shed to replace the old one that was outside there. It would cost a lot less and I'd be happy to anchor it down for you."

Ava's married brother jostled Nash as he strode by. "Stop flirting and keep working."

Instead of being embarrassed, as she was, Nash grinned. "Nothing wrong with doing two things at once." He gave her a nod to punctuate his point before continuing into the bedroom.

She liked Nash. He was easy-going, like Brody. Actually, all the men she'd met in town seemed that way. She must be meeting the right men. For the first time since her grandparents had become frail, she thought about dating again. What if she met the perfect man while living in Four Peaks? Surprisingly, the idea appealed to her, even if the town was tiny compared to Phoenix.

Then again, she was still new in town, and she was in what she'd call the honeymoon stage. That's how it had been every time her grandparents and she moved to a new apartment complex.

She looked around at the piles of boxes, some on chairs and end tables. The amount of work it would take to unpack should feel overwhelming, but she was actually looking forward to the task. Since her lease had been ending, she'd thrown all her and her grandparents' possessions into boxes and now she was anxious to go through everything.

"This is the last one, Ms. Kingsley." Stacy's tall, handsome brother set the box down on top of two others next to the kitchen counter.

His dark good looks and polite manners were appealing, but he was far too young for her. Obviously, Stacy must think her much younger than her twenty-seven years. "Thank you. If you wouldn't mind bringing the cooler in in from my Jeep?"

"Of course."

"Never mind, kid. I'll take care of that." Nash strode by and headed out the door.

She shook her head. The cooler had eight six-packs of beer in it. "He's probably going to need some help."

"I'm on it." The young man followed Nash out.

She had planned on opening the back of her Jeep and standing outside, but it was late afternoon, and the lovely fall day she'd started with in Phoenix had risen to scorching hot. Unfortunately, the casita didn't have air-conditioning or power yet. She had the generator hooked up, but the solar panels had not been installed yet. That's why she'd been anxious to get everything moved in before dark. But with three wonderful cowboys helping, she was done already.

Nash carried in the cooler on his shoulder. "Where would you like it?"

She pointed to the spot where her refrigerator would go when it arrived tomorrow. "Right there. The contents are for you all. I wasn't sure what you liked."

Stacy's brother, who'd followed Nash in, quickly lifted

the lid. "Nice." He grabbed one of the beers and twisted off the cap.

Ava's brother walked in from outside. He was almost as tall as Nash, but of Hispanic descent, with very attractive eyes. "Stand aside and let the old man have a look. Ah, now here's real beer."

She chuckled because she doubted he was any older than she was.

Nash turned to her. "What would you like?"

"Me? Oh, I only drink light beer. Never acquired a taste for full strength." She scanned the kitchen area looking for her tumbler. Spotting it next to a box on the counter, she picked it up. "I'm all set with my water."

Nash looked in the cooler and pulled out a beer different from the other two before twisting off the cap on the bottle. "Then you should come down to Boots n' Brew Saturday night. The Cattle Rustlers will be playing and there'll be dancing."

"Nash, are you asking the lady on a date?"

At Ava's brother's comment, she flushed.

Nash shook his head. "No. I was just being neighborly to a new neighbor." He turned back to look at her. "Unless you would prefer it be a date?"

She smiled kindly, though she knew her cheeks were red. "I think I'd like to settle in first, but if I have the evening free, I'll definitely check it out."

"How long you staying?"

She shrugged, not sure how to answer Nash since she hadn't thought any farther than Sunday. "I don't know. My grandparents asked me to stay a while. I'm not sure if they meant a week or a year or half my life. So I'm just taking it one day at a time."

"Cheers to that." Nash lifted his bottle, and she clinked her steel tumbler against it before lifting it to her lips.

Footsteps crunched the dirt just outside the open door before it was filled with a familiar figure. "What's going on here?" Brody stood in the doorway, clearly not happy.

Nash spun around. "It figures you would show up after all the hard work is done."

She could tell that didn't help Brody's mood at all, yet he didn't really change his expression. It must be that she was getting used to his body language. "Hi Brody. Would you like a beer?" She held her hand out toward the cooler.

"No. Thank you." His eyes widened as he took in all the boxes. "When you said you had a delivery, I thought you meant to the hotel."

"Oh, no. That's tomorrow. My refrigerator is coming."

His brow furrowed. "Refrigerator? But there's no electricity."

She bit down on a smile. The man seemed far too focused on electricity. "No, but I will soon. I'm having solar panels and a battery installed next week. In the meantime, I do have a propane generator, which I understand will enable me to at least run an air conditioning unit, the well pump, and my small refrigerator."

As if it had just dawned on him, his eyes rounded. "You're moving in."

Nash chuckled and patted Brody on the shoulder "That's generally what people do when they pack up all their belongings and transport them to another dwelling."

Brody frowned at Nash before looking at her. "When you said you would stay a while, I thought you meant as in a weekend here and there."

"Not at all. My lease was up for renewal. I see no reason to pay rent when I have this adorable casita all to myself." She smiled encouragingly, hoping he could see why it made sense.

He just shook his head as if she'd lost her mind.

Fine, she didn't need his approval anyway.

Nash held up the remainder of his beer. "Cheers to your new neighbor, Brody." He swallowed the rest and looked around for the trash.

"Over here." She pointed to a black trash bag next to her.

Nash dropped his bottle in on top of the tape and paper she'd already put in it. "I need to head out and run a few errands before dinner. Remember what I said about Saturday night."

"I will. And please take some beer with you. I won't drink it."

"Don't mind if I do." He strode over and lifted out the rest of the six pack. "Hey guys, you want yours as well?"

When the other two men nodded, Nash brought them the six packs to match their beers, then seemed to usher them out.

Hannah quickly followed them outside. "Thank you so much. I couldn't have done this without you."

After a few jokes about who was strongest, the three men left in their various trucks. Turning back to her house, she found Brody standing just outside the door. "How come you didn't ask me?"

She brushed by him, as much to get into the cooler interior of the casita than anything else. "Why would I ask you if I could move into my own home?"

He followed her inside. "Not that. It's your home. Of course, you can move into it. But why didn't you ask me for help moving? I would have helped you. And how the heck did you rope Nash into it?"

She took a swallow of water, not a little surprised by his tone. He sounded as if she'd hurt his feelings. "I didn't ask you because I took far too much of your time last weekend. I know you have a lot to do on the ranch. As far as Nash is concerned, I ran into him at the hardware store yesterday, and when he asked what I was doing in town, I told him I was moving into the casita today, and he offered his help. How come you didn't ask me about the other two men?"

He moved farther inside and leaned against the wall. "Because I know Ava and Stacy volunteered them. They do that a lot. You do know Stacy is trying to set you up with her brother. He's far too young for you."

Though she'd come to the same conclusion, she thought it funny that he mentioned it. "Really? I don't know. He's very handsome." She bit her lip to keep from grinning.

"Handsome? He's passable, but he's only twenty-two."

"Twenty-two. Hmm, and how old do you think I am?"

She could tell that he realized too late she'd set him up. Patiently, she waited for him to answer.

Finally, he grinned. "You're my age."

"Really? So you're thirty-two?"

His head jerked back. "You're not thirty-two. Even Tanner isn't thirty-two yet."

She laughed, pleased he at least thought her younger than that. "I'm twenty-seven, and I agree, Stacy's brother is too young for me."

As his shoulders relaxed, it made her wonder about his interest in who she dated. "Now Nash, he must be about my age, right?"

Brody pushed himself away from the door as he moved toward the kitchen. "Yeah, we graduated together." He headed for the cooler. "I think I will have that beer."

She waited while he chose one and twisted the cap. He looked around before spotting the trash bag and threw it in.

He took a swig then continued. "Nash and I have known each other since we were three, or so my mom told me. She was best friends with his mom. I think with both of us losing our moms at a young age, it made us closer. We'd do anything for each other."

"It sounds like you two really have each other's back. I never had brothers or sisters or even a friend that long. As for parents, my grandparents were mine, and they were wonderful." Even as she smiled, her eyes itched at her loss. Deciding that wasn't a topic she was ready to talk a lot about, she quickly switched her train of thought. "I lost my mom when I was two, so except for photos, I didn't really know her. When did you lose yours?"

"I was twelve." He paused to take another swig, his gaze no longer on her. "She died of chronic obstructive pulmonary disease. That's the fancy name for it, but she basically couldn't breathe. At first, she blamed it on not getting enough exercise. Then she said her heart was weak, but one day we came home from school, and we found her on the floor struggling to breathe. I'll never forget seeing my mom lying there. Of course, Tanner called Dad immediately, while Jackson and I helped her to sit up." He shook his head. "Never been so sacred in my entire life. Not even when I had an engine cut out in the Cessna Skyhawk I was flying."

Brody's gaze returned to her. "It's different when it's yourself and you think you're going to die. You can make peace with your life. But when it's someone you love, someone who is your whole world, your support, your cheerleader, and you can't do anything to help, it's terrorizing."

Her heart constricted at the pain in his face. She'd never come close to losing her own life, but she knew what it was like to watch someone slowly waste away. "I get that. My grandfather was my champion, and as his heart made him weaker and weaker, I felt my heart breaking a little more each day. I can't imagine what it must have been for you at such a young age."

A self-deprecating smirk appeared, not what she expected. "Oh, I was completely selfish, convinced that I alone could make my mom better. Only I could take care of her well enough for her to get well again. I refused to do my chores or ride my horse or even go to school. Dad put a stop to the staying home from school thing by the third day, but he gave up on everything else."

Brody took another swig of beer, clearly lost in his memories. "Mom and I had a special bond. Tanner was Dad's mini-me. He wanted to be just like him. But I always wanted to be something other than a rancher. Mom saw that in me. She told me before she died to pursue my dreams. She said I was like her. She told me I had skills that were yet to be developed, and I could achieve anything if I set my mind to it. She made me promise not to let my father ride roughshod over my goals." The self-deprecating smile returned. "I followed her advice, much to Dad's frustration."

Her heart melted into mush. There was so much more to the kind cowboy who had shown up at her apartment to buy her property, and she wanted to know more. She just wasn't sure where to start. "You seem to know a lot about ranching. Is there something about it you don't like, or is it that you want to explore other occupations?"

This time he laughed outright. "Both. Ranching is great if it's in your blood. But even then, it's a lot of hard work and tedious. You do the same thing every year. We're always fixing fencing, cleaning up after monsoons, moving the cattle, overseeing the breeding and birthing, negotiating the feed and the selling, and a million other things that keep the ranch running. It never changes."

"But you said the Rocky Road was turning into a dude ranch. Isn't that a change?"

He opened his mouth then closed it before shaking his head. "I hadn't thought of that. I guess you're right. But still, it's a one-time change. I'm sure it will be the same repetitive tasks only on more of a daily routine. You know, like Monday is trail ride day, Tuesday is barbeque day, Wednesday is target practice day, and so on. Just the thought of it gives me nightmares." He grimaced.

"That all sounds pretty fun to me. But then again, I've always been doing something different. The longest full-time position I held was as a clerk for the City of Phoenix in their accounting office. I love numbers. They helped to pay for me to get my degree in accounting."

"You're an accountant?"

His surprise was so complete that it made her laugh. "Not exactly. I have a degree in accounting, but I've mainly served as a budget analyst. The only actual accounting I've done per se is volunteer work. Right now, I'm temping. It was the best type of position while my grandparents needed me so much. Now, I'll have to look for a new position, probably closer to Four Peaks, since I'll need to pay for the solar grid being put in tomorrow."

As if he'd just realized how much the casita had changed, he looked around. "You've done a lot in a short time, and it looks like you're here to stay."

He didn't sound too happy about it. "Don't worry. I haven't made up my mind yet about whether to sell or not. However, I'm hoping all goes well tomorrow since I don't treasure the thought of unpacking all this in the heat."

"Did you get the propane back up like I suggested?"

"I did. The propane company found the old tank and lifted it out just to be safe and put in a larger new one. State of the art, they said, though from what I read online, a propane tank is pretty much a propane tank. They showed me where the switch-over is, but I'm not sure how it all works, so I didn't try it. I don't really want to blow anything up."

He seemed to perk up at her uncertainty. "Show me where the switch-over is. I'll take a look."

Not completely confident in his abilities, but hoping he'd be honest if he didn't know how it all worked, she walked over to the tiny pantry and opened the door. "This is the lever the installer said I should use. He said to make sure I wait a full minute between switching from solar to the propane generator."

Brody motioned her out of the way, as it was a very small space. Then he followed each line from the box. "Where's the generator?"

"It's outside behind where the couch is."

Without another word, he strode outside.

She thought about following him as she might learn something, but he was back in less than three minutes.

"You're all hooked up." He walked into the pantry and threw the switch up. Immediately, a soft hum could be heard through the adobe wall.

She walked over to the bedroom doorway and cool air began blowing from the wall unit toward her. "Oh, that feels wonderful." She moved to the front door and closed it. "I could almost stay here tonight."

He closed the pantry door. "Why can't you?"

She lifted both hands palms up. "No mattress. It's being delivered in a few days. I suppose I could sleep on the couch, but I've done that before and it's not that comfortable. No. I have a room for two more nights at the hotel. The mattress will be delivered on Monday."

He picked up his half empty beer bottle. "Well, if you need another night, I'm sure Ava has rooms. That place is only booked solid during Pioneer Days or when someone in town has a wedding."

"Really? It's such a unique hotel. I'd think it would be busier."

"If we get this dude ranch off the ground, then they might get a few more people who fly in a day early or decide to stay around an extra night or two. Speaking of that, I need to get back to the ranch and do more work on the website. We're doing a soft opening in a couple weeks, kind of a run-through with a select group of people to work out the kinks." He finished his beer and dropped the bottle into the trash. "But I will see you tomorrow morning, right? Seven a.m.?"

She stifled a groan at the early hour. "I'll be there. I'm very excited to learn how to care for horses."

He smiled. "And I'm happy to have the help." He touched the brim of his hat with his fingers. "See you then." He strode to the door and exited with a jaunt in his step he didn't have when he'd arrived.

There was something about Brody Dunn that made her sigh, and it wasn't just his good looks. Despite the fact he wanted to buy her land, he kept helping her to settle in. And even with all his work, he still made time for her. She hoped he wasn't just being kind so she would sell to him. She'd already decided that if she sold, it would only be to the Dunns. She just didn't know if she'd want to or not. She'd see how the next few months went.

In the meantime, with cool air streaming in, she could easily get a few hours of unpacking done before dark. What was she thinking? She had electricity, so she could turn on lights and continue. The question was where to start.

As she looked around, she noticed the pantry latch had come undone. She smiled, pleased that the casita already had a homey feeling. Not only was it a mess, but it wasn't perfect.

That's how she felt about her life right now. It was homey, almost perfect, except for the loss of her grandparents.

Yet she had so many new things to learn and explore and a hundred tasks ahead of her, but it just made her happier that she had purpose.

She started for the bedroom, then slowed. Brody had talked about not being a rancher, but he never said what he did want to do. She'd have to remember to ask him in the morning. She continued into the bedroom. He seemed to need a purpose in life as much as she did. Just another way in which they were in sync.

CHAPTER 7

BRODY COULDN'T HELP SCOWLING as he held the wheelbarrow while Hannah joyfully threw horse shit into it. How could someone actually enjoy cleaning up horse dung?

She leaned on the pitchfork as she examined the pile in front of her. "I think that's full. If I add anymore, it might slop over the sides when you wheel it out."

He gritted his teeth at her happy attitude and started through the stall door.

"Don't dally. There's more poop to scoop." She chuckled.

He growled low in his throat as he exited the barn to dump the wheelbarrow contents into the composting heap. The pile was high since the farmer in Cave Creek had yet to truck it away for his fields. With the sun beating down, the work was hot, tiring, and smelly. Yet he could hear her humming in the barn.

Tipping his load, he righted the wheelbarrow before grabbing his bandanna and wiping the sweat from his neck.

Was this how all the visitors would feel at their future dude ranch operation? The thought had him perspiring more.

Hannah seemed to be enjoying herself on the ranch, exploring Four Peaks, and settling into her little house. He needed to up his game if he hoped to convince her to sell soon.

He walked back to the barn with the empty wheelbarrow and stopped at the opening to the final stall. "I think this last wheelbarrow load should be yours."

"About time you let me chuck it. Here." She held the pitchfork out to him.

He took it from her as she moved behind the handles. "I'm ready when you are. Let's get 'er done."

"Right." It had been a lesson in patience to let her muck out three stalls. What took her an hour would have taken him a third of the time. Quickly, he picked up what was left and set the pitchfork against the stall wall. "Okay, it's all yours."

"Wow, you're fast." She lifted the handles and awkwardly turned the wheelbarrow around. "Now where do I take it?"

He pointed toward the barn doors. "Go straight out there, take a right and cross the dirt road. You'll see a large pile, though you'll probably smell it first."

"Got it." She pushed the wheelbarrow out of the stall and slowly through the barn doors.

He made himself stay where he was, afraid if he watched her, he'd be apt to take the wheelbarrow from her and dump it. Instead, he wiped the sweat from his neck with the bandanna in his back pocket again. He hadn't expected her to do all the stalls. She was definitely persistent, or stubborn. He wasn't sure which.

With the waiting getting to him, he moved out of the stall and put the pitchfork away. Purposefully, he moved to his horse, who'd been watching them all morning. "What do you think, boy? Would she make a good ranch hand?"

Chaos just looked at him.

"Yeah, I know. You want to head out. We'll have to wait until after lunch." He gave his horse a pat before walking toward the barn doors. She should be back by now, even if she did move slowly.

He stepped outside scanning the area, but she wasn't there, so he headed to the right and crossed the road. He didn't see her anywhere around the manure pile. Turning back around, he caught site of the empty wheelbarrow next to the back side of the barn. Worried now that something might have happened, he ran to it and looked around. Where the heck was she?

Moving quickly to the other corner of the barn toward the house, he stopped short. "What are you doing?"

She jumped before looking over her shoulder and bringing her finger in front of her lips. "Shh, you'll startle them."

"Startle who?" He strode forward, not a little irritated.

"Them." She turned her head back and pointed about five feet away where a covey of quail was walking down the pavers between the barn and the house.

She was watching birds? He stopped next to her. "Have you never seen Gambel quail?"

"No. They are so adorable." She smiled softly as she followed the dozen or so birds with her gaze.

He tried to wrap his head around the fact she'd never seen quail, a bird he ran into almost daily. He opened his mouth to explain that fact but closed it at the look on her face. It was as if she'd fallen in love. There was something about it that had him re-evaluating not only her, but himself.

Hannah was what his mother would have called 'a kind soul.'

As the birds hopped up onto the porch, she took a couple steps forward, never letting them out of sight. "Do you think they're lost?"

Her concern had him holding back a smile of his own. "No, they're not lost. They come around here a lot. In the spring, the pairs will find a place around the house for their eggs. Usually, it's that big planter over there, my mother's bougainvillea bush, or in the brittlebush along the eastern fence. Then when the babies hatch, we have to watch out for them walking across this area where we park, especially if we're going out in the morning."

She spared him a glance at that. "I would love to see the babies. Is it true they walk in a line behind their mom?"

"Yes, it's true. Though probably not as neatly as you may have seen in pictures."

The quail began to hop off the end of the porch to waddle across the desert to the bushes he'd mentioned. This time, she didn't follow, but turned to face him. "I'm sorry. I forgot you were waiting for me in the barn. We should probably go back and finish mucking out. Didn't you say we now have to add fresh shavings?"

"Yes, that's next. But if you're tired, you can rest."

"Absolutely not. I want to learn everything about horses." She cocked her head, her gaze turning serious. "Will you teach me how to ride? Nothing fancy, but I'd love to be able to get up on one and have it walk around. I'd even be happy in a corral, like I saw them do with kids at the Arizona State Fair. My grandmother wouldn't let me until I was ten, and by then they weren't offering horse rides."

Though he called her a City Girl, he hadn't truly understood exactly how small her world had been. "Did you never take any trips beyond Phoenix?"

"Oh, yes. We drove down to Tucson a few times. Grandpa was in a bowling league and sometimes they made the regionals. I also went to Disneyland when I was eight. We drove because Grandma was afraid of flying. But the place we went the most was Las Vegas. Grandma and Grandpa liked to play the slots. I think they used me to avoid playing too long. Once I was old enough, I told them they should go without me, but they refused. I think in some ways, they saw me as part of my mom and didn't want to leave me alone. I even tried to move out once, but they begged me not to, promising a bigger apartment even though I knew they couldn't afford it. I felt so bad that I never brought it up again. I didn't realize..." She pressed her lips together, stopping abruptly.

It wasn't hard to tell from her rapid blinking that she fought tears. His instinct was to comfort her with a hug, but that was hardly appropriate. However, he could offer understanding. "You didn't realize how little time you'd have with them."

She nodded, her lips still pressed together.

"I understand. I knew Mom was sick, but I thought the medicine was a cure-all. I guess I was too young to understand that there was no cure." He shrugged, uncomfortable now with his sharing as she focused on him. "It's easy to look back and wish we'd done things differently, but we can't and it's doubtful the outcome would be different anyway. I know it wouldn't have been with my mom."

"You're right. It wouldn't have been with my grandparents either. They were quite old, and even though I knew that, I think in my subconscious I refused to recognize it. But I've learned to be more observant and in touch with the moment."

He gave her a smirk. "Even when cleaning shit?"

"Absolutely. Look at all the exercise I'm getting and new knowledge I'm obtaining. It's also helping me to avoid unpacking more boxes." She shook her head. "Now, *that* is tedious work. Should the pots go here or here? Should this painting go over the couch or by the door? Should I put this shirt in the closet or a drawer? There are way too many tiny decisions that affect how I will live day-to-day. At least cleaning shit is straightforward."

He wasn't sure whether to laugh or argue. He decided on neither. "Personally, I find that kind of change invigorating. I agree that learning something new is far more enjoyable than the everyday monotony, which in my case is cleaning shit, or moving cattle, or ordering supplies."

Her eyes widened and she held her arms out. "But look at all this. You have so much to show for it. So much to be proud of. Your family has a legacy."

He stiffened, telling himself not to get pissed. She was new to Four Peaks. She had no idea how desperately he needed to do anything but ranching. "Yes, my family does."

"Well, I'm certainly not helping you much by talking about everything except cleaning the stalls, so I'd best do my part to be helpful."

Before he could respond, she strode past him back toward the barn. After a dozen or so steps, she stopped and looked at him. "You coming? I can't do it all by myself...yet." She grinned before disappearing around the corner.

He followed at a slower pace, not quite as excited as she. She'd make a great wife for some ranch owner even if she was a city girl.

What was he thinking? If she had to muck the stalls every day like they did on Rocky Road, the novelty would wear off in no time. She was more like him than he would have thought, always interested in something new. He'd thought trick riding would be his career, but soon learned how short a career it could be. Then he'd taken lessons and earned his pilot license. He loved flying small planes, but all the rules and regulations drove him crazy. He'd much rather be the one enforcing the rules.

That's what had him looking at the requirements for being a wildlife manager. He had all the qualifications now except the specific training. That and the special tests after he completed it. He'd always had a way with wildlife, maybe because he respected it. That was the career for him.

Walking into the barn he found her struggling to open a block of pine shavings. "Here, let me get that." Pulling his utility knife from his pocket, he cut the top open. "We'll need a bag of these for each stall. If it was Monday we'd have to clean everything, wash the stalls out and start fresh."

"How many bags does that take?" She pulled the bag across the barn floor, sweat trickling down the side of her ear.

"Usually, four to five, depending on the horse. My father's horse, Maximus, requires five." He pointed down the row to where the stall was. "He's being ridden by Tanner today. We take turns riding his horse and my brother Jackson's." He opened two more bags and dropped one at each stall door.

She stopped dumping the shavings. "Jackson? You mentioned him before. Why doesn't he ride his own horse? Was he hurt?"

His chest tightened as it usually did when he thought of his older sibling. "No, or at least I hope not. He's in the Army and was deployed to Syria. It's his third deployment." He attempted to smirk. "Sometimes I wonder if he'd prefer to be over there instead of here."

"I doubt that's true. This ranch is so amazing. I'm sure he loves it as much as you."

"No, he actually loves it even more. He's like my oldest brother Tanner, a cowboy through and through."

She stopped spreading chips and shook her finger at him. "You can tell me all day that ranch life is boring, but you are still as much a cowboy as they are."

Despite the fact he didn't want to be, and the fact she had no idea what she was talking about, he still felt a sense of pride at her comment. It felt as if she defended him even though she'd never met his brothers.

Since she'd gone back to spreading shavings, he lifted a

bag and swished it out across Fury's stall. When it was empty, he tossed the bag to the side and lifted the one for Harmony's stall, reliable Nash's horse. Once that one was empty, he grabbed up the other one and checked in on Hannah.

She was taking armfuls of chips and spreading them by hand. He would have laughed if he hadn't been so fascinated by her thighs in the tight jeans as she backed up closer and closer. He should move, but he didn't and eventually she backed right up into him.

"Oh."

He caught her about the waist, to steady her. Her floral scent filled his nostrils and his body reacted to her soft form in his arm. "You, okay?" He didn't loosen his hold. She was just too tantalizing.

She grabbed his arm and looked up at him over her shoulder. "Are you okay? I'm the one who ran into you."

He grinned. "So you did."

She squinted at him. "Then again I don't have eyes in the back of my head and you saw me coming."

He shrugged. "Maybe I did or maybe I didn't, because I just came in here to see how you were doing."

She appeared to think about that, but shook her head. "No, you knew I was backing up. You're way to observant to run into someone."

He laughed, enjoying the way she thought, and forced himself to release her. "You already know me too well. I better be careful around you, Hannah Kingsley, or you'll learn all my secrets in no time and I'll become quite boring to you."

She faced him, not stepping back at all. "Do you have so many secrets then?"

He nodded seriously. "I do. I have two."

Her hand found her hip. "Only two? Then you must tell me."

"Now what fun would that be? After all, I'm sure you'll ferret them out of me in no time anyway. Now, let's get the rest of these shavings spread, I think it's almost lunch time." As if on cue, his stomach growled.

She gave him the side-eye. "You do realize it's only after eleven."

"And you do realize I've been up and working since five this morning. Now get your little behind back to work."

"Little? Well, when you put it that way." She sauntered back to the bag of shavings, her hips swaying in exaggeration.

He meant to make a wiseass remark but it got stuck in his throat as he watched her. Shit. He spun around and exited the stall. The last thing he needed was to be lusting after his sexy neighbor, when he was hoping she wouldn't be his neighbor for long.

Scooping up the empty shavings bags, he strode out of the barn and stuffed them in the trash barrel outside. The morning was not going as he'd hoped. The chores on a ranch were far too new to her to be considered boring. In fact, she seemed to have idealized ranch life even more. But she wasn't running a ranch. She was living in a tiny casita in the middle of nowhere. Maybe leaving her alone would be the better strategy. Then she could see what it was like to truly live in the desert.

Yet even at the thought, his protective instincts protested.

A woman living alone in that casita was a catastrophe waiting to happen. Still, it was what she wanted, to live on the land for a while. That was the crux of his problem—exactly how long was "a while?"

"I'm all done." She strode out of the stable and found him. "Do you want this in there?" She held up her empty bag and pointed to the trash can.

"Yes." He lifted the lid and let her smash down the plastic she added.

She brushed her hands together. "Just two more stalls. We're doing great."

"They're all done."

"You did them already?" Her brow crinkled with what could only be disappointment.

He barely kept from shaking his head at her. "Yes. Now we need to clean the water buckets out."

She brightened immediately and set her hands on her hips. "Great. How do we do that?"

He smiled as he turned toward the barn. "I'll show you." Something about her excitement communicated itself, and he found himself looking forward to instructing her. She must be an angel to have made him happy to be washing horse buckets. Ranch chores were boring, but Hannah's outlook was anything but.

CHAPTER 8

HANNAH LOOKED past Brody to see a blonde woman. with her hair in a ponytail wearing scrubs. just exiting the house. Before the woman could close the door, a large white dog rushed past and charged Brody. Hannah held her breath.

Brody crouched and the dog tried to lick his face, but he turned his head away while trying to get the animal under control. The dog circled in his arms, its body almost pushing him over.

The woman approached them. "I'm sorry. She was whining at the door, so I thought we had a visitor."

Before he could respond, the dog succeeded in toppling Brody onto his butt. "It's okay girl, I'm right here."

The woman strode forward with her hand out. "Hello. I'm Amanda Dunn, Brody's sister-in-law. You must be Hannah."

Hannah shook Amanda's hand. "It's nice to meet you. Are you going to work?"

"Oh, no. I'm already at work. I'm working with Brody's

dad after his stroke. Though technically, I'm not 'working,' since I quit my last job to marry Tanner and help with the dude ranch. But I still wear my scrubs when making Jeremiah do his exercises." She leaned in and lowered her voice. "He listens to me better when I wear these."

"I get that. You look very professional in those."

"And you look like me when I'm not in scrubs."

Brody spoke from his position on the ground. "Last I knew, Mandy, your hair wasn't auburn, your eyes weren't brown, and you weren't five-foot-seven."

Hannah and Amanda looked at him as if he'd turned into a werewolf. Did he really think Amanda meant it literally?

"What?" He stood, one hand still on the dog.

She looked back at Amanda and laughed.

Amanda shook her head as if putting up with her brother-in-law was just part of being in the family. "Hannah, I know you've been working hard out here in the barn. Would you like to join us for lunch?"

"I'd love to." It would also take her away from the giant dog who seemed to think the world of Brody.

"Wonderful. I'm making it today and it's pretty good. Come on in."

She walked beside Amanda, feeling a little safer with her. It wasn't that she didn't like dogs. It was just that she'd been bit by a neighbor's chihuahua when she was little, so she kept her distance. She still remembered how much the little dog's bite hurt. She couldn't imagine getting bit by a large dog.

Just as they reached the porch, she halted. "Wait, I can't go inside with all this on me. Is there someplace I can wash up?"

Amanda turned around and looked her over. "Just drop your gloves and boots on the porch and you can use the bathroom inside to wash up. That's what my brothers did at home. I'm sure Brody will wash up out at the barn, and later he can take care of yours."

After doing as suggested, she followed Amanda into the coolness of the large adobe ranch house. Two things impressed her upon entering. First, the solidness of the structure from the adobe walls to the travertine floor, and second, the casual atmosphere. She'd never been comfortable around wealthy people, so it was a relief to find the Dunns appeared to be down-to-earth.

Amanda pointed down a hall on the right. "The bathroom is the first door on the right."

She headed straight for the room and quickly washed up. Feeling more presentable, she returned to the entry, where she found a wide archway leading to the kitchen.

As she walked in, Amanda turned toward her. "You can choose a stool. I hope you don't mind. We always eat at this island. Tanner and his brothers grew up here with their dad, so they don't have a formal dining area. From what Tanner told me, over there was where the table used to be, but Jeremiah turned it into a den, since it was never used." Amanda started laying out focaccia bread on a baking tray.

Hannah climbed onto a stool. "What are you making?"

"I actually made my husband's barbeque chicken salad." She lifted a forkful before heaping it on the bread. "However, I'm adding my own twist. These Dunn men get stuck in a rut sometimes, so I like to bump them out of it."

The front door opened and she heard Brody talking.

"Now Cami, we have a guest, so you need to be on your best behavior. Agreed?" He sounded like he was talking to a child, not a dog.

Despite her nervousness, she found his actions endearing.

He strode in without his hat and took a seat next to her. "Sit." The dog immediately sat behind his stool. He turned toward Amanda. "What are you doing? I hope you aren't going to ruin that barbeque chicken salad. Those aren't bulky rolls. That's not even brioche."

"Nope, it's not." Amanda turned to the refrigerator with no explanation.

Hannah swallowed a chuckle at how evasive Amanda was being.

Brody turned his head toward her. "You'll have to excuse her. She's starting to cook like Tanner, always experimenting. If you don't like it, I'll be happy to make you a normal sandwich."

She couldn't help observing that he was being both obnoxious and kind in the same sentence. "That's okay. I like trying new things."

Amanda turned back with cheese in her hand. "Brody, you stick to desserts and we'll handle the rest."

At Amanda's comment, Hannah laid her hand on Brody's arm. "Speaking of desserts, have you figured out Mama Juanita's Tres Leches cake yet?"

"Not yet, but I've only made one attempt. I know what I have to do differently, so I'm hoping I get it this time."

She released him, but patted his arm before setting her hand back in her lap. "That's okay. If you even get close, it would be amazing. I'm so pleased I'll be living nearby to try it." She leaned in closer and whispered. "You will let me try it, right?"

"I'm hoping you'll be the final judge." His gaze held genuine eagerness.

She smiled, very pleased that he still planned to work on it and would allow her to be a part. Even if it was just the tasting part, which was her favorite. "I'd love to."

"Good. I don't think asking Mama Juanita would be a good idea." He grimaced before turning back to Amanda. "Is my brother coming in?"

"He's on his way." Amanda took the cookie sheet of open-faced sandwiches and stuck them under the broiler.

Hannah's mouth started to water. "Amanda, those are going to be delicious."

"We'll see. I haven't made them before, so I make no guarantees."

The front door opened, and footsteps much like Brody's but far harder sounded in the entryway. Within seconds, another cowboy strode in. He was slightly taller than Brody, and his hair had no blond streaks, as if it never saw the sun at all. His facial features were much like Brody, revealing him as a brother, but where his were angular, Brody's were more friendly. "What's for lunch?" He moved to the sink and washed his hands, splashing water on his face as well.

Amanda answered him. "An open-face broiled barbeque chicken salad and cheese sandwich on focaccia bread."

The man, who had to be Tanner, dried his face and hands. Then he brushed a kiss on his wife's cheek before opening the fridge and grabbing a water bottle. "You want one—oh, hello."

She smiled. "Hello. I'm Hannah Kingsley, your new neighbor. And yes, I'd love a water."

Tanner handed her the water bottle. "It's nice to finally meet you. My brother seems to be keeping you busy."

Brody spoke up at that. "I'm just helping her learn what ranch life is like. I'll take one of those." Tanner threw one to him, and he caught it as it was about to go over his head. "Your aim is getting rusty."

Tanner took two more bottles out and set one next to his wife before unscrewing the cap on his own and taking a gulp. Setting the bottle on the counter, Tanner looked at his brother. "I meant to do that."

"Umm Brody, I think Cami wants something." At Amanda's observation, Hannah glanced behind him to see the dog had placed her paws on the cross-bar of his stool.

He immediately stood and walked around the island, the dog Cami following closely. "I promised her a bone."

"At this time of day?"

He grabbed a box of dog bones from a cupboard. "She still needs to gain some more weight."

Cami sat, but her tail swished across the floor as fast as a snake rattle. Taking a bone out, Brody held it as he placed the box back in the cupboard. "Hannah, would you like to give Cami her bone?"

She didn't move a muscle, but she managed to speak normally. "No. I'm good."

He must have sensed her hesitancy because he gave her a

questioning look before bending to hold out his hand. "Shake."

Cami lifted her paw into his.

"Good girl." He let Cami have the bone, and the large dog took it into to the den next to the sliding glass doors to enjoy.

"I don't blame you." Amanda put on a pair of oven mitts. "Cami can be too appreciative sometimes."

Tanner pulled out silverware for them all, as Brody returned to his seat. Amanda added sandwiches to plates, and once everyone had a plate and silverware, they gave the new experiment a try, she and Tanner standing on the other side of the counter opposite them though there were four stools.

Hannah took a bite. "Oh, Amanda, this is delicious. I need to try making these." The melding of different flavors was truly a treat. She rarely cooked anything so interesting, now that she lived alone. How different it was to be part of a family, specifically an adult family where everyone could share chores and enjoy each other's company. It was something she'd always envied, especially when she was in grammar school. Now she appreciated being a part of it, even if only for lunch.

"I saw you got the wood moved over to the boulder break. Thanks." Tanner gestured with his fork toward Brody. "I'd forgotten all about it. Between the building inspections and the new shooting range, I dropped that ball. I appreciate you picking it up."

Brody shrugged. "No problem. Once we get that repaired, we'll have to start on the birthing pen roof."

Tanner dropped his fork on his pate. "Hell, I forgot about the roof, too." He turned toward his wife, his green eyes wide. "I did it again. I told you I wasn't going manage the dude ranch and the cattle ranch at the same time."

She patted his shoulder. "You're doing fine. You're not doing this alone. We all have your back."

Though Tanner nodded, it was obvious he was kicking himself for his forgetfulness. Hannah tried to think of something encouraging, but since she was an outsider, anything she could come up with just sounded lame.

"Speak for yourself, Mandy. I've had his back for decades. I think it's time we took off the training wheels."

Surprised by Brody's statement, she stared at him as he grinned at his brother.

"At least I know how to ride. Still waiting for you to catch up." Tanner appeared completely serious.

"I can out ride you, out rope you, and out run you any day."

Tanner raised one eyebrow. "If you're so talented, why don't you oversee the rest of the details in making Dad's dude ranch a reality?"

Both of Brody's hands came up as if to ward off evil spirits. "Not a chance. You'll be running the show. I don't want to get blamed for any of the missteps you're sure to make."

"Coward."

Brody smirked. "No. Just smart."

Tanner pointed to Cami who still munched on her bone. "And keeping a half-starved abandoned dog is smart?"

Brody didn't even hesitate. "At least I have a dog for a pet, and not an obstinate, love-sick heifer."

Amanda laughed loudly. "You have to admit, Tanner. He's got you there."

"Hmph." Tanner shook his head, but Hannah could see he fought a smile.

The whole conversation was a revelation. Brody had purposefully goaded his brother to distract him from his self-doubt and worry. That Tanner didn't bring the subject back to his forgotten tasks on the ranch made it clear he was happy for Brody's help. Yet, the whole exchange had been one insult after another. She found the episode fascinating, especially because the basic motivation was their love for each other.

"What about you, Hannah. Do you have any pets?"

She shook her head at Amanda's question. "No. My grandmother was allergic to animal fur. I did have a goldfish when I was seven, but it didn't last long. I was so devastated when I came home from school one day to find it dead, that my grandmother swore to never have another pet in the apartment. She didn't like seeing me so distraught."

"Do you like animals?" Brody had turned, and though his question was casual, the focus in his blue gaze was anything but.

"I do. I love going to the Phoenix Zoo."

Tanner set his plate in the sink. "Speaking of a zoo. Amanda, did Dad tell you his idea about a petting zoo here at the ranch?"

Amanda rolled her eyes. "Seriously?"

"Yes, seriously. Let me show you what he was thinking. Then maybe you can find a good way to talk him out of it. Is he in the therapy room or the office?"

Amanda waved toward an archway on the side of the

kitchen. "He's taking his nap. Show me. I'll come back and clean up."

Tanner's whole body seemed to relax before taking his wife's hand and walking out of the kitchen.

It reminded Hannah of how her grandparents depended on each other, one always supporting the other, or being honest with each other even when it wasn't easy to do.

"Will you get a pet now to keep you company?"

At Brody's question, she turned back to him, having forgotten the original topic. "Actually, I was thinking about it. I'm nervous, though, that I might forget to feed it or hurt it in some way. I've never had another creature depend on me to live. It's a bit intimidating."

His eyebrows furrowed as he looked at her sideways. "Didn't you say you cared for your grandparents? It sounds to me like you have a lot of experience in that area."

"Oh, that's not the same. My grandparents could communicate with me. Boy, did they ever. But with an animal, you have to guess at what it wants and needs." She pointed toward the dog who lay with her head on the floor looking out the slider. "Like now, how would you know what your dog needs? Is she sad? Anxious to go outside? Does she want another bone?"

As if she'd said the magic word, the dog's head snapped up.

"Shh, don't say the word b-o-n-e. She knows that word and will come over to beg."

At the thought of the dog coming toward her, she stiffened.

"Are you afraid of dogs?"

His blunt question caused her to give a blunt answer. "Yes."

"I'm sorry. I didn't know. I can put Cami in my room if you're uncomfortable."

The dog had put her chin back on the floor as if she'd given up on her treat. "No. I don't want to disturb her. It's my hang-up, not hers."

"Did you have a bad experience with a dog?"

"I was bit." She waved her hand as if it didn't matter, even though it did. A part of her knew her fear wasn't fair to all dogs, but she couldn't seem to shake it. "I was ten and it was only a chihuahua, but it hurt, and after he bit my hand, he went after my feet."

"Didn't the owner stop it?" His tone sounded as if he were ready to punch the man in the face.

She shook her head. "It was my fault. I assumed, because it was a small dog, that it liked people. The teenage boy who was walking it thought it was funny that I was bit, praising his dog for protecting him. He said it served me right for touching his dog. I look at it as a lesson well learned."

"No one should own an animal and allow that to happen." The words seemed to issue from his clenched jaw.

"It's okay. The wounds healed. See?" She held up her right hand where there wasn't even a scar to mark that day's events. The only scar was in her psyche.

He took her hand in his and examined it. "I don't know. I see something on your index finger."

She grinned, loving how sweet he was being. "I was bit on the pinky."

"That's what I meant, your pinky." Though he said it

seriously, his lips fought a smile before he released her. "Then I would like to introduce you to Cami."

Her breath left her and her heart started to race. "That's okay. I'm fine."

He stood, shaking his head. "No, you're not. At just the mention of meeting my dog, your whole body turned as stiff as a fence post."

She forced a shrug. "Habit."

He studied her for a moment, and she was quite sure he could tell she was afraid. But he didn't say anything. Instead, he turned and walked to his dog.

"Cami, would you like to meet Hannah?"

The dog immediately rose, tail wagging and meeting him halfway across the room.

"Cami, sit." He pointed down at his cowboy boots.

The dog immediately turned around joyfully and sat her butt on his boots. Hannah smiled.

"She's still learning about personal space." He grimaced before patting Cami on the head. "I'm going to stay right here and you can come and meet her. She likes everybody, so hopefully she won't push you too hard. But I promise, she won't bite."

Hannah told herself she needed to get off the stool and try it, but her muscles wouldn't move. "She's a very big dog."

He looked down at the dog. "Is she? She seems small to me, because next to the cattle, she's a tiny thing."

She refrained from pointing out that such a tiny thing could push an adult to the ground. But he did have a point. The cattle were much bigger. Even the bull she spoke to. Why wasn't she afraid of the bull? Brody's dog was much smaller. She hadn't even been afraid of the horses in the barn, and they were much bigger.

Finally, she forced herself to stand.

The dog immediately stood and wagged its tail as it looked at her before looking at Brody.

"Cami, stay."

The dog's butt hit the floor next to him so fast, it looked as if he'd pulled a string.

"Hannah, walk over when you're ready and let her sniff your hand so she can learn your scent."

"My hand smells like my sandwich. She might bite it. I don't think that's a good idea."

Brody shook his head. "She'll more likely lick you. See?" He held his hand down, and the dog immediately butted her head against it before licking him.

Obviously, the dog was friendly, so why couldn't she move? Brody stood there patiently, no more than six steps away. The dog kept looking back and forth between her and him. More afraid the dog would lose patience with her than Brody would, she finally took a step.

The dog's butt came off the floor.

"Stay." Brody's command was immediate.

The butt dropped once more, but the tail didn't stop wagging.

She forced herself to take the next step. The dog didn't move this time, which made her more confident and she took two more steps. The dog looked at her. It lifted one eyebrow and then the other as if trying to figure out why she was hesitating. Of course, that was all in her own head, but it did make it easier to take the last step.

"Cami, this is Hannah. Hannah, this is Cami. Cami, stay."

The dog looked up at her, its dark brown eyes focused only on her.

Her pulse became erratic as irrational fear filled her, and she took a step back, trying to breathe.

The dog's head lowered and it lay down with a soft whimper.

She snapped her gaze to Brody. "Is she okay? I didn't touch her."

His gaze softened. "She's fine. Just disappointed. It's okay. You don't have to greet her today."

Disappointed?

She looked down at the dog, who kept her chin on the floor. Now she felt like she'd been mean. She couldn't handle that. "Cami?"

The dog's head lifted off the floor to look at her.

Taking a deep breath, she held her hand out. "It's nice to meet you."

Cami looked back at Brody, who nodded.

As if the dog understood, Cami stepped forward and sniffed at her hand then sat.

"She wants you to pet her."

Hannah wasn't sure how Brody knew what a dog wanted, but she trusted him, so she laid her hand on top of Cami's head and patted her. The dog's white fur was soft and silky. "Hi, Cami."

The dog lifted her head and licked her hand.

"Oh, that's wet." She wiped her hand on her jeans.

Cami stood again, turned around and sat with her back to her.

"Did I insult her?" She looked to Brody, who smiled.

"No. She wants you to pet her some more. But be careful. Once you start petting her, she'll never feel it's enough."

Hannah looked at the dog who lifted her head. Hesitantly, she patted her again and the dog tilted her head more.

"She likes her ears rubbed."

At Brody's statement, Hannah rubbed Cami's ears. The next thing she knew, the dog was pushing her whole weight against her, causing her to step back.

"Cami, come."

Immediately, the dog walked to Brody and sat facing him.

"Good girl." He gave Cami a pat. "She likes you."

The knot in her stomach seemed to unravel. "I'm glad. I like her, too."

"She's a great dog. I wish she could come outside with me more, but it's too hot yet. She has a double coat. Her breed is meant for cooler climes."

"Speaking of cooler, I need more water." She walked back to the island and opened her water bottle for a drink.

Brody grabbed his own bottle. "We still need to wash those buckets out. Are you ready for more work?"

She scanned the dirty dishes spread over the island. "Shouldn't we wash these first?"

"Nope. Today is Amanda's day. We each take a day to cook and do the dishes. Mine is tomorrow. Don't worry. She'll be back out to clean up before my dad wakes up." He opened his arm toward the front door.

Taking the hint, she took her water with her, noticing two cowboy hats on the entry table.

Brody snatched up his hat and set it on his head before opening the door for her. He hesitated before following her out, when arguing came from the other room. He closed the door and chuckled.

As they walked toward the barn, she had to ask. "What's funny?"

"My brother. He's hoping that Mandy will convince my father not to create the petting zoo. But I saw Dad's plans and Mandy is going to love them. Tanner's barking up the wrong tree on this one."

It was odd to her that he would find his brother's disappointment funny. "Do you think it's a good idea?"

"It doesn't matter what I think. But yes, I do think it's a good idea. Tanner just doesn't want another project to complete before the opening. He's already used to being in charge, and between Dad and Mandy, he's had to cave to everything. Dad's ideas are well thought-out."

"Why do you say it doesn't matter what you think?" She stopped just inside the shade of the barn, concerned by his comment. His opinion should matter among the family. He was an intelligent, experienced cowboy.

He kept going before halting and turning back to look at her. "I'm just one of the worker bees who plans to fly away as soon as I can. I do want my family to keep the ranch, but my interests lie elsewhere."

She stared at him, hoping he was joking, but was clear he was not. "Will you be leaving soon?"

"That's my plan." He gave her a grin before heading into the barn.

Surprised and unreasonably hurt, she remained standing where she was. Knowing that Brody planned to leave, go who-knew-where, undercut her contentment over discovering her inheritance. Suddenly, it didn't seem the slice of heaven she'd thought it, which made no sense. Brody was her neighbor and though he'd helped her, he'd also argued against her living on her own property.

She still had the rest of his family as neighbors and had already started making friends in town. If Brody decided to go off to pursue his goals, she should be happy for him. Yet as much as she tried to wish him well in her mind, she couldn't seem to manage it. She'd obviously been leaning on him a bit too much. She needed to learn to stand on her own two feet, because there was no one else she could depend on now.

"You coming, or are you going to stand there like brittlebush, looking pretty?"

She whirled around at his question and started into the barn. "Has anyone ever told you that you can be obnoxious?"

He laughed. "All the time."

CHAPTER 9

"BRODY, THE COWS ARE OVER HERE."

At Layne's comment, he turned Chaos around to face the ranch foreman. "Yeah, but they're fine."

The man, older by almost ten years, rode up next to him. "What's got you so focused to the northeast? Did you see activity out there we should know about?"

No. That was the problem. He'd seen no activity on Hannah's land for the last two weeks, nor had he heard from her. He'd forced himself not to contact her, but that hadn't stopped him from checking on her from the ranch, not that he could do it all day, but despite riding the fence that bordered her property, he hadn't seen her. The more concerning part was her Jeep was parked in the same spot, or at least that's what it looked like.

"Brody?" Layne waved his hand in front of him.

"What? I was just looking at the scenery."

Layne's eyebrow rose. "The scenery. You mean the scenery you've been looking at your entire life?"

Okay, so maybe that hadn't been the best answer. He shrugged. "I was just wondering if I was going to miss it when I land my first position as a wildlife manager."

This time Layne's eyes widened. "I thought you had to complete the training at the academy first."

"I do. But that won't take long, and then they might need me in Pinetop or Page or—"

"Or Bisbee, Ruby, or Nogales. Once you're accepted, they could need you anywhere."

He'd always assumed he'd be located north. Layne brought up a good point—that he could as easily be accepted for a position in a southern territory. "It doesn't matter where. I'll be happier than Cami with a new bone."

"That's all well and good, but I need to get that hurt cow and her calf into the trailer. Think you could focus on the here and now long enough to keep the other cattle from getting in my way?"

"I can do that standing on Chaos on one leg with him walking backward."

Layne's bushy black mustache twitched. "I don't need any trick riding. Just keep the cattle away."

"You've got it." He walked Chaos forward to stand guard.

As Layne circled the pair he needed, two heifers got curious. Brody tapped his heels and rode Chaos between the pair and Layne. They both gave him sorrowful looks as if all they wanted was a little gossip, but they turned back toward the rest of the herd. When the trailer back slammed into place, he turned around to find Layne dismounting.

Brody rode over. "When's the vet coming out?"

He looked up from tying his horse to the fence. "This

afternoon. I'm going to lock these two in one of the birthing pens. Now that we have a partial roof on, thanks to you, they'll be in the shade and I'll distract mama with some extra food. You'll bring my horse back to the barn?"

"Sure. Then I'm going to ride out and check on our new neighbor."

"Check on her? You make it sound like she's a heifer that's lost."

He smirked. "In a way she is. She's a city girl. She doesn't know jack about living out here. I'm sure she'll be moving back to Phoenix in no time."

Layne shook his head. "I feel sorry for her. Once you get something into your mind, you find a way to make it happen. Have you considered that she might enjoy staying here?"

"Staying where? On her property? What would she do with it? She's one lone woman."

Layne lifted one hand up. "That may be true now, but she might meet some cowboy and decide to marry and build her own ranching empire. Just sayin'."

He didn't like that idea on many levels. "Well, just say it somewhere else. I don't need anyone giving her ideas."

Layne shook his head before turning to the truck.

Brody rode to the gate and opened it, closing it after moving Layne's horse and his own outside. Hannah only had eleven hundred acres. It wasn't enough to support a large herd of cattle. But what if she decided she wanted a pig farm, or to bring in irrigation and grow cotton, or—he froze. What if she decided to build a paintball course? That would bring a bunch of people into their valley.

He mounted and clicked his tongue for Layne's horse to

follow. There were a number of men in town that he'd gone to school with who would love to get their hands on their own property, and Hannah was the perfect way. They might even try to manipulate her.

As he rode back to the barn, he imagined every worst-case scenario. He had to talk to her right away. Once he had the two horses settled in their stalls, he rolled the ATV out of the barn. He never should have left her alone. There were too many smooth-talking cowboys who might take advantage of her. He'd been honest from the start, but what if that backfired?

A bark from in the house gave him an idea. Walking back into the barn, he pulled out the wagon he'd built for Cami. It was big enough for a grown man, though no grown man would be caught riding behind an ATV. He hooked the wagon to the tow-hitch before opening the door of the house.

Cami bounded out, turning around to jump on him.

"You want to go for a ride to see Hannah?"

Cami barked as if answering.

He rubbed the dog's ear, then led her to the wagon. He opened one side and she jumped in without even being told. "Good girl." After securing the door again, he straddled the machine and started it.

Instead of driving down the rocky driveway, he cut across the desert. At least the Harpers' casita was directly north of his own home, making it easier to be neighborly. As he bounced across the desert, he tried to decide on an excuse for his visit. If he'd been smart, he would have tried making the Tres Leches cake again. He could always invite her over to try it on Saturday. He'd have time to make it by then.

Pleased with his reasoning, he pulled in front of the casita and turned off the machine. Getting off, he looked at Cami. "Stay." He didn't want Hannah to be scared, but if she interacted with his dog more, she might get over her fear.

He walked to the Jeep. Though he'd thought it hadn't moved, there were a number of tire tracks that showed she'd pulled in multiple times, which made him feel better. Walking up to the door, he knocked. "Howdy, Hannah. It's me, Brody."

He waited a minute or two before putting is ear to the solid wood door. When he couldn't hear anything, he knocked again, remembering how she hadn't opened the door of her apartment right away either. "Hannah, it's me!"

Again he waited. Could she be sleeping? He doubted it, as it was late morning. Was she out with friends? He didn't see her as the type to make a friend come all the way out to her property just to pick her up.

He walked around to a window, stepping past a newly planted agave plant and a small bed of dirt, obviously waiting for plantings. He didn't like the look of that. It shouted 'permanent resident' to him.

Knocking on the window, he waited to look in. He didn't want to scare her. When there still was no answer, he looked inside, the shade of his cowboy hat helping him to see the main room was empty. He quickly moved to the back window. This time he didn't need the shade of his hat to see she wasn't in there. The bathroom door stood open. Maybe she was showering. That would explain it. He pressed his ear to the glass, but didn't hear a sound. Then the air conditioning unit next to him clicked on, obliterating any hope of hearing anything.

Concern grew into worry. He went back to the door and knocked loudly, then tried the door. It was locked. Had she gone for a walk and been bitten by a snake and was even now lying on the ground dying?

He attempted to stifle his train of thought, but his worry grew anyway. He needed to put his emotion aside and focus on the facts. That's what a wildlife manager would do. He looked around the building for clues and found tire tracks leading away from the house toward the mountains. He crouched down and examined them. They were smaller than his ATV tracks. Confused, he followed them a few yards, but they continued.

Cami barked as if to remind him she wanted to come out.

He walked back and gave her head a rub. She could easily jump out if she had to. "I'll let you out in a few. First, we need to follow these." Giving her a last pat, he sat on the machine and drove next to the tracks. As he drew closer to the base of the mountain, he could see another machine parked up ahead. "What the..." It looked like a damn golf cart.

He pulled up next to it and got off to investigate. That's exactly what it was. He turned back to look at the casita which was quite small now. Was some golf course developer out here? He didn't like that idea at all. There was a towel covering the steering wheel, so he grabbed it and strode back to the wagon and let Cami out. "Sit."

Cami's butt hit the dirt.

"Okay girl, we need to find whoever used this towel. We've been practicing this, but now it's for real."

He let Cami sniff at the towel.

"Okay, seek."

Cami sniffed the ground for a moment then bounded up the hillside. He had no idea if she had the scent. When they practiced, she was only right half the time, distracted by the other smells of the ranch, but at least climbing higher he'd have a better view, even if she did just find a desert cottontail rabbit.

Cami stayed ahead of him about fifty feet, stopping once in a while to make sure he followed. The climb was getting long and he stopped for a moment to see if anyone was below, but there was no movement around the ATV or golf cart. He continued up. Who the heck brought a golf cart into the desert?

Finally, Cami halted, sitting, staring at a boulder they would have to climb around. Obviously, she'd just enjoyed the climb. Turning around, he looked out to see what was visible and sucked in his breath. Despite living under the four peaks all his life, he'd never climbed this hill. The whole valley was laid out before him and he could even see the town. From such a viewpoint, it was actually beautiful. But appreciating the view was his last concern. Now he was too high to see if Hannah had been hurt.

Turning to call Cami back, the dog barked before running around the boulder.

Shit, now the dog was after a rabbit. Hopefully, not a rattlesnake. "Cami, come."

Cami didn't come. In fact, she disappeared behind the boulder.

Not in the mood for games, he stalked after Cami. As he made it halfway around, he found her standing with her tongue hanging out. Immediately, his sense went into overdrive. "Cami, sit."

The dog did, as he walked past her to see what she'd found.

"Brody, what are you doing here?"

Profound relief washed through him at her voice, but it still took him a few seconds to find her in the shade of the large boulder since she sat on the ground. Worry returned in an instant. He immediately walked to her and crouched, ignoring the racing of his heart. "Are you okay?"

"I'm fine. Why?"

"Why? Because you're halfway up the mountain sitting on the ground. Do you have heat exhaustion?" She did look a little flushed, but it was hard to tell for sure in the shadow, plus she was wearing her cowboy hat.

"No. I have my lunch." She reached into a small backpack and pulled out a sandwich in a sealed plastic bag. "It's tuna fish. Why are you here?"

Now he felt like a complete idiot, which just turned his concern into anger. "I'm looking for you. I came by your casita and found your vehicle there, but you were nowhere to be found. When I saw the tire tracks leaving your place, I grew worried. I didn't know if you were abducted or lying on the desert floor somewhere, dying of a snake bite."

Her eyes widened at that. "I hadn't thought about a snake

bite. Maybe I can get some antivenom to take with me next time."

"Next time?" He had a hard time believing she'd be so foolish as to venture so far again. She had too much common sense, plus what she learned on the internet. "Why are you up here?"

She smiled. "Oh, I come up here about three times a week. It's so peaceful and the view is amazing. Did you see it?"

"Yes. It's nice." He couldn't seem to give her anything more than that. He actually thought her in her buttoned-down white shirt tied at her waist and jean shorts was a far better view.

"Nice? It's spectacular. When I first started up the mountain, I walked all the way from home, but then I was too tired to go very high. So I bought a used golf cart from Mr. Allen at the used car place in town. He said he knows you. He was very complimentary. He gave me a good price, too. So then I was able to ride to the mountain and climb. This is as far as I've gone. I need to keep doing it before I'll venture higher. I know not to go farther than I can handle."

"Alone?" He blurted it out before he could take it back. "It's dangerous."

Her smile disappeared. "No, it's not. I came prepared. I have water, food, bandages, in case I fall. I hadn't thought of the snake antivenom, but I will add that to my pack. Besides, if anything awful happens, I can always call someone." She pulled her phone out of her back pocket.

He crossed his arms over his chest. "Your phone. What

are you going to do with that—send light signals across the valley? Or were you planning to start a fire."

She rolled her eyes. "Duh, I'd call someone and let them know I need help."

"Really? Go ahead. Call me."

"You're right here. Why would I call you?"

He jerked his head up. "Humor me."

"This is silly." She clicked her phone on and dialed. Her brow lowered before she held her phone up.

"That's not going to help. There's no signal out here."

She rose, still holding her phone aloft. "How can that be? I can see a tower in town."

"Things appear a lot closer than they are in the desert. There's no signal anywhere in these mountains. They're state conservation land."

She brought her phone down and slipped it back into her back pocket. "So I wouldn't be able to call for help."

"No."

He watched as she cocked her head, probably trying to find a way to argue with him. Then, as if she'd reviewed all her options and realized he was right, her shoulders fell.

"Well, that sucks. I've really been enjoying my lunches up here, and I've been getting great exercise, too."

Her disappointment bothered him. He almost offered to accompany her, but he didn't have that kind of time. Besides, this was part of showing her why she'd enjoy the comforts of city life over desert life.

She finally looked at him, her brown eyes hopeful. "Since you're here now, would you mind staying while I enjoy my lunch? I'd be happy to share."

Cami chose that moment to push against the back of his legs, causing one of his knees to buckle a bit. "What? You remember Hannah."

Cami walked around him and sat, watching Hannah, who hadn't moved.

He really wanted her to not be afraid of his dog, and only for that reason, he made his decision. "I can stay. Do you have anything that Cami might like?"

"Um, I don't know. I have my sandwich and some individually wrapped cheeses, an apple, and a pudding cup. Oh, and a couple of granola bars. Would Cami like any of that?"

"What kind of pudding?"

"Chocolate."

"That's a no. Dogs can't have chocolate, but Cami does love cheese. Maybe you could give her the cheese, and I'll have a granola bar."

Hannah had leaned over to lift her backpack, but stilled halfway there, which showed him much more of her cleavage. He quickly lifted his gaze to her eyes.

"You want *me* to give Cami the cheese?"

"Sure. She'll be anyone's friend for life if they give her cheese."

Hannah finally snagged her backpack and stood upright. "Okay."

She didn't sound okay, but she did pull a triangle of cheese from her sack.

Cami's nose lifted, and soon her butt lifted as well, before she took a couple steps toward Hannah.

"When she gets closer, tell her to sit, then take the paper off and give it to her."

Hannah's brows rose. "Well, I wasn't going to leave the paper on."

He knew that. He wasn't even sure why he said that, except maybe because he wanted to protect Cami from suffering ever again.

As the paper was peeled, Cami walked up to Hannah, her tail wagging.

"Sit." Hannah's command was a bit weak, but Cami loved cheese, and her butt plopped down.

"Good dog. Here you go." Hannah held the cheese on her palm.

Cami's tongue came out and swiped the whole piece into her mouth.

"Oh." Hannah pulled her hand back then wiped it on her shorts. "I didn't expect to get so wet." She gave a small uncomfortable laugh. "Should I give her the other one now?"

"Sure. If you hold off until your done with your lunch, she'll look at you like she's starving the whole time. And she knows what starving is all about."

"Was she a stray that you took in?" Hannah pulled out the second piece of cheese and started to unwrap it.

Cami's gaze didn't leave Hannah's hands and her tail sped up as her butt lifted just slightly off the round.

Even as he thought of how he came upon Cami, he tensed. "Yes, she was a stray, in the worst way. Somone from up north had dumped her in the desert, and she was trying to survive. She must have been out here a month before I found her. She was skin and bones and her fur was matted and the color of the dirt. That's why I called her Cami, short for 'camouflage.'"

"Oh, the poor thing." As if the cheese was Cami's first meal since then, Hannah crouched down. "Here you go, girl." She held her hand out and Cami licked the cheese into her mouth. Hannah tentatively set her hand on Cami's back and stroked. "You won't ever have to starve again, now that you have Brody. He'll take good care of you."

He wasn't sure if it was Hannah's growing connection to his dog or her faith in him that had him straightening his shoulders. "No, she'll never have to worry. I think she knows that. She's very smart. She's the one who found you."

Cami turned her head to lick Hannah's face, and Hannah fell on her butt avoiding the kiss. "Does she think I have more in my mouth?"

He laughed. "No. She just likes to show her appreciation with a kiss." He wouldn't mind if Hannah had the same habit. Now where had that come from? "Cami, come. Let Hannah eat her lunch in peace."

Cami trotted over to him.

"You two can't stand there in the sun while we eat. Come sit."

Though there wasn't a large amount of shade, there was just enough if he sat right next to her, which he didn't mind doing. Walking around to sit on her right against the boulder, he kept Cami on his other side.

"Here." Hannah handed him half her sandwich.

"That's your lunch."

"No, it's yours. Mine is right here." She held up the other half. "I'm sharing my food and you're sharing your time."

"Thank you." He took a bite.

She grinned. "Besides, I know it's past your lunch time, and I expect your stomach to be growling any second."

He would have laughed, but he had tuna fish in his mouth, so he chewed instead.

"And since I'm not going to get to stay up here as long as I expected, I won't need all this food." Her lower lip jutted out just a bit, making her disappointment clear.

He felt like an ogre for ruining one of her new favorite pastimes. But it was for the best. It wasn't safe to be alone in the mountains, or the desert for that matter. "I know it's hard to adjust to new limitations. We're doing that now at Rocky Road. After my father had a stroke while riding the fences alone, Tanner won't let any of us ride out without a partner. Personally, I think he's going a bit overboard, but like I said, what I think doesn't matter. He can get very stubborn, especially when it comes to family. After my brother died, you'd think Tanner was my bodyguard." He shook his head as he took another bite, liking the bit of dill relish she had put in the tuna.

"Your brother Jackson died?" Hannah brought her sandwich down to her lap and stared at him wide-eyed.

"No, not at all. He's alive and well...as far as I know. He's in Syria, so it's a bit hard to tell." He tried not to think about Jackson too much. His mother always said that worrying accomplished nothing.

"Then who died?"

"My brother Devlin. I wasn't there, but all my brothers were in the hayloft and Devlin fell and broke his neck. It just about killed my mom." He took a deep breath as memories of coming upon his mother crying filled his head. "It was an accident, but Tanner blames himself as the oldest, while Jackson claims he might as well have killed Devlin with his own two hands. I wasn't there, but it messed up both of them. Just my opinion."

Hannah linked her hand with his. "I'm so sorry. I can't imagine losing a brother."

Her touch felt good, though he shrugged. "I was pretty young and it took me a while to understand everything. I hadn't been allowed to go to the barn without an adult, so I didn't see it happen. But I saw what it did to my mother, and like any little boy, I wanted to fix it. But I learned some things can't be fixed."

He'd also learned that waiting until someday was a waste of time. Someday wasn't guaranteed. He'd thought someday his mom would be super proud of him graduating high school at the top of his class. He'd expected her to be bursting with pride when he entered his career. He thought she'd cry at his wedding and insist on babysitting his kids. But none of that would happen. After she died, his motivation had left him, except for his search for a career that would satisfy the unnamable need inside him. That's what drove him. A need to succeed at whatever it was that he was meant to do.

His mom had told him to follow his passion no matter what his father wanted him to do. He didn't want to let his mom down.

CHAPTER 10

HANNAH OBSERVED Brody as he sat silent, no longer eating his sandwich. Even Cami had stopped leaning against him and lay down next to his outstretched legs. It was as if a deep sadness had enveloped him.

She didn't want to jar him from his memories. Despite saying that his brother's death didn't affect him, it did. Since Brody still held her hand, she sat in silence with him, happy to be of support. The fact was, she'd missed him over the last couple weeks, and as surprising as it was to have him show up on her mountain, she was thrilled he'd come looking for her... literally.

Though she'd thought she'd been depending on him too much because he had so much knowledge she needed and was the first she thought to contact on everything, it wasn't that at all. It was him in particular. The last two weeks had proved that, as she talked to other people in town, who were all pleased that she'd moved into Four Peaks. Everyone was so helpful, from Sheila at the Western clothing store, to Luke, whom she met at the hardware store and discovered he was Amanda's brother. He'd invited her to Boots n' Brew on Saturday, and though she declined the date, she planned to finally check it out, since Nash had recommended it, too.

Even after all that time, she'd still wanted to see Brody, always hoping she'd run into him. Obviously, she'd developed a crush on him without realizing it. That was no surprise. His bright blue eyes and dark hair with the blond highlights were enough to have any woman taking a second look. It wasn't even his build, which was a bit more muscular than some of the other cowboys she'd seen in town. She knew exactly what it was since she'd fallen for it once before, long ago. It was his kind heart.

As much as he complained about needing more than the ranch, he stayed for his family. Even him searching her out back in Phoenix was to buy her land for his family. Not to mention the dog sitting next to him, who needed him more than anyone. Was that why she found him irresistible and enjoyed every second he continued to hold her hand...as if he needed her?

Last time she'd fallen for someone like Brody, he had left to oversee the drilling of wells for a small town in Africa and ended up marrying a woman he met there. She didn't see Brody doing that, but he did mention that he flitted from one new experience to another.

Heck, he might not even think of her in terms of someone special. For all she knew, he was just being neighborly. She glanced at their hands entwined, his darkly tanned and rough from ranching, hers just starting to turn color but still soft, despite the papercut she got on her index finger two nights ago unpacking her last box.

His hand squeezed hers as he turned to look at her. "Are you ready to head down now?"

A vision of them walking down the mountain hand in hand filled her head. "Just as soon as I finish my sandwich." She held up the last bite in her other hand. "Unless you think Cami would like it."

He looked at the dog who raised one eyebrow at him. "No, I think she's had enough." He took the final bite of his own sandwich. Then as if it were as natural as getting up in the morning, he let go of her hand and stood. Cami immediately stood next to him, looking at him for what he'd want to do next.

Hannah popped the last bite into her mouth and added the granola bars back into the backpack with the apples. She still wished she could stay put awhile longer, but Brody was right about the safety issue. She'd just have to go online and research a safe way to hike alone, if there was such a thing.

Brody waited as she stood and settled the small backpack into place. She looked around to be sure she hadn't left any trash, then met his gaze. "I guess I'm ready."

He held his hand out for her to precede him. She walked by him and around the boulder. As she reached her self-made trail, she stopped. The view was spectacular and the reason she'd made the boulder her lunch place. The whole valley was spread out before her, with the Rocky Road to the right and empty desert to the left. From such a height, the power lines at the other end of her property were as impossible to find as was her casita. Yet, one road going into town was visible, as well as the various buildings on the north side of Main Street. She could almost distinguish the silhouette of the Lucky Lasso.

"Wow." Brody stopped next to her.

"Isn't it amazing? Have you never been up here?"

He shook his head. "I stopped to look about halfway up, but this reminds me of my view from a cockpit. Only I never flew over the ranch. I guess I was too busy exploring new places. I didn't realize how beautiful our valley could be."

He probably meant nothing by using the term 'our.' Or maybe he meant his family. She decided to take it as his family's and her valley. "You're so lucky to have grown up here. The desert has a beauty all its own that many people can't appreciate."

He turned to look at her. "That's true. And when the saguaro cacti blossom in May, it would be even more beautiful from this vantage point."

"I would love to see that."

Brody looked at her. "You would find it breathtaking."

Though he said the words about the desert, his gaze focused on her mouth, and her heart jumped in excitement.

"You're right. I would." Her words came out in a whisper, her body well aware that he leaned toward her.

"Yes, you would." His voice had lowered, and his lips drew closer until they touched hers in the softest of kisses.

She closed her eyes as his mouth moved over hers, sending tingles of excitement sparking down to her toes. She parted her lips and his tongue took advantage, deftly slipping into her mouth.

His hands cupped her face as he deepened the kiss,

causing her to clasp onto his arms as he explored her mouth. The scent of the ground after a hard rain filled her nostrils, as if he rose from the very mountain they stood on.

Tentatively, she tangled her tongue with his, and one of his hands pulled her closer. She leaned in, feeling protected and cared-for, despite the fact she was slightly dizzy as her body heated with desire.

Brody slowly ended the kiss, leaning his forehead against hers. "I hope you don't mind."

She licked her lips. "No, I don't mind."

He lifted his head at her answer and stared at her. "You are a unique woman."

"I'll take that as a complement."

His lips twitched up. "And well you should."

She gave him a soft smile, not sure what the kiss meant, but pleased nonetheless.

"We should probably continue down."

"Yes." She waited for him to turn and start down, but he remained where he was, looking at her.

Movement behind him caught her eye and she moved her gaze in time to see Cami disappear around a mesquite tree growing out of a pile of boulders. "Um, Cami just left."

"What?" He spun. "Cami. Shit, I hope she hasn't picked up the scent of a cottontail or we'll be here the rest of the day. Cami!"

The dog suddenly appeared around the corner, but then turned around and disappeared again.

Brody stalked off after her.

Hannah found the whole thing humorous. It was the way Cami looked at Brody, then quickly left as if she were egging him on that had the whole scene playing like a comedy.

"Cami!" Brody's voice sounded more than a little irritated. Unable to resist, she walked around the boulders and tree and at first didn't see them. Then she looked up to find Cami digging like her life depended on it and all the dirt and rocks were raining down on Brody who was getting closer.

"What are you after, dog?" He finally reached Cami, who suddenly stopped, lifting her snout from the ground with a bone in her mouth.

"What do you have, girl?" Brody's tone had softened.

Cami immediately sat and showed him her bone, though she wouldn't let go when he tried to examine it.

"I hope that's not a dinosaur bone or you'll be in big trouble. Now come on. You can keep the bone, but we need to head down the mountain."

As Brody descended, Cami followed obediently.

When they both reached Hannah, she called Cami. "Can I see?" She was a bit surprised when Cami came over to her. Hannah bent and looked at the bone. "I don't think that's a dinosaur bone. My guess is it's part of a burro."

"Up here?" Brody stopped next to her to have another look.

"If it was attacked by a predator, it could have been dragged up here. Either that or it's from another planet."

Brody chuckled. "I get it. You're saying it's not a big deal. But how do you know that?"

"The internet. Do you want to know why I was looking up dinosaur bones, or do you want to take my word?"

He looked from Cami to her. "I'll take your word."

She liked that. "Good. Now we'd best head down. I've hijacked enough of your day without meaning to." She looked out at the view and sighed before walking back around the mesquite tree. She could hear his cowboy boots crunching on the dirt as he followed her. They hadn't gone much farther when he touched her shoulder.

She stopped. "Are you okay?"

"I'm fine. Look over there." He pointed to an outcropping, where a bald eagle stood looking over the valley.

She sucked in her breath. To see one in the wild was breathtaking. They were rather large birds. She remained absolutely still, hoping it would see something. It was no more than a minute before the bird honed in on its prey, spread its impressive wings, and took flight. She watched, both hopeful it would succeed and fearful for whatever it hunted. It didn't even land as it snatched something off a large rock and flew into the air. As it came closer, she could see it was a snake.

"That should feed the whole family."

At Brody's statement, she tore her gaze from the bird. "What do you mean?"

Again he pointed. "See that dead tree about thirty feet up? I believe that's a nest. If there are any eaglets in that nest, they should be ready to fly out on their own soon."

Even as they watched, the bald eagle disappeared behind the branches. "Wow. The wildlife is breathtaking out here."

"At least that's one less rattler we have to worry about heading down. Do you want me to go first now?"

"Not at all. You might go off my path."

His brows raised, but he conceded with a lowering of his head.

She continued down, pausing every so often to enjoy the view. Brody didn't say anything as he waited patiently for her to continue. Each time she took in the view she was able to focus on the beauty around her, but with every step, she couldn't stop mulling over his kiss. Could he be feeling the same way she was?

They finally reached her golf cart and his ATV. She took off her backpack and laid it on the seat next to her towel. She draped the towel over the steering wheel. Though the days were cooling, the sun could be brutal.

Brody opened the wagon attached to his ATV. "Come on, Cami. In you go."

The dog obeyed him, finally dropping the bone as she lay down to enjoy her new find.

Hannah walked over and gave Cami a pat on the head. "Good girl." She looked to Brody. "She's very smart."

He beamed as if Cami were his child. "She is. I'm teaching her more and more commands every week. She loves to learn."

"I understand that. Thank you for showing me why I can't go up there again alone, and for pointing out the bald eagle. That's an experience I'll never forget."

His eyebrows lowered. "I'm sure you'll get to see more bald eagles. They like Four Peaks."

She gazed upward, not sure she would. She'd have to go with someone like him, which she certainly wouldn't mind, but if she sold the land… "Well, I appreciate it. I was so focused on my path, I would have missed it."

He gave a silent nod but made no move to leave. "Tonight, Tanner's making his mesquite-smoked chicken legs. Would you like to come over for dinner? I don't imagine you've had a chance to make those in your little kitchen yet."

Her heart leapt at the invitation before she came back to reality. "I can't. I promised Shelia that I'd meet her for dinner before going to Boots n' Brews. She says there's a great country band playing tonight." She didn't mention that Sheila had also said a lot of single cowboys would be there.

"Sheila? As in Sheila Langley who owns the country-western wear store in town?"

"Yes. She told me she dated you once."

Brody looked away, finding the grip on the ATV handles absolutely fascinating.

She grinned, not surprised he wasn't comfortable. "Don't worry. Sheila says you've dated just about every single lady in town."

His head snapped up at that. "I have not. There're just so many people in town, most of whom I went to school with. We don't get a lot of newcomers. I've dated maybe a handful and went out with a few more. She's exaggerating."

Hannah laughed. "I know. I noticed she exaggerates almost everything. Did you know a million people descend on Four Peaks during Pioneer Days?"

He closed his eyes as if looking for his patience and not finding it. He opened them again. "That's a crock. We're lucky if we get twenty thousand over the three days, and for some retailers, that business has to last them the whole year."

That wasn't much. The Barret Jackson car show in Scottsdale got hundreds of thousands. "That explains why

Sheila gives guitar lessons on the side. Anyway, I promised I'd go with her. Maybe I could come over another time?"

"Sure." He shrugged as if he didn't care one way or the other. "I'd better get back. I told Nash we needed to finish the roof of the birthing enclosure, but Layne just put our sick heifer in there." He turned on the ATV.

She wasn't sure how to read him. Did he really not care, or was he disappointed? She'd prefer the latter, but maybe he went around kissing women all the time. She'd have to find out tonight without asking outright. She had noticed that everyone knew everyone in town. She didn't want to start rumors about her and Brody. Her instinct said he wouldn't appreciate that. "Yeah, I better get back, too. I still have to finish reviewing a proposed budget and a few other items. Thanks again for a memorable hike."

Starting the golf cart, she waved at him before turning around and heading back toward her casita. Maybe he did go around kissing women when he felt like it or maybe he liked her. He did invite her to dinner, and as much as she wanted to accept, she never went back on her word.

She shook her head as she drove around a large barrel cactus. Nope, she wasn't going to drive herself crazy wondering. As her grandmother said, if things were meant to be, they would be. Right now she had some e-mails to send and a fun night at a country-western bar to get ready for. That was what being part of a community was about, and she definitely liked the feeling of belonging she had in Four Peaks. No wonder her grandparents asked her to stay a while. It had only been a month, and already she knew half the townspeople. It was a very special place. Maybe even one she didn't want to leave.

CHAPTER 11

HANNAH PULLED in next to Sheila and jumped out of her Jeep. She'd worn her cowboy boots, a denim skirt that didn't reach her knees and flowed out when she twirled, and a sleeveless white top with horses embroidered in russet colors on the back. Sheila had assured her when she bought it that it made her "look country." She'd pulled her hair back in a ponytail so at least part of the design could be seen.

The bar, however, looked more like something from two centuries ago. The wood on the two-story building was weathered to a grayish blue, at least in the fading light. The sign that had once proclaimed it 'Boots n' Brew' with a pair of cowboy boots and two beer glasses, had two letters missing making it 'Boos n' Bew,' perfect for Halloween she supposed, though that wasn't until next month. The four fake windows on the front boasted five shutters of the eight they should have had, with one still barely hanging on. Obviously, Sheila had exaggerated what a great place it was, though by the full parking lot, many people enjoyed it.

Sheila's arm linked in hers. "Let's get this party started."

Her new friend, who wore a straw cowboy hat, a leather half-top, a pair of jeans with studs down the side seams, and brown cowboy boots, pulled her toward the door. If she'd been in Phoenix, she'd have turned around by now, but this was Four Peaks. At least that's what she reminded herself when Sheila yanked open the door and the noise of loud conversation and music greeted them.

"This way!" Sheila pulled her along behind a row of tables that surrounded a large square dance floor with people moving on it.

Hannah couldn't quite see the dancers, so she looked up to find there was a balcony on three sides of the huge square room and a large stage at the back. The balcony appeared big enough to have at least two tables deep on it.

As they made their way through the crowd, Hannah noticed that there were all ages there. Though it was busy, it wasn't impossible to get through the crowd, as the high bar tables were spaced far enough apart so even if people ignored the stools and stood instead, there was still room to walk in between.

"Let's grab a table, if there are any left!"

Hannah just nodded, glad she hadn't come by herself like she'd been tempted to do a couple of weeks back.

"Hey, Hannah!" Ava, from the Lucky Lasso Hotel and Saloon, waved energetically as she was pulled onto the dance floor, probably by her husband.

"Score!" Sheila pulled out a stool at a bar table one row back from the dance floor. "The front tables are always taken first, but this isn't bad."

Hannah pulled out another stool and sat, looking around. Where they were was fairly close to the stage, but not so close they couldn't see the band from their angle. Also, based on where she was sitting, she could easily see the dancers, and she picked out Ava and her husband dancing with the others going around in a circle. She'd bet that was the two-step she'd read about on the internet when Sheila first suggested they go out.

"I'm going to the bar." Sheila hooked her thumb over her shoulder. "What do you want? First round's on me and you can take the second."

She wasn't much of a drinker, but she was in a bar, so she'd order at least one drink. "I'll have a rum and Coke."

"No, you won't. This place only serves beer. That's why it's called Boots n' Brew."

"I didn't realize it meant that literally. Just get me a light beer then. I'm not picky." Especially because she planned to make it last. Beer wasn't her favorite, but it would do.

The music played by the live band was definitely the toe-tapping kind, even if she didn't recognize the song. Besides the wood dance floor, there were large wooden beams that held up the balcony and the walls were wood, too, though in the darkened space with colored lights flashing, the wooden walls looked to be a warm honey brown, and not nearly as dilapidated as the outside.

As she scanned the people around her and on the dance floor, she recognized a few. Mrs. Silva, who owned the ice cream shop, and Mr. Hardy, who ran the hardware store, were both dancing with their partners. It looked like maybe Stacy, the waitress might—

"Well, look who finally made it to the Brew." Luke Hayden sidled up next to her, blocking her view of the floor.

She didn't mind as he was one of those cowboys with dark looks and a deep voice. Definitely a better view. "Hi, Luke. Yes, I finally made it. Sheila suggested we come."

He leaned his elbow on the table to face her. "I always said Sheila was a smart woman."

She clamped down on a smile because that wasn't even close to what Sheila said about him. He could supposedly charm a snake out of its skin and a sheriff into giving him her phone number instead of a ticket. He was also prone to getting in fights, but since she could see no bruises, she could only guess that was Sheila exaggerating again.

"You wanna dance?"

"I don't know how. I've never been to a country bar before."

His eyes rounded. "Well, it's about time then. I'll be happy to show you how to dance."

She so loved learning new things that she was off her stool in a second, but halted. "I can't leave. Sheila was very particular about getting this table."

He scanned the table top before nodding. "As I said, she's a smart woman. Since you don't have drinks yet, someone may swoop on in." He looked around. "I could show you a few steps to one of the easier line dances right here."

"I'd love that."

For the next ten minutes she followed Luke's instruction until Sheila arrived with their drinks.

"Luke Hayden, what are you doing?"

He immediately took his hand from her back and held

both up where Sheila could see them. "Just giving a little dance lesson."

"Dance lesson, my ass. You run along and bother someone else. Hannah's off-limits to the likes of you."

"Whatever you say, Shee-la." He chuckled before leaning in. "I'll grab you for that dance when they play it." He quickly spun around and headed onto the dance floor to seamlessly join the crowd line-dancing to a fast song about the Chattahoochee River.

She watched him dance. He was good, and she had to admit, she enjoyed the way all the men moved. There was a confidence about cowboys she found very attractive.

"Don't be getting mixed up with Luke there. He's not for you."

"Relax. I'm just out tonight for some fun. I'm not looking to take a stray home with me."

Sheila burst out laughing and held up her beer bottle. "Cheers to that, City Girl."

She clinked her bottle with Sheila before taking a sip, feeling much more comfortable. She gestured toward the dance floor. "How does everyone know how to do these dances? Do they take lessons or something?" She could imagine them teaching line-dancing in the schools in Four Peaks. Everyone was that good.

"Lessons? Not likely. We just go out there and follow everyone else until we figure it out. It's expected. We don't have many show-offs here, though there are a few, like him." She jerked her head up at a cowboy in all black who was spinning around when others were doing kicks. "Thinks he's better than the rest of us just because his daddy's a judge. That may be, but he's a worthless son-of-a-bitch, and I mean that literally. His mama is a damn bitch. Hopefully, you'll never need to make bail. That woman is the local bail bondswoman and as cold as ice."

Hannah barely kept from laughing. She was so pleased to learn Four Peaks wasn't as perfect as it first appeared. Perfect was boring.

A cowboy Hannah recognized stepped up to Sheila. "What do you say to a little two-stepping, Sheila?"

"I say bring it on." Sheila slid off her stool. "I'll be right back. I need to show Layne here how it's done."

Hannah waved Shelia off and took another sip of her beer. The band had started with an intro, probably to let people know what was next, went into the song, and the dancers began moving around the dance floor.

"Hi, Hannah."

"Hi, Nash." She smiled warmly as Nash stepped up to her table.

"Mind if I sit?"

"Not at all." She couldn't help looking over his shoulder to see if Brody was with him, but that was silly. They might be best friends, but they weren't attached at the hip. "How are you? I haven't seen you since last week at the grocery store. Did you ever find the fiber gummies your aunt wanted?"

He grimaced. "Yeah, I did. Did you find those weird berries you were looking for?"

"No. I substituted blueberries. They were close enough. How are things on the ranch?"

He shrugged. "The same old. Tanner is focused on

getting stuff ready for the dude ranch, using the service of the two new ranch hands while Brody, Layne, Ernest, Waylon, and I take care of the cattle. It's going to be quite the change when that thing opens."

"You don't look so sure about it."

He didn't answer at first. "I'm not, but I'm a bit old fashioned. It's the way I was raised. Brody thinks it's going to be very successful. I just wonder what that change will require of us. I'm much better with cattle than people."

It was obvious he really did feel that way. She set her hand on his arm. "I'm sure you'll be fine. You get along with everyone here, right?" She lifted her hand and held it out to the room in general.

"Well, sure. But these people all know me. I grew up with them. You wouldn't find me within a mile of this place during Pioneer Days, when all the city folk descend on Four Peaks. Not that I mean you. You're nice."

Even in the darkness of the bar, she could see the color rise in his face. Did all cowboys blush? No. She couldn't imagine Luke Hayden blushing.

"Hey, this dance is almost over. You want to dance?"

"I don't know how, though Luke taught me one line dance. If that's not the one, I'll be totally lost."

"We all have to learn somehow. Why not with me? I can show you the steps, once we hear what song it is."

"Oh, I'd like that. Everyone looks like they're having so much fun."

The song ended then, and some dancers left the floor while others chatted as the band counted down. As the music began to play, Nash's face lit. "This is a slow dance. You don't need to know any steps. What do you say?"

Though she'd rather be dancing with Brody, who was home with his family, she did like Nash, so why not? "Sure."

Nash took her hand and led her onto the dance floor. As he wrapped his other arm around her, she was acutely aware there was no chemistry. Nash would make a great friend. He was a nice guy, just like Brody, but different. No wonder he and Brody were close.

Brody walked into Boots n' Brew and immediately scanned the tables near the door before making his way to the bar. After ordering a beer, he turned to face the crowd, leaning his back against the stool he stood in front of. He knew everyone and everyone knew him. That was the problem with living in Four Peaks. He looked forward to moving north, or south, where he'd encounter all new people. Even if it was another small town, he wouldn't mind, because he hadn't grown up there.

He took a sip of beer and looked for Hannah. She wouldn't be on the dance floor. He doubted she knew how to dance, though she might have watched videos on the internet. He grinned as he imagined her following the steps in her little casita. The woman was definitely excited about learning, always satisfying her curiosity through research. His gaze swept over a tall, broad man in a white hat heading for the bar. It was Wyatt Ford from Cave Creek. He hadn't seen him in a couple of years. "Wyatt Ford."

Wyatt stopped in his tracks and stared at him a moment before he gave him a big smile. "Brody Dunn."

They gave each other a quick hug before he made a production of looking Wyatt up and down. "You've changed, but I can't figure out how."

Wyatt held up his left hand, which had a gold band on his ring finger. "I got married."

Though it made sense since Wyatt was supposed to take over his grandfather's ranch, it was still a surprise. "Last I knew you were talking up your neighbor and living the good life over on High Mountain Ranch."

Wyatt's smile disappeared. "Not any more. Grandpa died and never changed his will. I went with the last horses over to Last Chance Ranch, since it was the only place I could trust to care for them correctly, and while I was there, I met Alyssa Parker, a teacher in Canterbury. I'm in charge of Last Chance now. It's a horse rescue ranch. You wouldn't believe what idiots own horses. Alyssa and I are living on her father's place with a couple of our own horses. It's the sweet life."

"Wow. That's a lot. I need to buy you a beer." He turned and waved down the bartender, quickly snagging a bottle for his old friend. It helped to leave big tips when living in a small town. It guaranteed fast service.

"Thanks." Wyatt took a swig.

"I'm sorry about losing High Mountain Ranch. That had to have been a blow." He couldn't imagine losing the Rocky Road. It may not be where he wanted to spend the rest of his life, but he liked the idea of being able to go home when he wanted...if he could manage to get away.

Wyatt nodded as he wiped condensation from his beer with his thumb. "It was a shock that I didn't handle well, but I'm in a good place now. I just left Cave Creek, where I took Alyssa to show her my old hangouts. After seeing the development going up where High Mountain used to be, I decided we should stay the night at the Lucky Lasso, so I could show her where I went for fun when I didn't want my grandfather to know where I was."

Brody laughed. "If I remember correctly, you didn't always make it home."

"Yeah, well. Getting out from under the old man's watchful eye was always a plus, and the longer it lasted, the better. What about you? Last I knew, you were getting your pilot's license."

He filled Wyatt in on his various forays into other fields, but refrained from explaining his itch to attend the wildlife manager training in January. He didn't want to jinx it. He took another swallow of beer and lifted his bottle toward Wyatt. "How are those two sisters of yours? The same, or have things gotten better?"

"Both. Shaine, the bossy one, is having success in some sport. She's been making good money, or so she says. Madison is harder to keep up with. I'll suddenly get a call and she's in the Yukon, but her last e-mail was from down in Beliz. She seems to be trying her hand at all different professions, kind of like you."

"Hey, they say variety is the spice of life."

"Right. I better get another beer and get back to Alyssa, or she's going to think I forgot this is just a trip down memory lane."

"I gotcha." Brody waved his hand and had two beers for Wyatt in no time. "Where you parked?"

Wyatt grinned as he hooked his thumb over his shoulder. "My usual spot, first pole on the right."

"I'll come by. I've got to meet the woman that's willing to put up with you."

Wyatt's grin melted into a smile. "She special. There's nothing like finding that person who gets you. Thanks." Wyatt lifted the beers and made his way back to his old spot.

Brody took another sip of beer. With High Mountain Ranch closed, that meant the Rocky Road might be able to pick up some of the old ranch's business. He'd have to remember to tell Tanner.

So Wyatt was settling down into a whole new life, while he felt as if he hadn't started his yet. Then again, Wyatt was a few years older than he was. Where would he be three years from now? Hopefully, he'd be enjoying his career somewhere up north, or even down south. He really had no desire to own his own ranch, but he wouldn't mind a house.

He watched the dancers on the floor as he imagined what his house would look like. Just as he had the perfect image in his head, he recognized Hannah's cheek resting on a cowboy's shoulder.

Fucking-A, who was that? Anger churned in his gut as the couple turned away from him. He set his beer down on the bar and strode forward. He didn't give a shit who it was, he was cutting in. Walking through the other dancers, everyone he knew, he fixated on the cowboy's white shirt with the embroidered cacti. He knew that shirt from somewhere, but he couldn't concentrate, needing to get Hannah away from whoever it was.

He tapped the man on the shoulder who stopped and looked at him.

"Nash."

"Brody? I didn't know you were coming tonight."

Suddenly, feeling awkward, he shrugged. "It was a last-minute decision. Hi, Hannah. Nash, you mind if I cut in?"

His friend looked at him oddly. "Sure. The dance is almost over anyway."

As Nash stepped away, he took Hannah in his arms and everything felt right.

"Well, that wasn't very nice."

At her statement, his contentment evaporated. "What? People cut in on others all the time."

"First of all, he's your best friend, and second of all, we could have waited to dance later. I thought you were at the ranch tonight."

Shit, now he felt like a heel. How was he going to explain this to Nash? "I was, but when you said you were coming here, I thought, why not?" He gave her a half smile, but she didn't seem appeased.

Then the song ended on him.

"Thanks for the short dance." She slipped from his arms and made her way to the side of the dance floor.

As the intro of the next song started, dancers filled the floor and he moved off it. He didn't know whom he should talk to first, Hannah or Nash.

A tap on his shoulder solved his problem.

"What the hell was that? Are you jealous or something?"

Easy-going Nash looked ready to pound him into the ground. "It was just a dance she knew how to do. What's up with you?"

Shit, now he felt even worse. "Sorry. I didn't know it was you. She said she was coming here and when I noticed her, I thought it would be a great opportunity to talk to her, you know, when she's more relaxed. That's the best time to persuade someone."

"You've got to be shittin' me. You expect to charm her to your cause on the dance floor? Hell, Brody, when did you get so selfish?"

Before he could respond, Nash walked off toward the bar.

He rubbed the back of his neck, not sure how he'd screwed up so royally. The fact was, the last thing on his mind was persuading Miss Kingsley to sell her place. He'd just seen red at her being in someone else's arms. He really liked holding her in his...like he had earlier in the day when they kissed. Yeah, he kissed her, but she seemed to enjoy it.

"You better get your fanny over there and explain yourself, Dunn."

He whirled around at the sound of Sheila Langley's voice. "What?"

She pointed to the left side of the room. "Second row back, third from the stage. Right now she thinks you're the worst kind of friend."

Without thinking, he gave Sheila a nod and headed for Hannah. He had no idea what he was going to say, but anything was better than her thinking him disloyal to Nash. Even the truth, whatever that was.

As he approached, she was peeling the label off her beer in tiny strips, making a small pile of paper spaghetti. "I'm back."

She looked up at him, then went back to peeling her label. "So I see."

"I didn't know it was Nash." His mother always told him to tell the truth. He just hoped it worked.

She still didn't look at him. "So just because you didn't know it was your best friend, it's okay to interrupt my dance when it's almost over? It just so happens it was my first time on the dance floor and I was having fun." She punctuated the final word so much, he cringed.

"I'm sorry. I saw you there in the arms of some man and I just..."

Her head lifted and her gaze held his own. "You just what?"

"I just wanted you to be in *my* arms." He looked away, not even sure what had happened or why he said that. "I wasn't thinking."

"You were feeling?"

At her question, he looked at her. "Yeah. I was feeling..." Betrayed, angry, possessive. None of which made sense. "I was feeling like I wanted to hold you and kiss you again. I couldn't think."

She cupped his cheek. "Then I guess I can forgive you because I like you, too."

His chest tightened as realization dawned. How stupid could he be that he didn't even see how much he liked her. He'd been so busy trying to show why living in Four Peaks was not for her that he hadn't seen it. How could he be so blind? "I think I need a drink. Can I get you something?"

She gave him a crooked smile. "No, I'm good."

He walked toward the bar not seeing anyone, still trying to come to terms with the fact he liked his neighbor. What did that mean? It could complicate things immensely, especially since she said she liked him as well. When had everything gone sideways on him?

Making it to the bar, he ordered two beers and looked around for Nash. Spotting him on the dance floor, he waited this time until the song ended, then strode forward to intercept him. "Here."

"What's this?" Nash took the bottle.

"It's my apology offering. I was an ass, and I just found out why."

Nash eyed him skeptically. "Because you're so selfish you can't let anyone else enjoy their time?"

He cringed, but was determined to make things right. "That and I didn't realize how much I like Hannah. I just saw her in the arms of someone—I couldn't see it was you—and I needed to get to her."

"You were jealous?" Nash's eyes widened. "You're never jealous." His friend studied him, making him very uncomfortable. "You may have bigger problems than my forgiveness, Brody. Thanks for the beer." Nash lifted the bottle in the air in salute before cracking a smile and strolling away.

Nash was right. It complicated things. He needed her to sell, but he also cared too much for her now. Things could get unwieldy. At least he and Nash were good. Now to figure things out with Hannah.

When he got to her table, she wasn't there, but Sheila was.

"Now, I know you're not looking for me."

"I always said you were sharp."

"Really? Funny, I never said that about you."

"Thanks." He set his bottle down on the table. "Where'd Hannah go? Ladies' room?" Since the song playing was a line dance, and he was sure she didn't know any, that had to be where she'd gone, unless she had left thanks to his idiocy.

"She's out on the dance floor with Luke."

His whole body tensed, because while Sheila might give him shit about being a player, Luke actually was. He was no good for Hannah.

Sheila's hand clamped down on his arm. "Don't do it."

"Do what?" He was going out on that dance floor to protect Hannah.

"Don't make a fool of yourself twice in one night. First, Luke is your sister-in-law's brother, and whatever you're thinking of doing will not go down well with your family. Second, Luke is always looking for a fight, and even if you get into one, you'll look like an idiot in Hannah's eyes, and third—"

Friends of Sheila's tapped her on the shoulder and waved as they walked by.

He barely kept himself at the table, having already stood, notwithstanding any of Sheila's warnings. "And third?"

Sheila turned back to peer at him. "And third, she'd just finished telling me about a man she dated once who was jealous like you, but took it too far and she had to dump him."

He forced himself back onto the stool, the last reason holding more weight than any of the others.

"Smart decision." Sheila nodded, then looked past him.

He turned his head and found Hannah. She was dancing between Luke and Layne. He gritted his teeth and waited for the song to end. Luke walked her back toward them, his hand on her back, making Brody's jaw ache.

"That was so much fun!" Hannah greeted him with a kiss on the cheek in front of Luke.

That the man noticed was clear in his frown. "If you need any more dance lessons, I'll be happy to oblige."

Hannah laughed. "I'm good. Thank you." She slid onto her stool.

"So you're learning to line dance." He decided on a neutral topic, still feeling the effects of being claimed by her.

"I think you'll have to teach me more of these dances. I can see now why people come here."

He smiled. "If you want, I could teach you a few and we could come back next weekend."

"Would you? That would be perfect." She took his hand from his knee and squeezed. "Do you think I could learn to two-step?"

Feeling lighter than air, he nodded. "I know you can, and I'd be happy to teach you." He tugged on her hand and she slipped off her stool to stand next to him.

"Did you need something?"

He slipped his other arm around her and pulled her between his knees. "I need a kiss."

She looped her arms around his neck. "Oh, I know how to do that."

The second her lips touched his, his desire ignited, but he forced himself to keep it light, since they were in a bar. He didn't want her to get a reputation. But when her tongue slipped between his lips, it was everything he could do to stay controlled.

"Oh, get a room, will you?"

At Sheila's comment, he broke it off, happy for once at her brash ways.

Hannah laughed as she pulled her arms from around his neck and returned to her seat. Then she looked at Sheila and grinned. "Jealous?"

"Damn right. Now, where is that hunky cowboy I danced with earlier."

As Sheila slipped from her chair and left them alone, another slow dance started. He gave Hannah a sheepish smile. "Would you dance with me?"

"Of course, but if Nash cuts in, you have to be gracious."

"I promise." Standing, he took her hand and led her out onto the dance floor. As she came into his arms, his riotous emotions seemed to settle down. He didn't care why. All that mattered was that Hannah chose him.

CHAPTER 12

HANNAH LOOKED at the clock as her online meeting ended. She wasn't excited to have to go up to Prescott for two weeks to meet with the private college up there. She'd tried to trade the job off, but many of her co-workers had children who'd just started a new school year. At least she'd have paid time-off next month, since she'd be working full time while up north.

Her negotiations, though, caused the meeting to run over. Now she barely had time to change for what she considered a date. Brody was supposed to come over to teach her a few line dances beneath the shade of her new patio, though it wasn't exactly a patio. It was more two posts sunk in the ground to hold a roof up over the desert floor on the side of her house.

Since her front door faced east and she enjoyed the morning sun, she'd had the roof erected along the south side of the house, so depending on the time of day, she could sit outside in the shade. She'd eventually get some pavers and put them down. But it didn't appear she'd be learning line dances as she expected. All Brody said was it was a surprise and to wear jeans.

She hoped he planned a hike up her mountain, not that it was hers, but that's how she thought of it. Even though temperatures had fallen below a hundred, it was still pretty warm for jeans. But since Brody had given her no reason not to trust him, she pulled on a pair of white jeans that would reflect the sun. She added a sleeveless, light-blue button-down shirt, and slipped on her sneakers.

After throwing her sweats and blouse into the hamper in her closet, she walked into the kitchen/living room. Ever since the night at Boots n' Brews, Brody had texted her every morning and they'd talked at night. She was quite sure she had a new 'boyfriend,' though at her age, thinking of him that way felt juvenile. Someone needed to come up with a name for adults to call the person of interest in their life. 'Partner' didn't work, as they weren't living together, even if they were neighbors. 'Close friends' didn't really explain it either. Lover? Even at the thought, the butterflies in her belly that had started as soon as the work meeting ended seemed to multiply. She was getting ahead of herself.

Looking out the side window, she didn't see an ATV or truck, so she walked to the fridge and pulled out an ice tea. No sooner had she unscrewed the top and took a sip then a knock sounded on her door. She set the bottle down, surprised.

Quickly she moved to the door. "Who is it?"

"It's me. Why? Who else would it be?"

At the growl in Brody's voice, she yanked the door open,

only to find a smile on his face beneath his brown cowboy hat. Her butterflies went into overdrive at seeing him in a sleeveless, red-checkered shirt that showed off his rather large biceps.

She shrugged, holding back her own smile. "Well, I do have a gentleman burro who likes to visit me."

He laughed, causing her butterflies to crash into each other. "I was afraid I'd have competition for your attention. Luckily, I came prepared." He held up reins.

She stepped outside to see he had a horse tied to Chaos. "Oh, Brody!" She wrapped her arms around him in a hug before lifting her face to give him a kiss, which he willingly returned. As much as she enjoyed his mouth on hers, she stepped back, touched that he would teach her to ride. She didn't want to make it appear as if his thoughtfulness was not appreciated.

"Hmm, I may just need to bring horses over every day."

"I wouldn't mind."

His blue eyes appeared to darken at her comment. "I'll take that as an invitation."

Her heartbeat started to race at the look in his eyes. It made her feel completely desirable, as if he couldn't wait to make her his.

"But first, I believe you requested a ride a few weeks ago. So I coerced Mandy into letting you borrow Breeze. She's a good horse and can turn on a dime. Mandy uses her for barrel-racing exhibitions."

Hannah walked over to the pretty tan horse with the blonde mane and tail, letting it smell her. "She's beautiful." She stroked the horse's nose when it nudged her.

"What's important is she'll be good for a novice like you. Maximus is too large, and Havoc, my brother Jackson's horse, lives up to his name. You never know what he'll pull."

"I didn't realize horses had such different personalities, but it makes sense. I better change my shoes. After all, I do own cowboy boots." She winked at him before talking to Breeze. "I'll be right back."

She strode into her house and quickly changed. She was beyond excited. To be trying something she'd wanted to do since she was a child, with a man she was infatuated with, meant it was going to be one of her best days.

After putting on her boots, she locked the casita and in no time, Brody had explained how to guide the horse and had her in the saddle. "I didn't realize it would feel so high."

"You'll get used to it by the second mile. We're just going to take a leisurely walk like you wanted."

She was good with that. She liked learning new things in a safe manner.

Brody clicked his tongue and Chaos walked forward. When Breeze followed without being told, Hannah grabbed the pommel. But as the gait of the horse became familiar, she let go and held the reins loosely in her hands as Brody had instructed.

Luckily, Breeze didn't like being behind, and soon Hannah found herself walking next to Brody. She liked how it felt.

"I see you added a portico to the side of your casita."

Brody's tone was neutral, but for some reason she sensed he wasn't thrilled with that. "I did. I wanted a place to sit in the shade that didn't block my sunrises or sunsets. They are so much more brilliant out here."

"I imagine they are, without the tall buildings of downtown Phoenix obstructing the view."

"Exactly. I'm hoping as the weather cools some more, I can spend more time under it."

Brody didn't respond to that, but he did pick up the pace, which had her grabbing the pommel again. As before, she moved with the horse after a while, and felt more comfortable. When Brody turned to the right, she gave a small tug on the reins and Breeze turned, making her feel quite accomplished.

Soon they were at the base of the mountains and they slowed to a walk again. Brody finally stopped next to a shady outcropping. After dismounting, he came around and had her swing her leg over. She misjudged how far it was to the ground, and would have fallen on her butt if he hadn't caught her to him.

She laughed, perfectly happy to be in his arms, even if her back was to him. "Oops. You were right. I did get used to the height."

"I told you, you would." He didn't let her go. "You looked good up there." He spoke next to her ear, his breath sending tiny shivers up her arms. "Then again, you always look good."

The little zing of pleasure his praise gave her turned into all-out excitement as he finished his sentence with a kiss on the back of her neck.

Then he dropped his arms. "Let's bring the horses into the shade for a bit. There's some desert grass they can nibble on if they want."

Of course. She wasn't used to thinking of the needs of animals. Obediently, she walked Breeze over to where Brody stood, looping the horse's reins over a large rock. She found a similar-sized rock and did the same.

Brody pointed. "This appears to be a popular spot."

She followed his hand and saw two cottontail rabbits a few yards up the incline munching on grass. They were adorable. "Well, it is shady, and both man and beast appreciate a reprieve from the heat. Though it's definitely been pleasant the last few days."

He wandered along the edge of the incline as if looking for something. "It's amazing what you can find when you look. My brothers and I used to do scavenger hunts for fun. We'd start off with a list one of us made that had cactus needles and meteorite rocks, and we'd come back with snake skins that had been shed, desert mouse skulls, and eggshells."

"Ewww. If it was me, I'd look for flowers and pretty rocks."

He laughed. "That doesn't surprise me. Let's see who can find the better collectibles."

"You're on." It didn't take a minute for her to know she had a real challenge before her. The mountain base had some growth, but it was mostly rock and sand. Still, there had to be something pretty somewhere.

"Well, howdy." Brody's voice to her right had her looking over. He cupped something in his hand. "No peeking."

She rolled her eyes before resuming her search for something pretty. The first item she found was a rock. It was covered in mica and shined when the sun hit it. She dropped that in her pocket. Her next item was a brittlebush, though its yellow flowers were brown now. Then she spotted something white above her. Climbing up a bit farther, she discovered a broken bird egg of some kind. What would Brody think of that? Pleased, she picked it up carefully.

At that moment, the horses whinnied loudly and she looked down to see them tugging at the reins. She was about to descend when the rocks that held their reins rolled down as the horses pulled away and took off at a run.

"Hannah, don't move and don't say anything."

Her heart jumped into her throat at Brody's words, but she stayed still except to move her eyes to where he was, a little to her right and below her, which made it difficult to see him. Did he see a snake near her? Is that what spooked the horses?

He cautiously moved into her vision. He walked around, and in slow motion climbed higher. As he drew closer, she realized he wasn't looking at her but past her. What did he see? Sweat trickled down her back and her eyes smarted with unshed tears. Not knowing what threatened her was almost too much.

Slowly, so as not to startle whatever it was, she turned her head. As she lifted her gaze, she forgot to breathe. Just above her stood a mountain lion and he was staring right at her. Its ears were folded forward, and on meeting her eyes, it pulled up its upper lip and snarled.

"Don't move."

Brody's command hit her just as she was about to run. Though she didn't, her whole body began to shake and there was nothing she could do about that.

"Hey, you big cat. Git! Get out of here."

The mountain lion turned its head to look at Brody. Its whole body leaned back on its hind legs in a crouch.

Brody took two steps closer, coming into her field of vision as she kept her eyes on the hundred-pound creature. Brody's arms were raised above his head. "You want a piece of me? I guarantee you're going to have to fight for it."

The animal's ears flattened back on its head and a snarl issued forth that sent the hair on her arms to stand on end, her fear not about her but Brody.

"Didn't you hear me? I said get." Brody waved a broken branch of a mesquite tree.

Even as the big cat's weight started to shift forward, Hannah's muscles tensed as her heart stopped.

The animal jumped toward Brody, who swung the branch forward.

But the mountain lion landed higher on the slope and continued upward, obviously deciding that humans weren't worth it.

Her breath escaped in a whoosh as all her muscles collapsed under her and she lay on the slope as Brody reached her. His arms wrapped around her and he squeezed her tight, even as they slid downward a couple of feet.

"Shit, Hannah."

She grasped his shirt in her fists as she cried into his shoulder. She had no idea why she was crying. He was safe. She was safe, thanks to him. There was no reason to cry, yet the tears continued and her body shook.

Brody stroked her back. "It's okay. He's gone. I won't let anything hurt you."

At his words, her chest tightened with a yearning so

strong, it made it hard to breathe. No one had ever said anything like that to her. No one. Then, as if someone turned on a light in a darkened room, she understood. She loved Brody.

She'd been afraid of being attacked, but her fear escalated when the big cat looked as if he'd go after Brody instead. She'd wanted to pounce on it, however irrational that was.

"Hey there." Brody leaned away and used one hand to turn her face toward him. "You're okay."

She nodded, sniffing at the same time. "I know. I have no idea why I'm crying and shaking."

He gave her a soft smile, even as he brushed tears from her cheek. "Not shaking as much now though. It's the adrenaline rush, or rather coming down from it. Simply put, it's your body showing its relief."

"What about you then? Why aren't you shaking and crying with relief?"

"Oh, I'm crying on the inside. I wasn't so much afraid as pissed. First the horses run off with the only gun I brought, and then that mountain lion threatens my girl. I was having none of his crap." Brody shook his head, his brows lowered, but his lips twitched.

She pulled away. "Are you telling me you weren't even a little afraid?"

"Heck, no. I was shittin' in my pants that he'd attack you. But I was pissed because I also didn't want to hurt him. We're in his territory, and he had the right to be here. He's the very animal I want to protect once I become a wildlife manager. And yet the ungrateful ass wanted to go after you. That infuriated me."

She raised her brows, not because he was joking, but because he was serious and not making much sense. Her only conclusion was that he was afraid and angry at the same time. "A wildlife manager? You mean like the police of the animal world?"

"Something like that, but there's so much more to it. It's about being that buffer between the animal kingdom and mankind. I guess kind of like what just happened."

This was new information about him. She'd known he was honorable, but his future career proved he was a modern-day knight in shining armor...with flaws of course. She wasn't that love-struck. "That's very admirable. Is there a lot of schooling for that?"

At her question, his body stiffened. "Not too much. We should probably get down from here and get the horses."

She lay next to him, so she scrambled up. In her haste, she fell back on her butt. "Ouch."

He rose smoothly, moving like the big cat they'd just encountered. "Here."

He held his hand out and she took it. But as he pulled her up, he clasped her against him. "Hannah. I..." He stared at her a moment then cupped the back of her head and kissed her.

It wasn't a sensual kiss. It was demanding, claiming, and yet protective all at once, and she felt it right down to her toes. She met his need with her own, beyond grateful that he was unharmed and she was in his arms.

Just as she thought she'd have to break away to breathe, he did instead, but he didn't go far. He leaned his forehead against hers. "I want you."

His words were so soft that she wasn't sure if she hadn't simply read his lips, but his message sent a thrill down to her core. "Yes."

A quiet chuckle rumbled through him. "Good." He stood straight, separating them, but took hold of her hand. "Let's get you back."

They descended together and when they made it to the desert floor, he scanned the area. Both horses were within sight, but a long walk away. He let go of her hand. "You might want to cover your ears." No sooner had he said that than he let out a loud whistle and she did cover her ears.

Chaos lifted his head, but didn't move.

"Damn scaredy cat. We'll need to walk a little closer. Are you okay?"

"I'm fine." She glanced back up the mountain, just to make sure the horses didn't see something they missed. Not seeing the mountain lion anywhere, though it was the exact same color as the mountain and would blend in seamlessly anyway, she faced forward. "Let's go get our horses."

CHAPTER 13

BRODY FINISHED TYING the two horses to Hannah's new portico, letting them drink from the bucket she found for them. He had to re-tie Chaos twice because his hands shook so much. The last time he'd been so scared was when his mom had been in the hospital that last week of her life and he'd realized she wasn't going to get better.

All he could see was the mountain lion ripping into Hannah's long neck as if it knew exactly where to kill her. He had been fully ready to pounce on that animal and strangle it with his bare hands if necessary. Anything to protect her.

Patting Chaos on the back, he looked toward Rocky Road. When had his feelings for her grown so strong? He didn't like it. When she sold her land to them, she'd be free to live a comfortable life anywhere. What if she decided to live somewhere where he was assigned? Even at the thought, he knew it was a long shot. He couldn't be thinking about a future with her. She'd think him crazy.

First, he had to get her to sell, and then...and then what?

He walked to the door of the little casita. He didn't want to think of the future. Right now there was one overriding need above all else—make love to Hannah.

He opened the door to find her barefoot and pulling two water bottles from the fridge. She closed the door and held one bottle up. "Are you thirsty?"

The heck with the water. What he wanted was her. Still, he found himself moving forward and accepting her offer. Unscrewing the top, he was pleased his hands had stopped shaking. After taking a couple of gulps, he capped the bottle again and set it down on the counter behind Hannah.

She turned and put her bottle there as well, and as she faced him, he set his hand down on the counter on the other side of her, trapping her between him and the counter. Before he could say anything, she touched his cheek.

"Thank you for saving my life."

"You're welcome." He cupped her hand and turned his head to lick her palm. At her intake of breath, he looked at her. "I want you."

She didn't even blink. "I want you, too."

Her words sent desire slamming through him like water through a wash during a monsoon. Dropping her hand, he pressed himself against her, already growing hard. "Now."

Her eyes widened and the pulse in her neck increased. Unable to resist, he lowered his head to kiss that very spot.

Hannah bent her head to the side, giving him complete access as well as permission, and he took advantage of it, laying kisses along her neck and up to her ear. Her shoulder suddenly raised, impeding his progress. He pulled his head back to look at her. "What?"

"That tickles." She smiled apologetically.

"I don't want to tickle you. I want to make you hot. I want to feel your body on fire around me."

Her lips parted at his words, and he took the opportunity to kiss her. Not a delicate kiss, but one that let her know how much he wanted her. As her tongue tangled with his, she looped her arms around his neck, running one hand through his short hair.

He couldn't seem to get close enough to her. There were too many clothes separating them. Letting go of the counter, he allowed a small space to come between them to unbutton her shirt, pulling it down, forcing her arms to lower, and capturing them at her sides.

That's when he broke the kiss to taste the side of her neck, her collarbone, the swell of her breast. Reaching behind her, he unhooked her bra, even as he used his chin to push it down, so he could taste the rosy peak it revealed.

As his mouth clasped onto her nipple, Hannah arched toward him, offering herself for his pleasure, but it was her pleasure he was most concerned with. Circling the taut peak, he teased her before taking small nips, eliciting soft moans from her lips.

Even as he took her nipple into his mouth and sucked, he latched onto to the other with his fingers and lightly squeezed. Her hips bucked into him, hitting his erection, reminding him of his own need. Releasing her nipple to pay homage to her other breast with his mouth, he moved his hands down to her jeans, and with a practiced hand, had them open in a matter of seconds.

He stood straight once again, taking over her mouth with

his own. Her hips ground into him, so he used one hand to hold her against the counter even as his other burrowed into her jeans to the juncture of her thighs. Her skin was so smooth and soft, he almost forgot his target.

She turned her head away from his kiss and licked at his jaw before nipping at it, her hands finally slipping from her shirt to grab onto his biceps.

His own need spiked at her actions, and he slipped his fingers lower until he found the moist folds of her sex. Moving to the apex, he stroked the sensitive nub.

"Yessss." Hannah's breathy hiss, had his own control slipping.

He wanted to take her in the worst way. He wanted her to be his. But first he needed to give her the pleasure she deserved. He continued to stroke her, his erection growing harder as tiny squeals of excitement filled the little room. As the sounds came faster, he knew she was close, her hands gripping his arms as if she were falling.

Then her whole body stiffened and her pelvis pushed against his fingers as a loud scream filled the air. He held her to him as she bucked, his own heart racing at the ecstasy on her face. It was pure, honest, and absolutely beautiful.

As her breathing slowed, he continued to hold her, though her hands had dropped to her sides and she was limp. He barely kept from moving his fingers still pressed against her, but he wanted her to relax so she could enjoy the sensations all over again.

Her head lifted and she looked at him with awe. "Wow."

His ego grew bigger than it should. He shrugged and grinned.

Her tongue came out to lick her lips and his body tensed, including his fingers.

"Oh."

Carefully, he removed his hand from inside her jeans. "These need to come off."

She cocked her head. "So do yours."

Instead of answering, he unzipped his jeans. The release of pressure on his cock helped with the blood flow to his brain. Stepping back, he toed off his boots and pulled out of his jeans, throwing them on a chair she had set against the kitchen wall.

Hannah didn't hesitate either, and as he turned back, he found her clothes on the floor. He let his gaze follow her long legs to her shaved mons, over her stomach to her breasts, where he stopped. Her breasts were a perfect handful, but it was her areolas which were particularly large, as was her nipples that had his tongue aching to taste her once again.

"Don't forget your shirt."

At her voice, he smirked. "I forget everything looking at you."

A flush rose in her cheeks, which just made her look even more sexy.

Quickly, he unbuttoned his shirt a and threw it on top of his jeans. Then with nothing between them, he pressed her once more against the counter, enjoying the feel of her soft skin touching his. He set his hands on the counter on either side of her. "I'm going to take you now."

She shook her head. "No, I'm going to take you...all the way inside me." She punctuated her statement by wrapping her hand around his cock.

He forgot to breathe for a moment, letting the spike of excitement run through his balls and down his legs. Then he released her hand from him and lifted her onto the counter top. Spreading her legs, he stepped between them, his face at her chest. "Now this is so much easier." Without hesitation, he held both her breasts in his hands. He sucked hard on one nipple while his thumb stroked the other.

She didn't shy away at all. In fact, her hand held him to her breast as he sucked and released. When he moved to the other, he made sure to lightly pinch the one he'd left.

"Brody, I need you inside me."

He pulled his mouth away, trying to ignore his aching erection. "I know."

Her hand on his shoulder turned into a claw. "Really?"

"Yeah." He stepped back and placed his hands on her thighs, holding them in place as he did what he wanted to do since she'd come. Bending forward, he licked at her folds, pushing them apart with his tongue to taste the very essence that was her.

A shiver ran through her which had him intensifying his efforts until without thought he was back to her clit and licking her harder. The tiny squeals she emitted filled his heart before her loud scream filled the room again.

He couldn't wait any longer. Standing straight, he fit his cock to her entrance and pulled her ass toward him, sheathing himself in the warm pulsing of her body.

"Yes. Yes." She wrapped her legs and arms around him even as she tilted her hips, her pelvis continuing to push against him.

He didn't move, though he wanted to more now than

ever. He waited for her breathing to slow a bit. "Hold on." It was the most he could get past his throat.

Turning around with her, he then walked to her bedroom, thankful that the casita was so small. He sat down on her bed and lay back, taking her with him, only to roll her over and finally sink deeper into her hot softness.

"Oh, I like that." Hannah practically purred as her hands ran down his back to cup his ass. She squeezed his cheeks, urging him deeper.

He was more than happy to comply. Shit. She felt so good. She also smelled, tasted, sounded good. Everything about her was too good. He leveraged himself up on his hands and slowly pulled out, but not completely. He couldn't seem to make his hips go any farther.

Her hands came up to stroke down his chest and across his abdominals. "You're as hard as a rock, cowboy, and I love it." She licked her lips as her gaze followed her hands all the way to where they connected. Then her finger stroked down him to her entrance.

The shiver that ran through him had nothing to do with weakening arms and everything to do with the weakening of his control. Without a word, he sank back into her and her eyes closed as her hands came to rest on his arms.

Even as he pulled back again, the thought of having almost lost her had him pushing in faster than he intended, which sent a spike of primeval claiming running through him. As he slowly lost control of his body in the need to make her his, he had enough brain power to watch her as her lips parted, her breath increased, and the soft squeals he was already addicted to started.

At that sound, there was no more him and her, but them. They were one as they rocked together until her orgasm clenched at him and her scream sent him into the ecstasy he'd craved with her. Even as his body jerked to fill her, a contentment he hadn't felt since he was young enveloped him.

As soon as he was spent, he held her close, his head on her shoulder, not wanting to be parted from her, feeling as if he couldn't breathe without her. It was probably simply the aftermath of good sex, but he didn't care. It was a remarkable feeling to be so connected.

Finally, when he could tell her breaths were slower, he lifted his head to look at her.

Her eyelids fluttered open and a soft smile played about her lips. "That was wonderful."

He held back his ego. "You're wonderful."

She chuckled, sending new tingles of excitement through him. It must have been the same for her because her eyes widened. "You're not so bad yourself." She turned her head to kiss his forearm. It was such a simple gesture, yet it felt huge. He just wasn't sure why.

"Come here." Hannah lifted her hands to hold his face. "Kiss me."

He held back. "Are you sure?" He had tasted her ecstasy and wasn't sure if she'd like a kiss from him.

Her lids half-closed over her crystal brown gaze. "I'm absolutely sure."

A whole new jolt of excitement shot through him, and his cock jerked inside her. "Hannah." Her name came out on a breath before he granted her wish, kissing her like he'd never have enough of her.

Hannah stood in the shower enjoying the heat of the water, happier than she ever remembered being. She and Brody had spent the entire afternoon making love. She'd never done that before, and wouldn't be surprised if she was a bit sore tomorrow. She didn't care in the least. He was the best lover she'd ever had, not afraid to be strong but gentle at the right moments.

He brought her food and drink in bed, saying she would need her strength, which she found adorable. He encouraged her to ride him with what he said was her new horsewoman skills, and since he was a trick rider himself, showed her how she could ride him backward, a completely new experience.

In between, she told him about her grandfather teaching her math and supporting her in whatever she did. He, in turn, discussed his search for the right career, feeling a hundred percent confident in becoming a wildlife manager for the state of Arizona. From what she saw, he certainly knew enough about wildlife. She hadn't known that the worst thing she could do was run from a mountain lion, and the best thing to do was to make oneself appear bigger and confident. He was already saving lives, and he hadn't even started yet.

But it was the look of disappointment in his eyes before he left, since it was his turn to make dinner, that had wrapped around her heart and given her hope.

Finishing up, she toweled off and dressed to go over to Rocky Road. She was thrilled that Brody wanted her to join them for dinner. She'd finally get to see what kind of cook he was. She grinned as she pulled on a loose ankle-length skirt covered in Native American symbols, before donning a white blouse with short sleeves that fell past her waist. Then she added a belt that had one of the symbols the skirt contained. She by-passed her cowboy boots for a pair of flat sandals, and picked up her purse.

As she stood at her door looking back at the room to make sure she had everything, a sense of belonging filled her. This was the casita her grandparents honeymooned in. The place they came to be alone and enjoy each other. It was filled with their love, and now it was filled with hers for Brody. She'd even guess that he might be on his way to feeling the same about her. How could she sell it?

Maybe she could sell the land and keep the casita. She certainly wouldn't mind looking out her window to see cattle grazing in her front yard. Even as she imagined it, a rightness about the idea filled her. It could be the solution for Rocky Road and for her future income issue because she wouldn't have to find a full-time position. What was the sense in owning such a beautiful spot in the desert if she wasn't here to enjoy it?

Happy with her idea, she opened the door and stepped outside into highest heat of the day, just before sunset. Closing the door, she locked it and strode to her Jeep. She'd have to see what Brody's opinion was on her idea. If he liked it, it meant that he wanted her around longer. Then again, when they talked earlier, he said he wasn't sure where in the state they'd have openings in the wildlife management arena. He wanted to apply for the first available position. He said being picky meant he could wait years.

She headed to Rocky Road by road, even though the

direct route through the desert would be faster. She didn't treasure the idea of a flat tire in the middle of nowhere. As she entered the Rocky Road drive, she slowed. Last time she'd come down the rocky road a bit too fast and ended up biting her lip on a particularly rough bump. It was hard not rushing. She was just too excited to hang out with Brody, Tanner, Amanda, and finally meet his dad. This was big, at least to her.

Finally, she pulled in next to two pick-up trucks and got out. Immediately, she heard barking and stiffened. "It's just Cami. She likes you. Remember that." Stepping out of her vehicle, she was halfway to the door when it opened and Cami ran out to greet her.

She stopped as the dog circled around her, and did circles in front of her.

"Just give her a pet and she'll calm down." At Amanda's voice, Hannah took her gaze off the dog.

"It's just me." She put her hand out and Cami bumped it with her nose. Understanding what the dog wanted, she relaxed and stroked the pretty white fur.

"There's no 'just' about it. That dog loves you almost as much as Brody. She doesn't do that when I come home."

Her chest filled at that and she crouched down. "Is that true, Cami?"

The dog licked her face before she could turn her head and she shot up. "Ack."

Amanda chuckled. "See, I told you. Come on inside and I'll get you a wet paper towel to wipe off Cami's kiss before you kiss Brody."

Startled by Amanada's assumption, she was about to

question her, but the woman had already turned toward the house.

Hannah looked down at Cami, who sat staring at her. "Let's go in, Cami." As she took a step, the dog moved with her. The acceptance from the dog had her feeling as if she was wanted. She'd never had that with an animal and it felt special.

Once inside, Amanda handed her the promised wipe, and she quickly cleaned her face of Cami's lick. She was surprised to find no one in the kitchen, but something smelled good.

As if Amanda sensed her puzzlement, she pointed to the archway. "We'll be eating in there because Jeremiah can't sit on the stools...yet. I'm determined to get him up there eventually."

Since Amanda wasn't in her usual scrubs, Hannah was curious. "Do you not need to do therapy every day?"

"Hmph. Yes, we do, but the better Jeremiah gets, the more stubborn he gets. He spent the whole day in his office. I'm going to have to bring Tanner in to put some pressure on his dad."

"What about Brody? Can he help?"

Amanda waved off the question as she pulled glasses from the cabinet. "Brody has no sway with his father. I don't know if it's because he's the youngest, or because he always does what he wants whether Jeremiah likes it or not, but he really can't help with this."

It saddened her to think that the Dunn patriarch didn't care about what Brody thought. *It doesn't matter what I think.* Brody's words to her came back in a rush. Was his father's attitude toward him why he thought his ideas didn't matter? Even as her anger started to build, the sliding door in the family room opened.

"There she is. The person I've been cooking for." Brody strode across the room, pulled her in tight, and kissed her right in front of Amanda.

As he pulled away, Amanda shook her head. "Good thing Cami got her kiss in first."

Instead of being upset by Amanda's words, Brody laughed. "My dog knows a good person when she sees one." He gave her another peck on the lips, then continued into the kitchen to remove a large serving plate from a cabinet. "Chow's almost ready. You do like steaks, I hope."

She nodded, still a bit at a loss.

"Good." He walked by her and headed outside again.

Amanda handed her a pile of napkins. "You can put these by the plates." Amanda took her arm and turned her toward the archway. "This is a big deal, you know. Brody never invites a woman for dinner. I don't know what you did, but that man is happier than I've ever seen him. Now go."

She didn't move. "But I had lunch here a few weeks ago."

"Because I invited you. Trust me. Brody has never brought a woman home for his father to meet. Ask Tanner. Now go set those. Dinner is almost ready." Amanda gave her a nudge.

She walked into the other room where a table had been set, her heart racing. She was the first woman Brody had invited to dinner? That had to mean something. Hope for a future with him filled her, almost taking her breath away. She forced herself to fold the napkins in triangles and put them next to each plate. She shouldn't get ahead of herself. It wasn't as if he'd asked her to marry him or anything.

And if he did, would she accept? Hell yes. When had that happened?

Tanner Dunn walked in. "Hi, Hannah. Yes, my dad will need a napkin, too."

She blinked, not realizing she had one napkin left to place. She added it to the place setting that had no chair. Now that she knew how important her being at the table was, her palms started to sweat. What if the patriarch of the Dunn family didn't approve of her?

"You can sit there, next to Brody." Tanner pointed to a chair across from him.

She needed to do something until dinner. "I'll go see if Amanda needs any help." She took a step toward the archway.

"No need. She's not the one cooking."

"Did I hear my name mentioned?" Amanda came in with a pitcher of iced tea. "There you go. Help yourself. I'm going to get Jeremiah. If I don't, he's liable to miss dinner completely." She leaned in. "He expects his brain to work as well as it used to and it's just not there yet."

As Amanda left, Brody walked in with a large platter of steaks. "Tanner, want to grab the sweet potatoes out of the oven for me?"

Brody set down the platter as Tanner left, and pulled her into his arms. "I thought he'd never leave." In the next instant, she was on the receiving end of a breath-stealing kiss that had her feeling a little dizzy.

"Your vegetable casserole is still in there, or did you forget that?" Tanner bumped into Brody, forcing him to let her go.

Brody grinned, winking at her. "I didn't forget. I was just letting it rest."

Tanner snorted as Brody left to retrieve the dish.

"Okay, I'm here. We can eat now." Mr. Dunn rolled himself in.

Amanda shook her head behind him. "You're not the king, Jeremiah."

"Hey. Every man's home is his castle, so that makes me king." He rolled himself into his spot then looked at her. "Hello. Please tell me you're not another therapist Amanda ordered in."

She swallowed hard and forced herself to smile. "I'm pleased to say that I'm not, because I would be terrible at it."

Brody walked in just in time. "Dad, this is Hannah Kingsley. She's the one I told you about, who inherited the Harpers' property. I invited her to have dinner with us since I knew it was my turn to cook and I knew it would be good. Hannah, this is my father, Jeremiah Dunn."

"It's nice to meet you."

Jeremiah looked at Brody, then at her, then back at Brody. Finally, he looked at her. "Are you pregnant?"

"Dad!" Tanner frowned.

"Jeremiah." Amanda shook her finger at the older man.

"Seriously." Brody set down a casserole dish and took the seat next to her. "Mandy, I thought he was working on his manners."

Amanda frowned at Jeremiah. "He was supposed to be,

but those nuances take longer than others skills. I'm sorry, Hannah. It's left over from the stroke."

It was time to ease everyone's discomfort, though she wasn't pleased with Jeremiah's assumption. "I take no offense, Mr. Dunn. I am not pregnant. I'm Brody's girlfriend, not his one-night stand." She smiled to let him know there was no harm done.

"Girlfriend?" Jeremiah moved his gaze to Brody. "Is this true?"

"Dad, if Hannah says something then it's true. She's like Mom in that way."

Immediately, the older Dunn's face fell, making Hannah feel sorry for him. But then his eyes widened and he grabbed up his napkin, making a fist that he shook. "Who put these here?"

Afraid she'd done something wrong, she looked to Amanda, who patted Jeremiah's arm. "I asked Hannah to set out the napkins. Is something wrong?"

When the man didn't answer and Brody looked at Tanner, Hannah knew something was wrong, but she couldn't imagine what. "I'm sorry. Did I set them wrong?"

Tanner lifted his napkin and a sad smile played on his lips.

Brody pulled his out from under his dish, and his Adam's apple moved up and down twice before he spoke. "Mom folded our napkins this way."

Her stomach, which was hungry a moment ago, rolled in on itself, and she wanted to cry. "I'm so sorry. My grandma taught me to fold them like that. I didn't even think twice. I'm so sorry."

Tanner, Amanda, and Brody looked at her, and as if on cue, soft smiles appeared on each face. Amanda shook her head. "There's nothing to be sorry for. Right, Brody?"

Brody was practically beaming now. "Absolutely." He looked at her. "Don't ever change how you fold your napkins. This is perfect."

Not sure what to make of the whole thing, she glanced at Jeremiah, who was still staring at his napkin. She elbowed Brody.

Brody stood and lifted a large serving fork. "Hey, Dad. Which one do you want?"

His father's head jerked up. "I want the biggest." Jeremiah pointed to Brody but looked at her. "He'll eat two and so will Tanner. You just wait and see."

She smiled, pleased that everyone seemed normal again. "Are you saying I should take a big one, too?"

"Damn straight, I am." Jeremiah grinned before instructing Brody on how much he wanted of everything, which was a lot. Once his plate was set before him, he looked at her. "I knew your grandparents. They used to visit their land once a year. Nice people. Stubborn, but nice."

Surprised to learn her grandparents had spoken to the Dunns, she had to know more. "When did they come?"

Jeremiah squinched his face, making his rather large nose look more predominant "If I recall, it was in the month of May. They only stayed about a week and I'd ride over to say howdy."

"Oh, that was when they married. They said they had their honeymoon up here. I bet they came back for their anniversary."

"Well, they stopped coming almost thirty years ago."

That was when her mom and dad died. "That makes sense. I was a baby when my parents died, and it was around then when they took me in to raise."

Brody's hand grasped hers in a silent sign of support, and she found it much easier to handle the new information about her grandparents. Four Peaks truly must have been their happy place.

As everyone ate, the conversation flowed freely. Tanner updated his father on the next phase of the dude ranch build-out, Brody reported on what was happening with the cattle, and Amanda explained Jeremiah's latest milestone. Just like at lunch, the insults flew, with even Jeremiah getting a few in. She wasn't sure why, but it seemed as if being insulted meant that person was loved, and she found herself wishing she could be insulted.

Jeremiah pointed at Tanner with his knife. "You need to look at the spreadsheets. Something's not adding up. I thought you budgeted for everything."

Amanda put her hand on Jeremiah's arm to make him lower the knife.

"I did. I'll take a look tomorrow morning. I'm better at numbers after a good night's sleep."

Brody hmphed. "A good night's sleep isn't going to help any."

Seeing a chance to be part of the family, Hannah took the opportunity. "If you like, I'd be happy to review them for you."

"You?" Jeremiah frowned at her.

She gave him a smile in return. "Yes, me. That's my job. I'm a budget analyst."

That got Tanner's attention. "That's a relief. If I can't figure things out, I'll definitely accept that offer."

Pleased that she might be able to help, she took her last bite of baked potato.

Brody looked to his brother. "You know, when I told Hannah about the dude ranch, she thought it an excellent idea, just like Mandy. I wonder if we should try marketing it more to women. I know you were thinking families, but the women around this table are more enthusiastic about it than we are."

"Oh, I like that idea." Amanda gave a thumbs-up.

"What do women know about ranching? They'll probably break a nail or something."

"Jeremiah." Amanda actually tapped the man's arm. "You know very well that I can ride a horse better than most men."

"Yeah, Dad. And Hannah here had fun mucking out the stalls in the barn."

At Brody's defense, she piped in. "Yes, I did. Brody said the stalls had never been cleaner."

Tanner nodded. "I think this idea bears some research. Brody, you're the expert on the internet. See what you can find."

Jeremiah didn't say anything, instead he stuffed the last piece of his steak in his mouth and chewed.

Thrilled that Brody's idea was being considered, she beamed at him. It was good to see his family acknowledge his contribution.

Jeremiah's grumpy attitude actually didn't bother her. In fact, she felt more like part of the family. When eating dinner at people's houses, everyone was always on their best behavior, but Jeremiah Dunn didn't care that she was a guest. It may be because of his stroke, but it made her feel accepted. How lucky Brody was to have family dinners like this every night. She would so enjoy being a part of his family.

Brody set his silverware on his empty dish. "A meal like that needs a light dessert, don't you think?"

She lifted her brows, not sure how he could think of eating another bit. She was stuffed with his excellent cooking, and he had twice as much as she had. "Dessert? Now?"

He opened his mouth to answer when Cami started barking so loudly, the two brothers both stood.

Brody started forward. "Someone must be here, and they must be strangers or she wouldn't be going so ballistic."

Jeremiah backed up his wheel chair. "Well, let's see who it is."

They all filed out of the room and into the entry. Brody grabbed Cami's collar just as Tanner opened the door and strode out. "What the hell are you doing here?"

CHAPTER 14

BRODY STARED UNBELIEVINGLY at the man standing in front of a truck, in tan camouflage with short-cropped brown hair and no hat, before he let Cami loose. "Jackson!" With relief plowing through him, he strode past Tanner and gave Jackson a hug, a little taken aback by how stiff his brother was. Cami ran around them both. "Cami. Sit."

Jackson looked past him and pointed. "What the fuck is *she* doing here?"

Not a little shocked by his brother's language in front of Hannah, Brody stepped back. "You better watch it, Jackson. That's Tanner's wife."

Jackson let out a slew of expletives under his breath that didn't bear repeating.

Tanner walked over. "It's a long story, but suffice it to say that what we thought about Handy Mandy was wrong. She saved Dad."

Jackson's dark brows lowered ominously. "What happened to Dad?"

"I'm right here." Dad rolled himself over from the bottom of the ramp they'd put in. "No need to talk about me when I'm sitting right here."

"Dad?" Jackson stared, his mouth slightly open, a small tick under his right eye noticeable.

That was new. Maybe it was the stress of war and would fade after Jackson was home awhile.

"Can you give an old man a hug?"

At his father's words, Jackson appeared to snap out of it and bent to give Dad a hug, but like with him, it seemed stiff. "What happened?"

Dad shrugged. "Had a stroke out on the west line. It was bad. But Amanda here is getting me back into shape."

At the mention of Amanda, Brody noticed both women hanging back. He was having none of that. Striding back to Hannah, he took her hand and brought her forward. "This is my girl, Hannah Kingsley."

Jackson looked at Hannah, but didn't seem to really see her.

She smiled tentatively, her hand reaching down to touch Cami who sat next to her. "It's nice to meet you."

His brother gave a short nod before turning his gaze back to Mandy, who strode up.

"I'm very relieved you're home safe."

Brody felt for Jackson. A lot had happened in the year-and-a-half he'd been deployed in Syria, or wherever the government had actually sent him. It was a lot to take in.

Hannah gripped his hand, obviously aware of the tension, but she couldn't begin to understand it all. Then she cocked her head. "Is that a baby crying?"

"Oh, crap." Jackson spun on his heel and headed for the truck, then stopped and turned back to them all. "Literally. She's a pooping machine."

Brody looked at Tanner, who shook his head. A baby? What the heck was Jackson doing with a baby?

His brother stepped away from the truck with a baby in a car seat, one of those ones that hooked into another piece. The baby stopped crying at the movement. Jackson strode forward, his jaw filled with tension. "This is my daughter, Tabitha."

Brody liked other people's children, but didn't see himself having any. But if he did, his gut told him he would never present his child like Jackson was, holding the baby in the seat like she was week-old gym clothes that hadn't been washed. The child was tiny. Then again, anything would look tiny next to Jackson. He was taller than Tanner and broader than Brody was.

Dad recovered first, rolling his wheelchair closer to take a look. "Hah. I should have known Jackson would be the first to give me a grandchild. Well done, son. Where's her mom?"

"Dead."

The word was stated with no emotion whatsoever, sending a chill through them all, if the silence was any indication.

Hannah's free hand came up to her chest.

He understood. She'd lost her mom at about the same age.

This time it was Mandy who came to their rescue. "It sounds like you have a lot to share with us. Why don't we go inside. Has Tabitha been fed?"

Jackson shook his head.

"Then Tanner, why don't you and Brody help Jackson with his belongings. Jackson, I'm sure you're tired after traveling with your daughter. If you can set her on the island in the kitchen, I can see about getting her some food. Did you bring any formula?"

Jackson nodded, obviously still unsure what to do around Mandy.

Letting go of Hannah's hand, Brody walked over and patted Jackson on the shoulder. "Go ahead. She won't bite."

Jackson grumbled under his breath. "That makes one female." But he did finally move toward the house.

Tanner headed for Jackson's truck.

"Brody, I think I should go."

At Hannah's statement, he pulled her into his arms, her light floral scent enveloping him. "I don't want you to."

"That makes me feel good. Thank you for saying so, but I think your brother needs his family right now. Maybe you could come over to my place for dinner tomorrow night. It seems only fair that I reciprocate."

"I would like that."

She smiled at him, that open, caring smile that made him feel like everything was right with the world. "Excellent." Her smile faltered and her gaze shifted to the house behind him. "I hope your brother is okay."

"Jackson? He's okay. He's always okay. He's as tough as the boulders that roll down the Four Peaks."

She didn't look convinced. "Boulders like him then find themselves out of place, and as we both know, they can break in two, or a million pieces."

Her words struck a pocket of uncertainty inside him. It was an uncomfortable feeling that Jackson wasn't the person he'd grown up with anymore. "Did anyone ever tell you that you're incredibly observant?"

"Why yes. I believe you have."

He gave her a soft smile. "See, I knew I was smart."

She batted his shoulder with her hand as she stepped out of his embrace. "I'll see you tomorrow."

"Brody, I'm going to need your help." Tanner punctuated his statement by slamming one truck door and opening another.

"Go." She gave him a little push before turning to walk to her Jeep.

Her hips swayed with her natural gait, but in the skirt, it had him mesmerized.

"Brody."

He turned at Tanner's command. "I'm coming."

Tanner stood next to the truck with a tan duffle bag the size of a calf on his shoulder, and it looked about as heavy. "There's a diaper bag and cases of formula in there."

Brody walked past his brother and peered inside. "Cases? It looks like he bought out the whole damn store. No wonder his daughter poops so much. Is that healthy?" He slung the diaper bag over his shoulder and grabbed three cases of formula.

"Hell if I know. We'll have to make a second trip."

They walked back into the house in silence. Tanner dropped the duffle bag on the floor in the family area, and Brody set the formula on the kitchen counter.

Mandy immediately took the diaper bag from his shoulder. "We'll get this little one some supper."

As he and Tanner walked out, Brody noticed that Jackson watched every move Mandy made. He felt for his brother. To have his newborn daughter being cared for by someone he thought their worst enemy had to be hard to process.

Once outside, he couldn't keep silent. "He's changed."

"Yeah, I know. I expected it the first time he was deployed, but when he came back twice the same wiseass we always knew, I didn't worry about it this time. Looks like I should have."

"Mom always said worrying doesn't accomplish anything. But a kid?" He was still trying to understand that Jackson was a father. It was the last thing his brother had ever wanted.

Tanner pulled out four more cases of formula. "Maybe being back here will help him. We can put him back out with the cattle. It may make him feel like himself again."

Brody pulled out the last four cases, ignoring the additional packs of diapers, and hip-checked the door closed. "I hope so." Even as he said the words, the concept that Jackson was really home sank in. If Jackson was home and back out on the range, then maybe, just maybe, Dad would release him from his promise and he wouldn't have to sweat attending the academy in a couple of months.

The thought had his spirits rising, and with them, the realization of what Jackson's daughter meant to them.

Tanner set his cases down on the nearby bench on the porch to open the door.

Brody stopped to hold it open while Tanner lifted his

load again. He grinned at Tanner. "You know, this means we're uncles now."

"Hell, you're right." Tanner broke into a wide smile. "And maybe Dad will stop pressuring Amanda and me about having a kid."

As Brody followed Tanner in, he shook his head. "Don't bet on it."

Tanner set the cases down in the family area and Brody piled his on top. He'd have to rearrange the kitchen to accommodate the new addition to the family. The broom closet no longer housed brooms, so if he cleared out the junk in there, he could add some shelves and make it Tabitha's closet.

Mandy had the baby feeding from a bottle while Jackson looked on. It was obvious he wasn't happy with the arrangement, but he didn't move forward to intervene either. Brody found the whole situation odd.

Out of the blue, Jackson turned to Dad. "Is my old room still mine, or has that changed, too?"

Brody didn't like his brother's tone and opened his mouth to tell him so, but Dad answered first. "Yes. Your room is exactly as you left it."

Jackson didn't acknowledge the statement. "I've got more stuff in the pickup bed. I only need one thing tonight, and that's the playpen so she has a safe place to sleep."

Brody found the phrasing odd.

"I'll find it and Brody can set it up." Tanner strode outside once again.

Taking the opportunity to leave the awkward silence of the room, Brody walked down the hall to Jackson's room to make room for a playpen. The door to his brother's room was always open and it was included in the vacuuming, but he'd never thought about it in terms of a nursery. It was beyond ironic that Jackson would be having a baby sleeping in his room.

Brody eyed the space. Depending on the size of the playpen, there'd be no problem fitting it in any number of places. Jackson had always been the neat brother, everything in its place.

"Here it is." Tanner strode in. "You lucked out. It looks like it folds out."

Brody took the contraption and unfolded it on the side of the bed against the wall. There were small locks that had to be flipped to keep it in place. "Shouldn't she be in a crib?"

"I wouldn't be surprised if he has one of those in the back of his truck as well."

"Good point." They stood staring at the pink-and-purple playpen next to the bed, with the cornflower-blue blanket and dark walnut headboard. To say it looked out of place would be an understatement.

"I better get back out there. I don't want Jackson saying anything nasty to my wife."

Brody nodded. "It's weird you are thinking that, but I agree."

After Tanner left, Brody remained where he was. He'd never wanted children, preferring to hand them back over to their parents when they got cranky. Did Hannah want children? The answer came immediately. Yes. And she would make a great mother.

He shook his head. What was he thinking? It's not like he and Hannah would be together forever...or was it? No, it couldn't work. He had a career to pursue and once she sold her land, she could go wherever she wanted.

But then she could go with him.

He tried to brush away the thought. He really liked Hannah. He could even see a long-term relationship with her, but marriage was not on the table. Comfortable with his decision, he left Jackson's room to see how things were progressing in the kitchen. At least his life was much less complicated than his brother's.

Jackson was a father. He shook his head. That was an even a bigger surprise than his brother marrying a Hayden. He was quite content that his life had no such drama.

Brody strode toward the house whistling. He couldn't help it after spending the night with Hannah. Plus, after a week, Jackson had finally been convinced to leave Tabitha with Isaac, who was Dad's CNA, a few days a week. It turned out the big guy loved babies, and boasted seven nieces and nephews.

Mandy had offered, but that had gone nowhere. As far as he was concerned, how Jackson dealt with Amanda was between Tanner and Jackson. The important part was Jackson was back out with the cattle, which meant Brody wasn't needed anymore.

Brody opened the front door and stepped inside. The temperature difference was much less, now that autumn had truly come to the valley. After dropping his hat on the side table near the door, he ignored the kitchen, where he would be making lunch, and strode down the hall to his dad's office.

The fact that his father was able to do some computer work now had made him a much happier person. Mandy said it was because he felt productive and like he was contributing to the ranch again. So this was the perfect time to talk to Dad about leaving the ranch.

The door to the office was open and he stepped inside to find his father pulled up to the computer. "How's it going in here?"

His father didn't look up. "It's a trainwreck."

Surprised his father even knew that expression, he walked around the desk to see what the problem was. As the youngest son, he was usually the one everyone came to when having computer problems. "What's wrong?"

"The damn numbers are adding up wrong. It's not balancing."

Brody grimaced. If it was a computer user problem or a writing problem, he was the man for the job, but he and numbers didn't get along at all. "I know someone who could help you with that."

His father finally looked at him. "Who?"

"Hannah. She's some kind of financial wizard. I bet she could make everything come out smelling like roses."

"Son, it's a balance sheet, not a garden." His dad looked at the clock on the wall, one of those old-fashioned ones with big numbers and hands that his father swore was the only reliable type. "It's not lunch time yet. Why are you here?"

Brody set his hip on the corner of the desk. "I wanted to see how you're doing."

"Bullshit. Out with it, son. I have numbers to force into place."

He chuckled. Sometimes it was nice to be known so well. "Okay then. With Jackson home now and the two new ranch hands working out so well, I'd like to be released from my promise to help with the ranch. The Game and Fish department has accepted me for their next training."

"No." His father turned back to the computer.

Stunned, he stared at his father in disbelief. "No? Why not? You have plenty of help now, and even you are working again. You don't need me anymore."

His father spoke to the computer. "A promise is a promise."

He stood and set both hands down on the desk. "I know that. It's been drilled into me since I could walk. But you can release me from my promise, so I can finally be free to pursue my dreams instead of yours."

That got his father's attention. Rolling the wheelchair back, his father faced him fully. "I told you I'd release you from your promise if you got the Harpers to sell. But you aren't doing that are you? No, you're too busy dating the owner of the property to talk her into selling. That tells me she's more important than pursuing your so-called career."

His father's emphasis on the last two words had him gritting his teeth. He forced himself to keep his cool. "The extra land is a moot point now, since you have moved forward with your dude ranch. It appears that's more important than remaining a cattle ranch. Therefore, buying her property is no longer important." He almost added 'like me,' but held back.

"One has nothing to do with the other. I told you once we have the land you could leave. You'd think I was torturing you or something. You should be happy you have a ranch to call home. We could still lose it if the dude ranch isn't successful. I'd think you'd want to be here to help out."

That was it. He was done sacrificing his life for the ranch. Tanner loved the place and would inherit it one day. Jackson got to pursue his military career. As the youngest, he'd been the only one forced to sacrifice for the family, and he was done. "Then if you won't release me from my promise, I'm going to have to break it."

His father's eyes rounded and his face turned red. "You can't."

"I can. Mom told me long ago that I was different. That I should pursue my dreams no matter what you wanted, and I plan to follow her council. At least she was one person in this family who gave a shit about what I thought."

"Don't you dare bring your mother into this!" His father's yell reverberated through the room.

"Why? Because you're the only one who's allowed to talk about her? She was *my* mother and I'll bring her into this if I want. Out of respect for you, I've stayed, but for the love I'll always have for her, I'm leaving, just like Jackson did. If you could let him leave you when you didn't have enough help, you can let me go when you do. It's not like you even need me around. You have Tanner and Layne backs him up. What do you need me for?"

"You...made...a promise." His dad's words were ground out between his teeth.

"Yeah. That was my first mistake. I see no reason to

compound it by keeping it." He turned on his heel and headed for the door.

"You break your promise, you won't be welcome in this house ever again."

He halted in the doorway and turned to look at his father. "Why would I want to come back?"

His father's mouth opened, but nothing came out.

Brody strode out the door, only to find Mandy and Isaac waiting for him in the kitchen.

"What happened? We could hear the yelling from outside." Mandy gave him an accusatory look.

"That would be him." He hooked his finger over his shoulder. "I'm going for a ride—alone."

Mandy's eyes widened, as the rule was no one was to wander the ranch alone since his father's stroke. "What about lunch? It's your day for meals."

"I quit." He strode through the entryway and grabbed his hat on his way out, not caring if anyone ate. His own stomach was so tense he'd be sick if he even smelled food.

He let the door slam behind him as he headed for the stable. Unlooping the reins from the hook, he walked his horse outside and mounted. "Okay, boy. We're living up to your name today. Let's go wherever you want." He clicked his tongue and Chaos headed for the mountains, which was just fine with him.

CHAPTER 15

HANNAH SET out the last piece of glassware on the counter. She'd finally emptied the last box from her move over two months ago. She would have had everything organized earlier if she hadn't been distracted by Brody. But what a yummy distraction.

She grinned as she set the empty box on the floor and surveyed the variety of glassware. It was all odds and ends she used once in a blue moon, as her grandmother used to say. Opening the cabinet before her, she frowned. It was packed. She moved to the next one. It was packed, too. Opening the last cupboard, she smiled. The top shelf was empty. "Perfect."

She pulled over the chair she kept against the wall to use for just such a purpose. The dust and dirt on the shelves had been heavy, but she'd ignored the top shelves, erroneously thinking she wouldn't need them. How wrong she was.

Wetting a paper towel, she climbed on the chair and looked at the inches of dust on the shelf. With no help for it, she carefully wiped one side, only to have a folder fall onto the counter sending up a cloud of desert dust all over her clean glassware. "Great." Not happy she'd have to wash everything by hand, she went ahead and wiped down the wooden shelf.

It would need two or three wipes. She stepped down and moved the glassware to the sink, but only half of it. She wet another paper towel and moved back to the chair when she was struck by the handwriting on the folder. It looked like her grandmother's. Far too curious to wait, she cleaned off the folder before opening it.

Her breath caught. It wasn't her grandmother's. It was her mother's! Her mother's name was printed on a label on the front—Monica Harper Kingsley. The 'Harper' was crossed off and 'Kingsley' added in a different color. If her mother was married at the time, that meant she was already born. Her parents had died in a car accident on their way home from their honeymoon, so she was told. What was something of her mother's doing in the casita?

She sat in the chair and quickly opened the folder. There was an odd assortment of paper. A couple of receipts, a grocery list, a picture of her parents next to a saguaro cactus, a pressed flower, an image of a black horse ripped out of a magazine, and a folded piece of paper. As she put the receipts aside, a name caught her attention. Though the ink was faded, it was definitely from the Lucky Lasso Hotel and Saloon.

Her parents had been in Four Peaks? In this very casita? Her hands trembled at the thought. She lifted the picture and studied it. She'd seen pictures of her parents before, but this one was different. If she wasn't mistaken, the mountain behind them was one of the Four Peaks. Reverently, she tucked it in the pocket of the folder.

Opening the folded piece of paper, she found a list of days with activities next to each. There was shopping, dancing, horseback riding, hiking, and even swimming. Under each were phrases like 'amazing view' and 'delicious breakfast.' At the bottom of the note were the words *Best honeymoon ever*!

The paper dropped from her fingers. Her parents had honeymooned in the casita, just like her grandparents! Tears formed in her eyes and she wiped them away as she tried to focus on the inside of her casita. She imagined her father carrying her mother over the threshold. She could envision them laughing together on the couch. They probably—her throat closed.

Setting aside the folder, she rose. She walked into the bedroom and touched the quilt. Her parents had slept in the very bed she now used. She grasped the footboard with both hands, the tears falling freely now. Not tears of sadness, but of happiness. It was as if her parents were here, with her. The last place they had spent time together full of joy.

She moved around the bed and sat in the middle of it facing the headboard, willing herself to feel them. She couldn't, but it didn't matter. They had been here, as had her grandparents. This was truly her home. Her heart filled with love and she smiled through her tears. For the first time in three generations, she had what no one else had—a place. She hadn't realized how important it was to her until now.

All she'd known was apartments, some better than others,

but all with shared walls and rent to pay. The little casita was *hers*, her family's. She belonged here. No one could take it from her because it was paid for.

Except for the solar panels, new roof, and end-of-year taxes. The thought brought reality back and she moved off the bed. If she was going to afford to keep her family inheritance, she needed to get the glassware washed and the cabinet ready, so she could get back to work. She may be an emotional mess, but luckily numbers were logical, and she had no online meetings.

She quickly got everything done for what was supposed to be her lunch break, then moved to the desk she'd set up next to the couch. It took less than ten minutes, and she was back on an even keel with her work. There were figurative fires to put out and numbers to crunch, so the rest of the day flew by. When next she looked at the time, she'd gone over her work hours.

Standing, she stretched her back, the muscles happy to move. Checking her phone, she was surprised there were no texts from Brody. Usually he sent one in the afternoon, asking if she had plans. Then again, they may need him at the ranch, as they were getting very close to opening their dude ranch.

She shut off her computer and went back into the kitchen to put the now clean and dry glassware on the top shelf. She'd just put away the last glass, when someone knocked on her door. She stepped down from the chair and moved to the door. "Who is it?"

"It's me. I need to talk to you." Brody didn't sound happy.

Quickly, she unlocked the door and let him in. "Hi." As

he brushed past, she noticed his truck parked next to her Jeep. Usually, he used the ATV.

He hadn't even given her a kiss hello, which he always did now. Something must be seriously wrong. Closing the door, she waited for him to speak.

He stood staring at the couch, his hands rolled into fists.

She wanted to give him a hug, but anger seemed to radiate from him. Then he turned around and faced her.

"I need you to sell your place."

She felt as if someone had punched her in the gut. "What?"

He walked into the kitchen and leaned against the counter as he spoke to the titled floor. "It will take some time. There's paperwork and credit checks and numerous other hurdles to be jumped, but I'm sure it could be accomplished in a month. I know my father will approve a generous offer." He finally looked at her. "Have you thought about what you want for it?"

She'd never seen this side of Brody. He was neither the polite cowboy nor the attentive lover. He was a businessman, who wished to conduct business. But she was having none of it. "Brody Dunn, what are you talking about?"

He stiffened as if ready to do battle. "I think I've been very clear. I'm talking about you selling us your property. You said your grandparents asked you to stay a while. It's been a couple of months, so that constitutes a while, though I imagine they hadn't expected you to actually live here. Who would expect a single woman to live out in the middle of the desert?"

This was not Brody. Something had to have happened.

She couldn't accept that he could be so heartless about her inheritance. "What happened? Why all of a sudden do you want me to sell my land?"

He pushed away from the counter and walked to the couch, where he turned and faced her. "It's not all of a sudden. I told you the first day we met that my family needed to buy your land to survive in the cattle business."

He wasn't being honest with her and she didn't like it. "But the Rocky Road Dude Ranch opens in just a few weeks. Amanda and Tanner believe it will save the ranch."

He shook his head. "My father isn't so sure. He's the one managing the finances now, and he's worried. We went into a lot of debt to build the infrastructure for this venture. It's not like Four Peaks is a vacation destination to begin with. The only way to secure our future is to buy your property."

She'd never thought of Brody as selfish, but he was sounding that way now. "What about *my* future? This is the first home I've ever owned. It's my legacy from my grandparents, and—" She wasn't going to share her discovery with him right now. "I enjoy living here." Secretly, she hoped he'd offer for her to keep the building and give her an easement, what she'd come up with before finding her mother's folder.

He spread his arms wide. "This is so small. With all the money we pay you, you could buy a big house. You could even stay in Four Peaks if you wanted to."

Disappointment wafted over her. "We've had this conversation before, but you still haven't told me why today. You didn't text me as usual, didn't even kiss me hello, but came storming in demanding I sell now. Why?" She crossed her arms over her chest, partly to cover how hurt she was at his actions.

Brody rubbed the back of his neck, the first sign that he was the man she knew. But when he still didn't say anything, she was done being nice. "Either tell me why I need to sell right now, or leave."

His head jerked up. "You want to know why?"

"Yes." She scowled at him, unable to think of any reason that would excuse his behavior.

"I'll tell you why. Because my father won't let me out of my promise to stay at the ranch while he needs me unless you sell. If he doesn't release me from that, then I'll miss the wildlife manager training in January. They only offer it once a year. I don't want to lose another year of my life to the family ranch. I've already given him more time than I expected."

She wasn't sure whether to laugh or scream. He had to be kidding. She shrugged. "So break your promise."

"That's exactly what I told him I would do. But I can't. Everything in my DNA is against breaking a promise. I gave my word. A man's word is his bond."

She would have admired his integrity if she wasn't so pissed. "Let's see if I have this right. You gave your father a promise. He told you he'd release you from that promise if you got me to sell. So now you want to ruin my life so you can start your own with a clear conscience?"

"No. That's not it. Your life wouldn't be ruined. It would be better. Certainly a lot bigger than this." He held his arms out to encompass her casita.

She was beyond thinking straight. "Believe it or not,

bigger is not better. However, caring, compassion, and honesty *are* better, all qualities I thought you had. But I was wrong. You also can't see beyond the obvious." She strode forward into his personal space. "You could have just as easily waltzed in here, swept me off my feet, told me you loved me and asked me to marry you, and all your problems would have been solved. But you blew it. Get out of my tiny house. It's obviously not big enough for you, being as how you are used to such comfortable living." Though she pointed toward the door, she didn't break eye contact.

Brody's eyes widened in shock before he turned on his heel and brushed by her, leaving the casita with a loud bang as he slammed the door.

Shaking, she listened for his truck to let her know he left. She couldn't hear it through the thick adobe walls, but the rocks hitting the outside wall as he peeled out told her he was gone. Just to be sure, she opened the door and stepped outside to see the large dust cloud following him down her simple driveway. Closing the door behind her, she stepped under the shade of her portico and sat on the new glider she'd bought just last week. The same glider she and Brody had sat on just two evenings ago, talking about the history of the town of Four Peaks.

She wanted to cry because the hurt in her chest was causing her physical pain, but no tears came. Had their relationship all been part of a plan he had to get her to sell? She didn't want to think that of him, but the man who just left her house, was not the man she'd come to know over the last few months. Maybe she'd only seen what she wanted to see. She'd never had a real cowboy interested in her. Or maybe he'd just hit his breaking point.

Did he want to become a wildlife manager more than he cared about her? It appeared she had her answer. Deep down she understood his need to leave his family, but only on an intellectual level. Her family had been so small, she'd love to have what he had. Maybe humans were meant to always yearn for what they didn't have.

Staring out at the desert, she could see a handful of wild burros munching on the autumn grasses in the distance. Even they had each other. Maybe her heartache was partly her own fault. She'd wanted to be a part of Brody's life. She'd yearned for family and maybe, just maybe, she'd not given his ambition the attention it deserved.

She rose from the glider and turned toward her front door, temporarily blinded by the bright sun just setting beyond a peak. She held her hand up to shield her eyes. At least she still had her home. She opened the door, stepped inside, and quietly closed it behind her, leaning back against it. But she had no one to share it with, no one to tell about her parents' honeymoon, no one to let know when she got back from Prescott safely, and no one to wake up next to in bed.

A single tear fell from her eye, and she brushed it away. She'd known when her grandparents had passed, she would be alone. She'd just been able to forget that for a while, thanks to Brody. But now, she'd have to get used to it. She'd only delayed the inevitable.

Brody had no idea had good he had it.

CHAPTER 16

"BRODY!"

Nash's voice interrupted his dark thoughts. "What?" He looked over his shoulder.

"The gate!" Nash pointed to the open gate where two heifers had already meandered through.

"Shit." Urging Chaos forward, he rode through the opening, only to cause the two cows to split. "Shit!" Herding one back in, he then went to round up the other. When they were both safely inside again, he jumped from his horse like any good trick-rider and slammed the gate shut hard, letting out his frustration and anger, which broke the latch.

"Goddamn it!" He kicked the gate against the latch, jamming it in.

"Whoa, Brody, take it easy on that thing." Nash rode over and dismounted. "What's up with you?"

He kept staring at the latch, mentally daring it to let go. "Damn ranch." Finally, he glanced up to find Nash looking at him as if he'd turned into a burro. He rubbed the back of his neck before climbing up on the fence and jumping down on the other side to gather his horse. He walked Chaos back to where Nash stood patiently waiting for an explanation.

He didn't have one. Not a good one. "What?"

Nash crossed his arms over his chest. "Come on. I know you. I know when you're pissed off about something. What's going on?"

He leaned back against the fence. "Everything's gone to shit."

"Okay. Why?" Nash calmly expected an answer. The man was always calm. It was irritating.

"It must be me. I must be cursed."

Nash's lips quirked up. "Now that's a new one. Usually, the world is against you or you suck."

His gut tightened, a sinking feeling that it may very well be the second. "I asked Dad if he'd release me from my promise since Jackson is home and helping out again."

"He said 'no,' right?"

"He did. He said he'd already told me if I got Hannah to sell then I could be released, and not until then."

"Hmm, and I'm guessing you didn't tell him that you were accepted into the training and it only happens once a year?"

Brody stared at Nash as if he was a mind reader. "How did you know? Did you talk to Dad?"

Nash laughed. "Hardly. I just know you."

He shrugged. "I told him I'd been accepted for the next training. Same thing. It's not like it would matter. Dad's hell-bent on getting that land. Suddenly, he's having second thoughts about the dude ranch saving Rocky Road. He was doing finance stuff on the computer and not happy with the numbers, so it was probably just my luck, or should I say my curse, that I walked in just then."

"So ask again at another time. He's turned you down before, but I know you can get him to come around. You can convince anyone to agree with you eventually."

"Not Hannah." He clenched his jaw, not meaning to say the words out loud.

But Nash was too damn observant. "What about Hannah? No, wait. You went to Hannah and tried to talk her into selling her land now, so you could leave your ranch duties in time for the wildlife manager training. Was she impervious to your persuasion?"

He ignored the exaggerated look of surprise on Nash's face. "There was no persuading. The curse was at work again. I was so furious with Dad, I just told her she needed to sell now."

Nash's brows lowered, all hints of humor gone. "You didn't say that."

Brody turned and started to walk Chaos away from the gate.

Nash grabbed his arm as he passed. "Brody, you're a great guy, but sometimes you can be so damn immature. What did she say?"

He pulled his arm away. "The same thing as Dad. So I'm stuck here for another year." He kept walking, his gut feeling like one of the Four Peaks boulders had come to rest inside it.

"Brody, what did *you* say?"

At Nash's question, he stopped, but he couldn't face his friend. "I told her she could have a better life in a nice house with the money she'd have." Even as he said the words out loud, he cringed. Hannah wasn't about money. Even in his anger, he'd known all she wanted was a place to belong, with people who cared about her.

Nash let out a low whistle. "She loves that casita."

He finally turned around. "I know. I knew that. I was angry."

"So go apologize." Nash shrugged his shoulders as if it was that simple.

But that was the crux of his pain. "I tried."

"She wouldn't listen?"

"No, she's not there. As in, not in her casita anymore. I've been checking for the last three days now. She's left. No new tire tracks and the door hasn't been opened. She's...gone." He swallowed the lump in his throat as he said the word. Voicing it made it so final.

"But where would she go? A friend's place?"

He shook his head. "She didn't have any close friends in Phoenix. I know she's not at Sheila's or Stacy's or even Ava's hotel. That's the problem. She doesn't have anyone. And now I've scared her off." He was twelve times a fool and he knew it, which just made everything harder to bear. He had no one to blame but himself.

How had he *not* known how much he cared about her? Was his Dad right? Was she more important than his career? The tightness in his chest said she was. When did she become the most important part of his life? When did he fall in love with her?

The truth hit him like a charging bull. Shit. He loved

Hannah Kingsley and had just run her off. He was an idiot, who didn't deserve her.

Nash chuckled before mounting up again.

The sound grated on his nerves. "What are you laughing at?"

Nash turned his horse to face him. "Hannah may be nice and pretty and kind, but you didn't scare her off. That lady has a backbone, and I guarantee you, she'll be back." He chuckled again. "And I wouldn't want to be you when she does come back. Come on, Mr. Heartbreak."

For the first time since he'd stormed into Hannah's casita, hope filled his head. Nash was right. Hannah was sweet and sexy, but she didn't let anyone steamroll over her, not even him.

He swung up on Chaos to follow Nash. "Come on, boy. You don't want Harmony to think she's better than you."

If Nash was right, which he probably was, that meant it was only a matter of time before Hannah returned. Brody wasn't sure how much time he had to figure out what he was going to say then. He'd have to convince her he was sorry. He'd have to admit she was more important than even his future career, though he wasn't sure how that had happened. It must have been when he'd fallen for her. Even as he acknowledged that fact, his gut loosened.

He loved Hannah Kingsley. The admission lifted an invisible weight from his back. He loved her. It was both a freeing and terrifying feeling. He had to win her back. When he set his mind to something, he always found a way. Yet a whisper of doubt swept through his head.

Part of him hoped she didn't come home soon because he

needed to think. But the other part of him wished her back tomorrow because he didn't want to spend another day without her.

Shit. He just hoped she'd forgive him. His biggest fear was that he killed her feelings for him. It scared the hell out of him to tell her he loved her. He'd never said those words to a woman before and these were not the best circumstances.

He straightened his shoulders and turned Chaos toward a wandering cow. Somehow, he would convince Hannah he was worth taking back, not with his proven methods of persuasion, but with his honesty. That, and a truckful of luck.

"I have concerns about the development office completing this campaign. Could you take a look at what it could mean to our budget if we don't reach our goals and e-mail me?"

At Travis Ingram's question, Hannah pulled her sweater closer together. The breeze had picked up as he walked her back to the Earp House Bed and Breakfast. "I can tell you right now. The school won't be able to build the theatre."

The assistant treasurer for the college halted.

She stopped and looked back at him. He was a pleasant man who rarely showed emotions in the meetings, but whom she found to be quite witty during lunch. He was tall and lean, much thinner than Brody. He also sported a blond mustache that complimented his wavy, short blond hair, the opposite of Brody. Most of all, he didn't have a confident cowboy's swagger. "What is it?"

He smiled. "I appreciate how you get right to the point without sugar-coating things."

She shrugged. "That's what's great about numbers. They're black and white. There's no gray about them. If you don't have the money, you can't buy something, unless you get a loan. That's when you add red to the equation, but not gray."

This time he laughed. "Exactly. I've been in the red a few years now from buying an old Victorian here in town. 'Old' being the key word."

She grinned. "Actually, I don't think they are building new Victorian houses these days."

"Good point. Bringing an old house back to its original glory while adding modern electricity and plumbing is far more complex than any balance sheet."

As much as she liked talking with him, it was getting rather cold for a desert dweller and she was anxious to get back to the fireplace in the sitting area. She shivered as the breeze from a passing truck hit her.

Travis appeared oblivious, but at least he started forward again. "Have you ever thought about buying an old house?"

A pang hit her chest as she pictured her casita. "Actually, I inherited my family's home."

His brows raised. "Really? How nice that you don't need a mortgage. That debt hanging over my head is like sleeping on sandpaper."

She did have house debt of sorts, which is why she continued to work and had recently contemplated the offer of a full-time position with her company. After moving to the casita, she hadn't given it a second thought, but now, what else did she have?

Travis pointed. "My house is a bit like this one."

She turned to politely to look at the Victorian that had been completely restored. It now was a lawyers' office. "Is yours this size?"

He practically grew an inch with pride. "Mine is five-hundred square feet larger."

She frowned, a bit puzzled. "And you're the only occupant?"

"Yes. I'm hoping to restore it and sell it, maybe to a firm like this one."

"So it's actually an investment, not a home."

He nodded. "If I wanted a home, I would have bought one of the new houses that went up on Sunset Peak Road. But what's the fun in that?"

He really was a black-and-white type of guy. Were there only two types of men, black-and-white, or gray? Brody was definitely in the gray area.

They finally reached the Earp House, and she halted at the start of the walkway. "It's been a pleasure helping Verde Canyon College. I do hope your school will call upon our company again."

He looked toward the bed and breakfast as if he expected her to invite him in. "I'm sure we will. I don't have much say in that yet, but I know my boss was very happy with your insights on our budget. Next time I'm in Phoenix, I'll be sure to stop in and say hello."

She wasn't about to tell him she worked from home.

Besides, she didn't much want someone showing up at her door saying 'Howdy.' "It was nice working with you. I wish you luck on your house."

He chuckled. "Thank you. I appreciate it. It feels like a never-ending project."

She gave him a quick nod and headed down the walkway, not interested in talking in the cold any longer, and definitely not interested in inviting him in. When she reached the door, she looked back to see he still stood there.

Mr. Travis Ingram waved.

She waved with one hand as she opened the door with the other. Once inside, she made a beeline for the fireplace in the sitting room. The house had a Victorian feel and reminded her of her grandmother for some reason. Most likely it was the flowered drapes and the tiny leaf-print on the couch. Two items her grandmother would have liked.

Holding her hands out to the warmth, she hoped that Mr. Ingram had continued on to his house. His interest in her hadn't been obvious until just that afternoon. She'd might have contemplated dating him if she'd met him while her grandparents were alive, but now that she'd fallen in love with Brody, she wasn't sure any man would live up to her new expectations.

How was she going to continue to live in the same town with him? How long would it take to fall out of love with him? If she told him she never planned to sell, his reaction might help that process. Would his father then never release him from his promise, forcing him to break it or be trapped?

Even at the idea, she felt herself softening toward him,

but then she straightened her shoulders. No. She wouldn't feel bad for him. There were worse fates than helping one's family. She'd helped her grandparents her whole life. How would he feel if he lost his whole family in a couple of years?

She shivered despite the warmth of the fire. She sincerely hoped that wouldn't be the case. No doubt his father would come around in the next year and release Brody from his promise, when the dude ranch was successful. If it was successful.

In the meantime, she'd have to live with Brody being angry with her, and her hopelessly in love with him. If she took the full-time position, she would be out of town more, so that might make things a bit easier. She wasn't ready to see him in person yet. Maybe—

Her phone vibrated in her sweater pocket. Pulling it out, she looked at the caller. "Hello, Sheila."

"Hey, lady. Where are you? I haven't seen you around."

Pleased to hear a familiar voice, she moved to the couch and sat. "I've been up in Prescott for work, but I'm coming home tomorrow."

"Really? And you didn't tell me? Honey, you need to let me know when you're leaving town. Everyone's been asking me where you are. Amanda and Tanner stopped in yesterday wanting to know if I'd heard from you. Nash came by the day before, and Mr. Hardy was wondering why you hadn't been by for popcorn."

Her eyes started to water. "They were all asking about me?" She couldn't say any more as her throat closed with emotion. Why would they ask about her? She'd only been in Four Peaks for a few months before she'd left for Prescott.

"Of course they were. We're a small town and we look after our own. You need to promise me that you'll tell me if you have to leave again."

She sniffed, swallowing hard at the same time, her heart filling. "I promise."

"Good. Now tell me what's going on with Brody. Brody hasn't been in town at all, which in itself is odd. Nash let slip that Brody was moping. You wouldn't know something about that, would you?" Sheila's voice was filled with curiosity.

Brody wasn't in town? Did that mean something? "I'm not sure. Last I saw him I told him to get out. Not the most polite thing to say, but he was being an ass."

Sheila laughed. "All men are asses at one time or another. And women are bitches at one time or another. It's just human nature. Is it anything you'd like to talk about?"

Did she? She'd always talked to her grandmother about important things in her life. She'd never had a good friend to share confidences with because she'd never needed one. "I don't know."

Sheila laughed again. "Lady, we need to go to dinner and have a long chat."

"I'd like that." Though Sheila was a bit older than she was, and much brassier, the woman's big personality made her feel comfortable.

"Good. In the meantime, you need to get your ass back down here ASAP."

"I do?" She rose. "I was planning to leave tomorrow."

"Oh good." Sheila sounded relieved. "You have to come to Boots n' Brew tomorrow night with me. Roadhouse Tricksters are playing and they are the best. They only come once a year because the lead singer has a sister in town. Everyone goes."

That must mean Brody would be there. "I don't know."

"Why not?" Sheila got quiet for a moment. "If you're worried about running into the ass, don't. Like I said, he's staying on the ranch these days. Besides, everyone has been looking for you. You have to make an appearance."

She couldn't hide forever, and if others in town were wondering about her...

"Hannah, you still there?"

"Yes, I'm here. Just thinking."

"Well, don't think so hard. I'm sure Luke will teach you a new dance, and I could introduce you to the base guitarist. He's pretty hot."

Hannah laughed. "Please don't. Now that I have a home, the last thing I want is to hang out with someone who travels."

"Okay, then. If you promise to swing by my house and be my designated driver, I promise not to introduce you to the guitarist."

"Hmm, why do I think you're getting the better deal?"

Sheila hummed. "Because I am, honey. See you tomorrow. Oh, and wear that cute white skirt you bought in my shop."

Before she could ask why, Sheila hung up. She set the phone down next to her and looked at the fire, feeling much happier than fifteen minutes ago. People had missed her. Her! She shook her head, still having a hard time believing it. It seemed like she not only had a home of her own now, but she also had a hometown.

Tears of happiness filled her eyes. She really did have a place she belonged now. Which meant she couldn't let her failed relationship with Brody or his father's need for her land to keep her away. Even if she couldn't have the man her heart had fallen for, she'd gained a home.

She rose and headed up the narrow staircase to her room with a Blue Heron on the door. She stepped inside and looked around. There really was no reason to stay another night. Four Peaks was only three-and-a-half hours away. If she packed and checked out, she could be home before midnight.

She wanted to go home. She missed her casita and her open desert, and now that she was a part of the community, she couldn't wait to return. Quickly, she threw her suitcase on the bed and opened it. In no time, she was packed and on the road.

It grew dark before she was halfway through her trip. She was navigating the descent and switchbacks of Route 87 after Payson when her headlights flashed across eyes in the dark. Slamming on the brakes on the curve, her Jeep tilted as her passenger-side tires left the road. It seemed like she hung there forever as the vehicle continued its forward motion. Finally, it righted itself and she came to a stop before a large male elk.

With her heart beating her breath away, she struggled to take in air, her fingers locked around the steering wheel in a death grip. The bull elk continued across the road and she followed it with her eyes, though she couldn't seem to move. It lifted its head and let out a loud bugle sound before continuing into the wood.

She glanced in her rearview mirror for headlights, but thankfully there were none. With sheer will, she managed to let her foot off the brake, and gravity rolled the Jeep forward as she steered it to the side of the road onto a narrow strip of underbrush against the mountain wall.

Her body started to shake even as she gulped in air. Leaning her head against the steering wheel, she focused on her heartbeat, trying to get it to slow. Just as she thought she'd made progress, tears started to flow. Releasing the steering wheel with one hand, she wiped away the wetness.

If she had hit that elk, she'd be dead. The reality of that thought made her shake harder, but her tears dried. She didn't even have a will. Who would she leave her casita to?

Brody.

Her heart squeezed at how much she loved him, even if he was an ass on occasion. It sucked to be in love with someone who didn't feel the same way. If he did, he would have put them first, not his career dreams. But he wasn't there yet, and now he never would be. Still, she'd give him the property because it meant so much to him. She just wished she meant so much to him, too.

Uncurling her other hand from the steering wheel, she let it drop in her lap as she put the Jeep in park. She still needed a couple more minutes to get her equilibrium back before she could continue home. She'd get a good night's sleep in her family's bed and start her new life without Brody tomorrow. It wasn't perfect, but life rarely was. At least she had friends who cared about her and a hometown to return to. It was far more than she used to have, and she'd treasure it. Hopefully, her feelings for Brody would fade with time.

Her chest squeezed at the thought, but she was determined. As her grandparents had said, she was a peach with a hard pit at her core. If she decided on a plan of action, no one would keep her from it, even if she did feel like mush at the moment.

CHAPTER 17

BRODY FINISHED RUBBING CHAOS DOWN, then gave him some oats. "You worked hard today. I appreciate it." Giving his horse a pat, he stepped out of the stall.

He was covered in dirt, and his own sweat made him feel like he was a walking mud man, like the one he'd seen on one of the old B horror movies he'd watched as a child with his mom. He'd never thought he'd turn into one.

Striding out of the barn toward the house, he had only one thing on his mind—a nice hot shower. When he reached the front door, it opened before he touched the knob.

"Oh, Brody. I was just coming to see if you'd come in yet." Mandy backed into the house.

He strode through the door and dropped his hat on the entry table, while she closed the door behind him. "If you need my help, you'll have to wait until I shower. I've got dirt on top of caked-on mud."

She smiled. "Good. Then go shower. We're all going to Boots n' Brew. Roadhouse Tricksters is playing tonight."

"Roadhouse Tricksters?" They were the best band to step foot in Four Peaks, and only came through once a year. But he'd catch them next year. "You guys go ahead without me. I'm not in the mood."

Mandy set her hands on her hips. "You can't just mope around the ranch forever."

"Actually, I can. I'm bound to the ranch, but nothing says I have to like it." He turned on his heel and started down the hall.

"You know your brother is going to make you come."

He waved his hand as if it didn't matter, but if Tanner really got it in his head, they were bound to get in a fight. It never failed. Not even caring about that, he went straight to the bathroom, turned on the shower, and toed off his boots. Stripping down in record time, he stepped beneath the warm water and sighed.

Mandy might say he'd been moping, but he'd thrown his all into the work around the ranch just to pass the time. Nash had given him hope that Hannah would return, but after fourteen long days, she still wasn't home. He'd checked just the night before last. It was making it damn hard to keep his hope alive. The last place he wanted to be was with a crush of people at Boots n' Brew, watching as couples two-stepped around the dance floor or held each other close in a slow dance. He was tough, but not that tough.

The hot water felt good. He shampooed his hair and lathered his body. Suddenly, the water stopped. "What the heck?"

A pounding on the door had him frowning.

"Brody, time's up. Get your ass dressed."

"Go to hell!"

The door opened, and Brody spun around.

"Dad wants to have a private talk with Jackson, so get dressed and be in the truck in fifteen minutes."

"I'm full of soap you asshole."

Tanner grinned. "I'll give you five minutes to rinse off if you promise to get dressed and come with us."

Asshole. "The heck with that. I'll just go in the pool and rinse off."

"Sure. But be sure to dry off before walking through the house. Dad will have your head if you leave a trail of water."

He gritted his teeth, more than pissed at Tanner. "Fine. But I want ten minutes to rinse off and ten minutes to dress."

"I can live with that." Tanner closed the door.

Brody waited for the water to turn back on, the soap starting to itch. Finally, it sprayed out, and he quickly made sure to get the soap off everywhere. After turning the water off before Tanner could, he stepped out and dried himself. He wrapped the towel around his hips, grabbed his dirty clothes and boots, and left the bathroom.

Once in his room, he threw on a pair of jeans, socks, and pulled on a blue t-shirt from a drawer. After grabbing his black hat from his closet to match his mood, he headed down the hall. He'd be damned if he was going to dress for the evening. He planned to sit at the bar with his back to the dance floor until he could make his escape. Nash would give him a ride home if necessary.

He'd just reached for the front door when his dad spoke from behind him. "Have fun."

Unable to manage a polite response, he nodded without

looking back. He stalked across the dirt yard to Tanner's truck and opened the back door. "I can drive myself."

"Get in."

He hesitated for a moment, then figuring he could drink away his sorrows and not have to drive, he got in.

It didn't take long to reach Boots n' Brew, where the parking lot was half full already and they were early. As soon as they entered, he went straight to the bar, taking a seat with his back to the dance floor. Once he had his beer in hand, he just watched the bartender as more and more drink orders came in.

About an hour later when the band was announced, he turned around to look as the crowd erupted into applause. At least he could listen to good music. He turned back and finished off his beer.

"What are you doing here?"

At the sound of Nash's voice, he turned around. "Tanner made me come." He waved to the bartender to let him know another beer was needed.

"Good. It won't kill you."

He frowned, not liking the smirk on his friend's face. "No, but it will strain my patience. Let me know when you leave because I'm going with you."

"Only if I'm alone." Nash reset his hat on his head. "I may be lucky tonight. You never know."

"What are you going to do, take her back to your place with your aunt sleeping in the next room?"

Nash shook his head. "Of course not. Any woman who comes home with me would never pass her inspection." He grinned. "I'll go to the lady's place."

"You sound pretty confident. You have anyone in mind?"

Nash looked toward the dance floor where a line dance had started. "I do. Stacy's cousin is in town. Met her at the grocery store yesterday. She made me promise her a slow dance."

He forgot his own pique in light of Nash's possible relationship. "That sounds promising. Which one is she?"

Nash pointed to a woman with long, straight black hair dancing beside Layne. "I'm not really expecting anything, but a few dances, drinks, and conversation would be a good start."

Brody smiled for the first time in a long while. He lifted his beer. "I'll toast to that."

They clinked beer bottles and he swallowed, then almost started to choke as he saw Hannah at a table off the dance floor.

"Hey, Brody." Nash pounded him on the back. "You okay."

He coughed to get the clogged feeling in his throat to go away. "Yeah. Yeah." Swallowing hard, he nodded in Hannah's direction. "Hannah's back." He couldn't take his eyes off her. She looked like an angel to him. Dressed in a short white skirt, pink tank, pink cowboy hat, and her auburn hair plaited in a braid down her back, she looked good enough to eat, or kiss, or lick, and everything else he wanted to do.

"What are you going to do?"

Nash's question brought him back to reality. "Whatever I need to do. Excuse me." He handed his empty seat to Nash and slowly made his way through the crowd on the far side of the stage from where Hannah sat. If he went to her, then Sheila and whoever else saw him would be sure to add their two cents. He wasn't putting up with that. Hannah was far too important.

When he reached the door to backstage, he didn't hesitate to open it and step into the small stairwell. It was only five steps up and he was in the wings. Motioning over a roadie, he explained what he wished to do. Then he waited, hoping his request would be granted.

His hands started to sweat because he didn't have any back-up ideas. Even as he ran scenarios in his head, they all failed miserably. This one could fail too, and if it did, he'd just have to keep trying. With that determination in place, he steeled himself as the roadie came back to him.

"They're cool with it, cowboy. Good luck." The man gave him a thumbs up as he listened to his instructions on his head set and disappeared.

Brody's hope soared. Then he spent the next two songs the band played thinking about all the ways his actions could go terribly wrong. But then the band announced their first break of the night and walked off the other side of the stage to applause and cheers.

The roadie appeared out of nowhere. "Here's your mic. Just turn it on here."

He held the microphone for a moment, feeling frozen to the spot, but all he had to do was picture Hannah sitting out there, thinking he was an ass, and his feet took him across the stage. When he reached center stage, he stopped and searched for her in the crowd. He finally found her. In the bar lighting, he couldn't see her expression, but he could see her pink hat and top, so he clicked on the mic.

"Hey, Brody. What are you doing? You can't play."

He had no idea who it was, but he didn't care. He was there for only one person. "Hannah Kingsley."

He kept his eyes on her as she chatted with Sheila.

"Hannah Kingsley!"

This time half the crowd quieted, and she finally turned toward the stage.

"Hannah, I need to say I'm sorry for being a jerk."

"So what's new?" He recognized the voice, but ignored an old high school friend as the room filled with low chuckles.

He didn't care what anyone thought of him. Only what Hannah thought. "I didn't realize how much you meant to me."

The entire crowd quieted.

"I thought I needed to fulfill my destiny, to be something meaningful off the ranch to make my mother proud. I knew in my gut that I would make a great wildlife manager. So much so that I had blinders on. My mind was set on a goal with no deviation."

He took a breath, ignoring the fact that there wasn't even the clink of glasses being washed behind the bar. "But then you came into my life, or rather, I came into yours. You look at everything I find tedious as an adventure. You never cease to amaze me with how quickly you embrace the unknown to make it known. That's what you did with me."

He shrugged his shoulders. "You came to know me better than I knew myself. And when I continued down the wrong path, you called me on it. But I had those blinders on. Like a horse, only worse. I couldn't see what was right in front of me, either. You."

He took a breath to gather his courage. "It wasn't until you left and I couldn't understand why I felt like a javelina caught in a horse stall that I finally understood nothing was right and everything was wrong without you. Even the pursuit of my career was wrong. If you want, I'll give it up and stay on the ranch for you. You mean that much to me."

There were a few gasps in the crowd, which he ignored to focus on making her understand. "Hannah, I love you. Nothing can ever be right in my life without you. Please say you'll forgive me. I was a jerk, and as much as I try not to be, it happens sometimes. Please say that I haven't ruined the best thing I ever had in my life. Most importantly, please say you'll consider, maybe down the road when I prove myself and you can forgive me, that you'll be my wife." His heart pounded in his chest as he waited for a reaction.

She hadn't moved an inch, and he wished he could see her expression. What he could see is that everyone had turned to face her. Then, as if on cue, a stagehand turned one of the lights on and moved the beam to Hannah. It was an orange light, which put her in a pretty glow, and most importantly, he could see her face. Unfortunately, she looked stunned.

Was he too late? Had he killed her feelings for him? Was she completely embarrassed now? His chest tightened at his thoughts, making it difficult to breathe.

Sheila nudged Hannah with her elbow.

As the woman he loved walked forward with no expression on her face at all, his heart seemed to slow until he forced in a deep breath to keep it going.

When Hannah reached the stage, she lifted her hand for the mic.

Begrudgingly, he crouched down and gave it to her, wanting to know and yet not wanting to know what she would say.

Her brown gaze didn't leave his face as she lifted the mic to hold it before her mouth. "Brody, I understand your frustration. However, I will never understand why you wish to leave everything you have, everything I didn't have until now. Can you honestly tell me you can be happy on the ranch?"

He nodded emphatically. He could be happy anywhere as long as she was with him.

She opened her arm toward the room before turning back to him. "And can you be happy with your neighbors and friends you've lived with your entire life?"

He looked out at the crowd, for the first time seeing their faces in the orange light. They were all grinning at him. They seemed happy for him, even though for years he told everyone who would listen that he couldn't wait to leave. He was an idiot. He really hadn't understood how lucky he was to be part of a community. He turned back to Hannah and nodded.

Then she smiled widely, crinkling the corner of her eyes. "Then yes, I'll marry you in a bit when I forgive you, even though you're an ass sometimes."

His heart filled with love as relief powered through him and he knelt before her.

The crowd erupted into cheers, but he only had eyes for

Hannah, even if she seemed a bit blurry. Cupping her face, he gave her the gentlest of kisses before whispering against her lips. "I love you."

She set down the mic, before whispering in his ear. "I love you, too."

He needed her in his arms, so he sat on the stage and threw his legs over, intending to jump down, when two people lifted him in the air before setting him next to Hannah.

He grabbed her to him as everyone converged upon them, not letting go of her for even a second. And there they stood for the rest of the band's intermission, accepting well-wishes from everyone there, or almost everyone. He did notice the Hayden brothers didn't come up, but he was fine with that.

As the band came back on stage, he was finally able to pull Hannah to the side as the dancers flooded the floor. "Did you want to dance?"

She shook her head and gave him a secretive smile. "No. I missed you. I want to ride."

His body reacted immediately, but he held it in check. "As long as I can make love to you, I don't care how we do it."

Looping her arms around his neck, she bumped her hat against his. "And I want to wake up next to you tomorrow morning and every day after that."

He didn't know if he deserved her, but he'd damn well work to prove he did for the rest of his life. "If that's what you want, then that's what we'll do."

Her eyed rounded as her brows raised. "Even in my tiny casita?"

"Even in your tiny casita...until I can get an addition built."

Her face turned serious. "What about your dad wanting my land?"

Now that he planned to marry her, he found the idea of letting his father buy the land not so much to his liking. "I'm sure we can come to an agreement of some kind. I'll talk to Tanner. I see no reason why you should sell."

"Oh, Brody." Her lips came up to meet his and he kissed her back, slipping his tongue between her lips to taste her sweetness.

"Hey, get a room."

At Tanner's comment, Brody broke a kiss that promised a lot more. "You should talk."

His brother pulled his wife closer at the waist. "I am. I heard my name."

As Hannah cuddled against his side, she nodded. "Yes, we were just discussing how to make your dad happy that we aren't selling my land."

"Ah. I'm sure we can come up with something. Let me think."

When Mandy started adding her ideas, he knew his hope to take Hannah back to her casita would be a long time coming, but since he'd promised to wake up next to her tomorrow morning and every day after that, he found some patience. This was important, as it would affect their future together.

Their future. He gave her a small squeeze, still stunned she would be his forever, something that had scared him with other women. His mother had always said he was like her, and he'd know his soulmate when he found her. Now he truly understood what she meant.

Hannah looked up at him. "What do you think about that idea?"

"I will go with whatever you decide. It's your land."

She shook her head. "No, it's ours."

He knew he'd catch crap for it, but he couldn't resist. He titled her chin up and kissed her with all the love flowing through him.

Mandy laughed. "Come on, Tanner. I think they can take it from here."

And that's exactly what he would do, take Hannah from the bar so he could show her fully how he felt. Scooping her into his arms, he headed for the exit, surprised as everyone parted to allow him easy access.

"Make her proud, Brody." Sheila yelled, as they passed by her table.

Hannah giggled. "Oh, I'm already proud."

Humbled by her faith in him, he quickly got her outside and to her Jeep. Setting her down, he had to give her one more kiss. "Would you like to drive?"

She shook her head and handed him the keys. "No, I told you. I want to ride."

This time a completely different part of his anatomy reacted and he held his hand out for the keys. "Then ride you will."

CHAPTER 18

HANNAH PINCHED herself just to be sure she wasn't living a dream. Nope, it hurt, so this was real. She had a handsome, naked cowboy approaching her bed, more than ready to make love to her, by the looks of it.

She sat on her bed still in her skirt and top, her arms wrapped around her knees as she watched Brody undress. It was probably silly, but she enjoyed watching him toe off his boots with such ease. She'd tried it with her own and had little success. He'd been more than happy to help with that as well as with her short socks. "I think I might be a bit overdressed."

He took the two steps to the bed. "I agree. Lean back. I'll be happy to help you with that problem."

"You're so helpful."

He gave her a devilish grin. "I try."

She leaned back against the headboard and he sat on the bed at her feet. As his hands ran up her legs, a shiver of anticipation raced across her skin. Then his fingers hooked onto the sides of her panties.

"Lift."

She leveraged her hips up and he pulled her panties down. After he pulled them past one foot, she lifted the other and flung her underwear across the room to hit the wall and land on her dresser. She grinned. "Perfect."

"I agree." His gaze wasn't on her clothing, but on the juncture of her thighs which she'd exposed when she'd lifted her leg.

That he thought her perfect there had her blushing. Luckily, he didn't expect a response, because as he leaned forward, lifting her short white skirt, her thoughts jumbled around in her head like lottery balls.

His tongue licked at the inside of her thigh, and her leg moved to the side as if on its own accord. When he licked at the other thigh, she moved that leg away as well. Not because she didn't want his touch, but because she did, but not there.

She needn't have worried because he inched his way closer, his breath passing over the entrance to her sheath.

"Hannah, you're so beautiful, and kind, and intelligent, and tasty." His tongue licked across her folds and up to her sensitive nub.

Though she expected it, the intense feeling that one stroke sent had her lifting her hips.

His hands immediately cupped her butt and he held her to his mouth as he began to explore her folds. She gripped the pillows on either side of her and she let her head fall back. His attentions made her feel valued while at the same time exciting her. She forced herself not to move as he paid homage to every inch of her, adding extra licks to her clit.

Just when she thought she'd have to move, he stopped, his breath touching her wetness, cooling her heated skin, yet sensitizing it even more before his hands slipped out from beneath her.

She opened her eyes when he moved, to find he'd pulled back and sat on his haunches.

His hands rested on her ankles. "I don't think I deserve you, but I promise I will spend my life trying."

Her heart melted. "I just want you to be you."

He shook his head as if he couldn't believe it. "You amaze me, Hannah."

She smiled. "You amaze me as well. That you would give up your dream career for me is too much. I could never do that to you. I want you to be happy."

"You make me happy."

"Maybe for now, but eventually you would wonder *what if*. I want you to pursue your goal to become a wildlife manager." She winked. "You know a girl can't resist a man in uniform. Though to be fair, this isn't bad either." She laughed as he pulled back his head as if insulted.

"You little—" His hands locked around her ankles and he yanked her toward him.

"Ack!" Caught off guard, she found herself flat on her back with him leaning over her.

"Just for that, I'm going to have to determine if I like you better with this pink tank or bare."

She sincerely hoped he preferred without. Thinking he'd

like to pull it over her head, she started to leverage herself up, but his hands came down on her shoulders.

"Nope. You stay right where you are."

Curious what he was about, she lay back.

His hands moved to the neckline of her tank and before she understood his intention, he'd ripped it apart.

Her breath left her at the deliberate act, causing her heart to pound as adrenaline rushed through her, spiking an excitement she'd never felt before.

He scowled at her bra, which was a lacy white thing, as her breasts weren't so big that they needed an underwire. He hooked one finger under it between her breasts. "This isn't even a challenge."

She shrugged her shoulders, anticipating another rip and excited by it.

He gave a nod. "This is an improvement over the tank, but I need to see more. Unfortunately," he flicked his finger beneath the bra, pulling her breasts closer together at the action and causing her nipples to perk up, "I like a challenge."

As Brody appeared to contemplate his next move, he idly pulled at the bra as if testing its strength. Then, as if he'd decided what to do, a sly smile curved his lips.

She cocked her head. "What are you thinking?"

"Oh, I have a lot of thoughts running through my head at the moment like how good your nipples will taste once they're uncovered and how much I want to sink my cock deep into your body, but first I need to remove this barrier... with my teeth."

Her body heated with yearning at his words, so she wasn't sure she'd caught the last ones. "Did you say teeth?"

He didn't answer as his head lowered and his teeth found her right nipple through the lace. His love bite sent excitement straight to her core and her hips bucked of their own volition. He simply moved to the left and did the same to that nipple, which caused the same reaction.

Then before she knew what he was about, his teeth slipped from her hard peak, caught the lace, and ripped it open. Her breath caught as he blew against her wet nipple.

When he moved his head, she looked down to see her areola and nipple sticking through the lacy material. It was so erotic that she was surprised by the yank on her other nipple when he did the same to her bra there.

He leveraged himself up and looked at each breast purposefully with pride. "I like this much better."

Her need spiked at his look, and she lifted her hips against his erection.

His cocky look changed at her touch and he moved his gaze to her. "The fact is, I love you no matter how you look."

She would never tire of hearing him say those particular words. "Make love to me, Brody."

"With pleasure." His hips lowered and his cock found her opening. With deliberate slowness he entered her, filling her until he could go no farther.

She wrapped her arms around his neck and pulled him down for a kiss, showing him without words how much she loved him.

He kissed her back with equal tenderness and passion, until she angled her hips and he sank deeper into her.

His mouth left hers as he exhaled. "So good."

She whispered against his ear. "So right."

He lifted his head and smiled at her even as he pulled his hips back and pushed into her again.

He filled her completely and she moved her hands down to his butt, holding him to her, but then he pulled back again. Each time he slid into her, he came out a little faster, building the friction that sent shocks of pleasure through her entire body.

Soon she was tilting her hips, grasping onto him as he brought her more and more pleasure, raising her higher until she burst into ecstasy. All the colors of a sunset shot through her, joy holding her with him as he came inside her, his shout filling the casita.

Slowly her body calmed, and she could feel him holding her tight as if she was his anchor in his greatest moment of bliss. The thought made her proud that she could be for him what he had become for her. She gave him a comforting squeeze.

He lifted his head and smiled. "When will you marry me? Please tell me you really won't make me wait 'a bit.'"

Her heart filled at his hurry. "I would marry you tomorrow, but maybe it would be nice to marry at Rocky Road in the new club house?"

His gaze softened. "It should be ready in about two weeks. Don't you need to make all kinds of preparations?"

"Well, I have no family to invite, so I don't have to worry about invitations." The practical thought saddened her.

"No family? What about Sheila, and Stacy, and Ava. And don't forget Mr. Hardy, and Mrs. Barker and Mrs. Silva.

Surely, you want her ice cream with our Tres Leches wedding cake."

She laughed. He was right. She had a big family now. "Yes, I would love Mrs. Silva's ice cream at our wedding, specifically her Churro ice cream. It would go perfectly with the Tres Leches cake."

"Sounds good to me. You're right though about the invitations. We won't need invitations. We can just tell Mr. Hardy and everyone should know by the next day."

She grinned and nodded. He was absolutely right. There was a reason the hardware store owner always had free popcorn. He liked being the hub of town news. "I only have one request."

"That we wait until you can order the perfect dress? You know, I don't care what you wear."

"Yes, I know you prefer nothing at all or this fancy new bra I'm wearing."

He gave her a shit-eating grin.

"No, it's not about what I'm wearing. Sheila has a beautiful country-western wedding dress that I'm sure would do nicely."

"I'll buy it for you if you wear this bra under it."

"Brody, will you be serious?"

"I was." He tried to look affronted, but his lips kept quirking up.

"Do want to hear my request or not?"

His eyes widened. "Hmm, now I know when to be serious. Please, tell me your one request."

"Maybe I'm being sentimental, but my grandparents spent their honeymoon in this very casita. And a couple of weeks ago, I discovered that my parents spent their honeymoon in this casita as well. I would like to carry on my one family tradition and spend our honeymoon right here."

"I would be honored to spend our honeymoon here. We'll have a lifetime to experience new places and adventures. Starting our life together here will give us our own anchor."

Her eyes started to water at how wonderful he was. "Thank you. I know it may seem silly to you since you—"

He set his finger against her lips. "It's not silly. It's perfect. Just like you."

As he lowered his head to kiss her, she grasped him closer, beyond thankful that she discovered her hard-as-a-rock cowboy had a soft heart.

EPILOGUE
ONE WEEK LATER

BRODY HELD Hannah's hand tightly beneath the table in the den as his father read the lease agreement they'd had drawn up to allow Rocky Road use of Hannah's land for cattle grazing. Many arguments and conversations had led to this moment, and if his father didn't accept it, their relationship was going to be rockier than it was already.

As his father turned over the last page and set aside his new reading glasses, Brody's gut tightened, and instinctually, he reached down to rub Cami behind her ear. She'd become his shadow whenever he was at the ranch since he'd moved in with Hannah.

"This seems fair. I'm guessing that if I sign this, you plan to attend the academy in January." His father frowned, obviously not excited by that idea.

He wasn't backing down. "Yes, I will."

His dad surprised him by turning to Hannah. "And you're okay with him taking on a new career away from here?"

She smiled confidently. "I am." She turned to look at him. "If he gets a position in another part of the state, we'll move there. We can always move back if we retain the land. And if we leave, it wouldn't make a difference to the cattle."

"Hmpf." His dad lifted the lease agreement and continued speaking just to Hannah. "And you're in agreement with this too?"

She nodded. "I am. This will give us time to decide what we want to do with the property, and you a chance to get the dude ranch profitable."

"I have one last requirement." His father set the agreement down and sat back in his wheelchair.

His gut twisted. "Dad, we talked about everything. You can't suddenly add more requirements"

Hannah squeezed his hand tighter. "Hold on, Brody. Let's hear him out."

"I want grandchildren."

"Dad! You go too far."

"No, I don't. I'm in my fifties and Tanner has no children yet."

Brody was done with living by his father's needs. "You have a grandchild. Jackson brought you home a granddaughter. Be satisfied with that. Hannah and I will have children if and when we want to. Now sign the lease." He let go of Hannah's hand and flipped the pages over, leaving the final page with the place for his father to sign facing up.

His dad sighed, but didn't balk any longer. Leaning forward, he signed his name, or the best he could since the stroke. "There." He set the pen down.

"And you'll release Brody from his promise, right?"

Hannah's back was straighter than a pitchfork handle as she looked his father in the eye.

"Yes. At the end of the year, I release you from your promise, Brody."

Relief swept through him as if he'd just passed his final exams. "Thank you." He rose. "We thank you."

His father waved him away. "Go on. I expect there will be a celebratory dinner tonight. I'll have Amanda make a copy and get it to you."

His dad didn't smile, but he sensed a feeling of relief from him as well. "Don't worry. I have steaks and sweet potatoes planned for dinner tonight."

His father just nodded before turning his wheelchair around to face the television.

Having been dismissed, he took Hannah's hand and left the house. Once outside, he grinned. "We did it!"

She gave him a big hug. "We did! You're free and we still own my land. We're going to have to get Tanner a thank-you gift for his idea." She let go of him, smiling as wide as he was.

"I agree. After talking with my dad, maybe we should get him some Viagra."

"Brody!"

He laughed, too happy with the outlook of his future to let anything bother him. But then he sobered as he realized something was missing. "Where's Cami?" He'd been leaving her at the ranch house at night because he didn't want to crowd Hannah's casita.

Hannah looked around, then pointed to the house. "Did you leave her inside?"

He turned on his heel, concerned. Cami never let him out of the house without begging to go too, especially now.

He opened the door expecting her to greet him, but she was nowhere to be seen.

Hannah stepped in behind him. "I'll check the den."

"I'll take the bedrooms." As they split up, he thought about calling her, but was far too curious to find out where she'd gone. Two of the bedroom doors were shut, his dad's and Jackson's, so he checked Tanner's then his own at the end of the house. That's where he found her.

Cami lay on his bed, her head between her paws as she looked up at him. "Ah, girl. Do you miss me?" He sat down next to his dog and stroked her, his heart aching that she had to stay at the ranch. He really needed to get the addition to the casita started soon.

Hannah peeked her head in. "Oh, you found her." She walked closer.

Cami lifted her head for a pat, and Hannah didn't hesitate.

He liked that she was far more comfortable with Cami. "I think she misses me at night, even though I've been able to have her with me during the day now that it's cooler."

Cocking her head, Hannah lowered her brows. "Why don't you bring her home at night? I thought it was because she likes being here."

Surprised, he shook his head. "No. I was keeping her here until I get the addition done. She's a big dog and the casita is, well, small."

Hannah squeezed herself in on the bed at Cami's head. "You mean like this."

He grinned. "Yes, exactly. Could you imagine walking around her, or sleeping with her?"

"Yes, I can. And we can always get her a doggy bed."

He pointed to the one on the other side of the room. "I tried that already."

Hannah shrugged her shoulders. "So we try again. Our bedroom is a lot smaller. She's part of our family. I think we should take her home."

If he didn't already love Hannah, he was certain he would have fallen in love with her right then. How the heck had he gotten so lucky? He pulled her toward him over Cami and kissed her.

Cami lifted her head and licked at their chins, and he pulled away laughing. "Yes, girl. You can come home with me."

As if she understood him, she jumped off the bed and stood looking at him with her tail wagging.

Hannah stood, then walked over to the dog bed and picked it up. "Would you like that? Would you like to come home?"

Cami turned in circles before giving a short bark.

He rose and wrapped his arm around Hannah. "I swear I'm the luckiest cowboy in the world to have two such lovely ladies in my life."

"Yes, you are. Now let's go home and celebrate."

They headed back out with Cami in tow. He opened the door to his truck and Cami jumped in the front passenger seat. "Sorry girl. You can come, but you need to sit in the back now. He pointed to the back seat and Cami jumped over the center console. "Good girl."

He stepped back to allow Hannah to enter, then closed the door for her.

As he walked around to the driver side, he caught Jackson standing just outside the barn watching them. He turned toward his brother, but Jackson disappeared back into the stable. He hesitated, not sure what to do. The Jackson who had left Rocky Road on his last deployment was his fun self and even more adventurous, but the Jackson who came home was sullen and angry at the world. Hopefully, he just needed time.

Knowing how he himself felt when he was pissed, he decided to go home instead. Jackson wasn't ready for his little brother to be bothering him. Still, as he got behind the wheel, he looked back at the barn where Jackson had stood, wishing he could help.

"It's okay Brody. When he wants to talk, he will."

He gave Hannah a nod and started down the rocky driveway. Halfway down, he turned to her. "Maybe Jackson needs a pet."

She laughed. "He has a daughter. The last thing he needs is something else to take care of."

"You're right. I was just thinking about what makes me happy. If he doesn't need a pet, then maybe what he needs is a wife."

Hannah shook her head. "Don't go there. Your success rate as a matchmaker is zero."

"Hey, I've never tried to match two people up."

"See, so why ruin a perfect record?"

He grinned, even as he slowed for a particularly large

bump. "I understand what you're saying. Stay out of Jackson's life until he invites me in."

"You're so smart. That's why I fell in love with you."

"And here I thought it was because of how handsome I am."

She coughed as if choking and he stopped the truck. "What?"

She rested her hand on his face. "You are handsome, but that's not why I fell for you. You make me feel safe and like I belong somewhere."

He turned his face to kiss her hand. "You belong with me always. Now, let's go home. I have a special treat to celebrate."

She wiggled her eyebrows. "Oh, I bet I know what it is."

He laughed, "Well, that too, but that is a special treat every night. This is something else."

Despite the myriad questions she asked him all the way back to the casita, he wouldn't tell her. It needed to be a surprise.

Once inside, Hannah brought Cami into the bedroom. He went into the kitchen where he'd hidden the Tres Leches cake he'd finally perfected at the ranch the day before. Pulling it out, he set it on the small table they had added to the kitchen since he'd moved in.

"We'll have to use some of the dishes for food and water for Cami. I'm sure—" Hannah halted. "What's this?"

He held up two forks. "It's Mr. Dunn's Tres Leches cake."

"Oh, you did it?" She moved forward and accepted a fork.

"Yes. Or at least, I believe so. Sit." He held out the chair for her. Then sitting across from her, he held his fork above the cake on his side.

"We're not going to cut it?"

"Why? It's just the two of us. And if it's as good as I think it is, we may just eat the whole thing."

Her eyes sparkled with excitement. "I can't wait."

"Ready?" He held his fork just above the cake and waited for her to do the same.

"Ready."

They both took a forkful into their mouths. Shit, it was really good, but he enjoyed watching Hannah's eyes close in delight even more.

Her eyes opened and she gave him a big smile. "It's perfect. No, better than perfect. I think it's even better than Mama Juanita's!"

Her compliment made him feel invincible. "Thank you."

She rose and pulled her chair next to his. "We need to practice for our wedding." She took another forkful out of the cake and held it up.

Understanding dawned. "I don't think I need any practice." He dipped two fingers into the cake and held it before her mouth.

"Oh, I like this." She opened her mouth and he gently inserted his fingers.

As she sucked the cake off, he felt himself harden.

"It's even better that way. Now your turn." She held up the fork.

Obediently, he opened his mouth.

She started forward with the fork, and then with her other hand, smashed the cake off it onto his face.

Immediately she jumped up to run, but he grabbed her hand and spun her around and onto his lap. He grabbed a handful of cake and stuffed it down her button-down shirt.

She squealed. "That's cold."

"Is it? Then allow me to wipe it off." As he unbuttoned her shirt, she remained still, until his tongue found the cake and licked at her skin. When he'd cleaned everything off, she cocked her head at him. "I think I like it this way best. There's only one other place that might be better. On you."

His groin reacted to her suggestion. "Since you are the bride to be, I am at your service."

She rose and with one hand took a handful of cake before kneeling before him to unzip his jeans with her other hand. "Now, cowboy, let's see who does it better."

Even as the cold cake hit him, he was sure she would do it better. Her tongue took its first stroke and he gave himself up to her ministrations, content at last.

She would always be his better half, the best part of him. All his life he'd looked for the career of his dreams when all along all he needed was Hannah, the woman of his heart.

ALSO BY LEXI POST

Rocky Road Ranch

Between a Rock and a Cowboy

Hard as a Rock Cowboy

ABOUT THE AUTHOR

Lexi Post is a New York Times and USA Today best-selling author of romance inspired by the classics. She spent years in higher education taking and teaching courses about the classical literature she loved. From Edgar Allan Poe's short story "The Masque of the Red Death" to Tolstoy's *War and Peace*, she's read, studied, and taught wonderful classics.

But Lexi's first love is romance novels, so she married her two first loves, romance and the classics. Whether it's sizzling cowboys, dashing dukes, hot immortals, or hunks from out of this world, Lexi provides a sensuous experience with a "whole lotta story."

Lexi is living her own happily ever after with her husband and her two cats in Florida. She makes her own ice cream every weekend, loves bright colors, and you'll never see her without a hat.

[Visit her Website](#)
[Lexi Post Updates](#)
[Email Lexi](#)